Let Go

A Simple Love Story: Book 7

Dana LeCheminant

Cover design copyright © 2021 by Sheridan Bronson
Guitar element © 2021 by Vecteezy.com

This book is a work of fiction. The characters, names, incidents, places, and dialogue are either products of the author's imagination or are used fictitiously. Any resemblance to actual persons, living or dead, events, or locales, is entirely coincidental.

First Printing: March 2021

ISBN: 978-1-951753-07-8

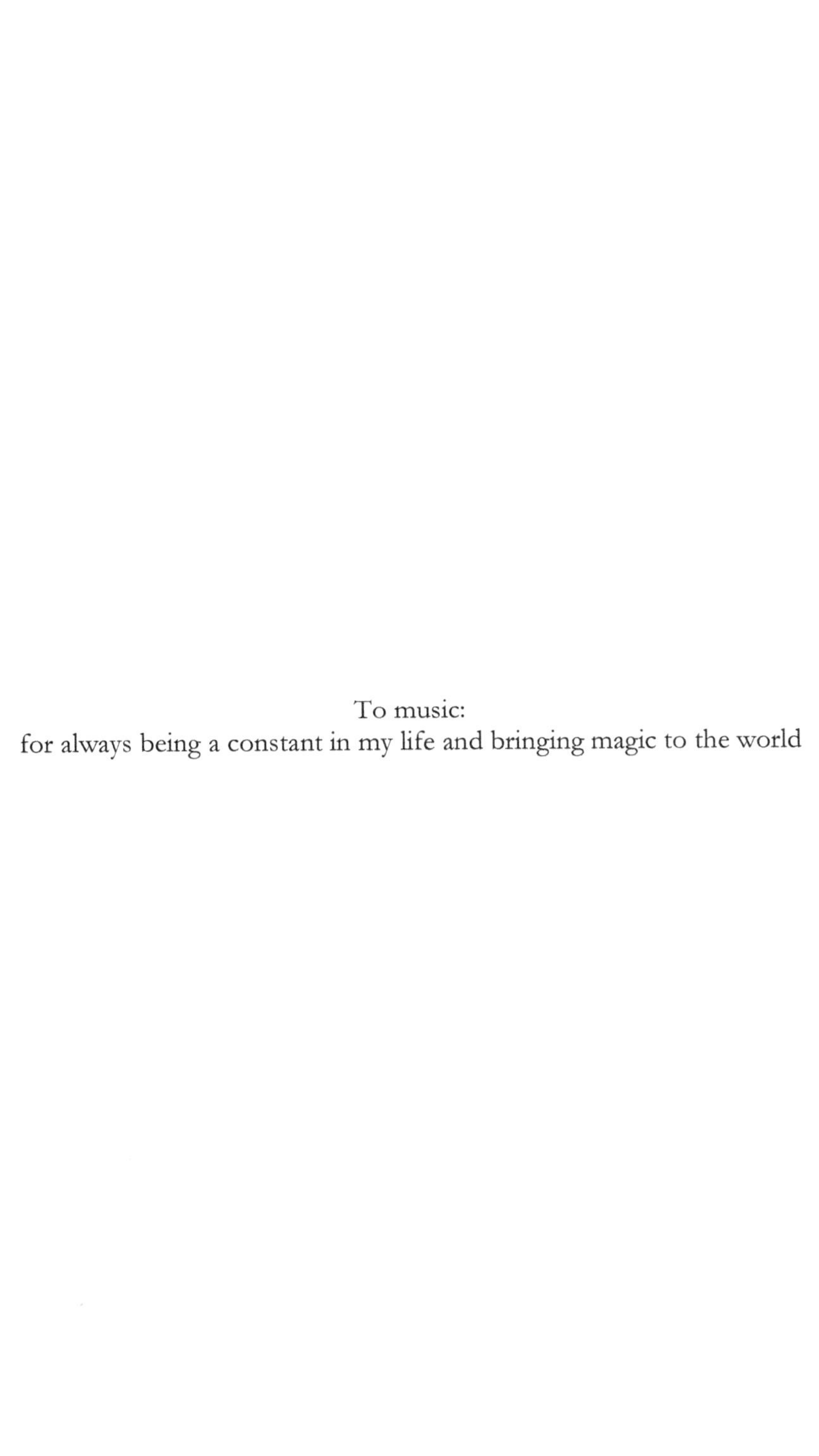

To music:
for always being a constant in my life and bringing magic to the world

CHAPTER ONE

I was okay with the divorce. Honestly, I'd seen it coming for a while, and Jordan was nice about the whole thing. Yes, he got the house and the furniture and the dog, but I got to keep my car. He worked hard, so it only made sense that he got most of the things. And I could handle losing my job. I was the newest on the team, and the company was struggling. Logically, if they had to get rid of anyone, I was the best choice. I was even fine with my parents moving to Denmark on a whim. I might not have seen that one coming, but I would still be able to video chat with them, even if the hours were a little off. They deserved to do what made them happy, and I couldn't argue with their decision. They promised to come back for Christmas in a couple of years, at least, so it was fine. I was okay with all of that happening over the last week.

But the flat tire was too much.

It happened just outside of Kansas City. The car suddenly jerked away from me, and I might have screamed a bit as I pulled over to the side. Thankfully, I managed to get to the curb without too much careening back and forth like I always saw in the movies. As clouds built overhead in the late afternoon sky, I sat there for a minute just trying to catch my breath.

"This is what happens when you aren't paying attention," I told myself and unbuckled my seatbelt with shaking fingers. At least there wasn't a lot of traffic going past, so I didn't feel like a complete idiot when I got to the passenger side of the car and frowned at the completely mangled front tire.

What had I hit? A chainsaw?

I took a deep breath and shivered as a bit of wind cut through my sweatshirt. I just had to think this through. My dad had taught me how to change a tire when I learned to drive, and yeah, okay, that might have been fifteen years ago, but how hard could it be? I had a spare in the trunk, and Dad had drilled it into me to always be prepared for this kind of thing, no matter what.

My first instinct was to call Jordan, and I might have actually done it if my phone wasn't in the car. Never mind he was way back in Chicago—calling my ex-husband was a terrible idea no matter what. I knew better than to bother him with something I should be able to handle myself. So instead of crawling into the car to get my phone, I rolled up my sleeves and pulled open the trunk.

"Well," I huffed and stared down at the complete mess of junk inside.

That was the problem with moving across the country without renting a van; I had a lot more stuff than I realized, and I wasn't so great at the whole block puzzle game thing, so it was all just piled in there and shoved into every little nook and cranny, wherever stuff could fit. It would all have to move if I wanted to get to the tire.

"We'll be smarter this time around," I told myself and started digging.

Half an hour later, I managed to clear out the trunk just enough to hoist open the floor mat and hold it up with my shoulder so I could grab the spare tire. Dang, were tires always that heavy, or was it just this particular one? I needed to go to the gym more often, apparently. Though, now that I didn't have a fancy one down the street from my house—the house that I no longer had—that wasn't likely to happen.

If I was being honest, it hadn't happened anyway.

"New Year's Resolution," I muttered then heaved the tire out with a grunt. "Never mind it's July."

By the time the tire was out and waiting, and I had grabbed the thingy to lift the car up, I was exhausted, and I hadn't even gotten to the fixing part of all this. I had no reason to be tired just from moving things around.

"Don't lie to yourself," I said, frowning down at the mess of tools I didn't know how to use. "You were exhausted to begin with. At least it can't get worse."

I should have known not to say those words out loud.

Kansas rainstorms were a whole lot worse than Illinois storms. Or maybe it was just this particular storm. It didn't matter which was true, because I was still soaked within minutes, and the second I bent down to try to lift up the lifter thingy, my feet slid in the mud and sent me sprawling.

And I cried.

I hadn't even cried the night Jordan handed me the divorce papers, but I sat there in the mud, huddling against my pathetic little car, and sobbed as the rain kept pouring buckets down. I missed my job, even if I hadn't been doing much marketing despite that being my job title. I missed my parents, even though I had just barely spent a day and a half with them.

I missed Jordan.

His little good morning kisses and the way he smiled when I gave him his coffee in the morning and the way he breathed when he was deep asleep. I really hadn't been able to sleep over the last week without him next to me, which was why I was so tired.

I wanted my life back.

I wasn't sure how long I sat there and cried in the rain, but it was long enough that I was starting to feel a little ridiculous. I was thirty years old, for goodness' sake. I was crying over a *flat tire*, and there were people out in the world who would kill to have a car at all. People probably *had* killed for a car like mine.

I gulped. "Don't think about that, Amelia," I said and brushed my wet sleeve over my face to dry my tears. Metaphorically. "You've had your cry, and now you can get back up and get to work. A pity party won't do anyone any good, and Amelia Blake does not sit in the mud and wait for Prince Charming to come to her rescue."

I would probably have to change my name, wouldn't I? Jordan was pretty clear about wanting everything that was his, and that included his last name.

What would I change it to? Go back to being Amelia Carter? That felt like a step backward, a return to the girl I used to be. There was a letter sitting on my dashboard that had another suggestion, but even thinking that one made me shudder. No, I wasn't brave enough for that name. At least not yet. I would have to look somewhere else, because it wasn't like people just walked around offering up names to share.

"Do you need some help?"

I shrieked and slipped in the mud again, sliding onto my backside and giving myself a pretty thorough view of the man who stood over me with concern. I hadn't heard a car pull up, but then again the rain was loud enough that I probably wouldn't have. But given the guy's level of soaking, I was pretty sure he'd been walking down the road, not driving it.

"Oh." I struggled to my feet, though the mud made it difficult. He was a pretty young guy, and by the looks of him he had been walking this road for a long time. Days, probably. "No, I'm…" I glanced at the tire and the lifter thingy that was still just sitting next to the car because I hadn't even gotten it underneath. "I'm fine."

His lips quirked on his thin face as he took me in. I must have looked terrible, covered in mud and soaking wet. Then again, he was just as soaked, so I was only half terrible. "You sure?" he asked, and one of his black eyebrows rose higher up his forehead than the other. His eyes were such a bright, icy blue that they seemed to glow through the storm, and I couldn't look away.

"Oh yeah," I said and tried to sound confident as I smiled at him. "I don't want to bother you, and I'll figure it out. How hard can changing a tire be, right?"

The quirk turned into a smile to match mine, and he glanced up the empty road, as if waiting for someone else to come along so he could be off the hook. But then he slid his shoulders out of what I realized was a guitar case and held it out to me. "Hold this," he said, and the moment my hands grasped the guitar, he dropped down to his knees and slid the lifter a few inches deeper under the car.

I stood there somewhat dumbstruck as he worked, maneuvering the thingy and twisting the x-shaped tool until the car started to rise on one side. He didn't have the problem of sliding around in the mud like I had, though I wasn't sure why it was so easy for him when he wasn't exactly a big guy. His worn black t-shirt did nothing to hide how slim he was, and though he was taller than me, that wasn't saying much. I was average at most, so this guy couldn't have been more than five foot nine. And yet he worked the tire off without much issue and was already lifting the spare into place before I was even aware he was doing it.

That was when I realized what I was holding. And that it was getting completely wet. The hard guitar case was old enough that I had a feeling it wasn't exactly waterproof, so while the stranger fixed my tire for me, even though I hadn't asked him to, I hurried to my pile of wet stuff behind the car and dug through it until I found a blue tarp that had sat in my trunk for years. It wasn't the prettiest solution, but at least it would keep the guitar dry. Drier than it was at the moment.

I probably should have used it to cover my own possessions before now, but clearly I hadn't thought that one through.

By the time I came back to the side of the car to see if the guy needed help, he was on his feet with the lifter thing in one hand and the ruined tire in the other. "You'll probably want to buy a new one," he said, lifting the tire a little before tossing it into the trunk. He was nicer with the lifter, holding it out to me so I could put it where it belonged. "Jack."

"Oh yeah!" I said. "*That's* what it's called."

He laughed, and water dripped from his dark, too-long hair as he shook his head. "No. I mean, yeah, that's what it's called, but I meant… I'm Jack." And he held out his greased and muddied hand.

Suddenly the rain didn't feel quite so cold as my face burned with heat. "Oh."

He pulled his hand back, apparently thinking I didn't want to shake it, which wasn't at all the truth. I was about to, but now he probably thought I was both pathetic and rude. I liked to think at least the latter wasn't true.

"Thanks," he said and nodded to the tarp covering his guitar. "I've been meaning to get one of those."

"You can keep it," I replied before he tried to give it back.

Smiling again, he tucked the tarp a little more securely around the case then lifted it up and slipped it back over his shoulders. "Well, don't drive too fast on that spare. You should be able to make it back to Kansas City to get yourself a new tire. Ideally you should get four, but the others don't look too old, so you might be okay."

My heart seemed to sink into my stomach. Needing to buy one new tire—let alone four—was going to be bad enough, but I hated the idea of backtracking, even if it was only twenty or thirty miles. This drive was pushing my bank account's limits as it was, and gas wasn't exactly cheap.

"Thanks," I said and started running through my budget again, trying to see where I had some extra money. I stared at the spare tire that looked so innocent but wasn't as helpful as it wanted me to believe.

Jack was already a good thirty feet down the road before I realized he'd started walking again.

"Wait!" I shouted and nearly slipped in the mud again when I dashed forward to stop him. "You're going to walk in this rain?"

He glanced up at the sky as if he hadn't even noticed the water pouring down. How could he smile at a time like this? I was legitimately waiting for the floods to come, and he didn't seem bothered in the least. He even managed to grin. "You know, it's not too bad. At least it's summer, right?"

Looking back at my repaired car, I knew I couldn't just let him wander off into the storm looking like a drowned rat. The man had fixed my tire, for crying out loud, and I was taught better than to let him go without something to repay him. "Come with me back to Kansas City," I said. "Let me buy you lunch."

My budget screamed a little.

But Jack smiled again, and the expression was so warm that I knew I couldn't rescind my offer. "I can't argue against free food," he said and wandered back to the car. And before I could stop him, he slid the guitar off his shoulders again and began reloading my trunk.

I thought about arguing, but I was too tired for that and simply joined him, handing off my little possessions as he placed them with a lot more care and deliberation than I had. Clearly this guy was a lot better at that one game with the falling cube shapes than I was. Within ten minutes, everything I owned was back in the car—soaked but intact—and Jack was squished in the front seat with his guitar between his legs as we drove in the opposite direction of where I wanted to go.

Weirdly, it felt almost normal to have him sitting next to me as I drove, and at first I chalked it up to familiarity. I'd been married for several years, so it wasn't like I spent a lot of time in the car by myself. But then I considered the fact that Jordan was always the one who drove, and I couldn't remember the last time I had had a passenger when I was behind the wheel.

Something about having Jack in the car with me after my little breakdown made all of this feel better somehow. In the middle of the worst rainstorm I'd ever seen, Jack was almost like his own source of calm as he looked out the window and silently watched the plains go by. Sure, I'd hit rock bottom. When it rains, it pours, all of that. But I had a feeling everything would be okay.

I had no idea what it was, but something about Jack felt important. Like we were meant to cross paths on this highway in Kansas.

I wondered if I would ever figure out why.

CHAPTER TWO

Thank the heavens for the existence of kind people in the world. The man behind the counter at the tire shop took one look at my muddied and wet clothes and offered to rotate my remaining tires, free of charge. He said it was a special, but I could tell he pitied me. And while I hated the idea of charity, I couldn't bring myself to refuse. My budget probably would have murdered me if I tried.

Another bright spot of the afternoon was the cheap-looking diner across the street, so we didn't have to go far to find food. Jack grabbed us a booth, and I slipped into the bathroom with a change of clothes to try to rectify my horrible state. Until I got somewhere with a shower, I wouldn't be able to get rid of all the mud, but at least I could get most of it with some paper towels and the sink.

By the time I got cleaned and changed, a waitress was at our booth and chatting with Jack while she poured him a cup of coffee I wished I didn't have to pay for.

Don't be so rude, I thought, imagining what my mother would think if she knew I was considering not paying for a measly cup of coffee for the guy who changed my tire for me.

"Hiya, hon," the waitress said as I slid into the seat across from Jack. "Can I get you something to drink?"

"Water," I said without hesitation.

I accidentally met Jack's eye, something I would have liked to avoid before I died of embarrassment, and he leaned over the table and whispered, "Coffee's free with a meal," so the waitress wouldn't hear.

"And a coffee would be great," I added, hoping he was right.

His smile had a bit of laughter in it, and I hoped that was because I spoke so quickly, not because he had tricked me.

I ordered the cheapest thing on the menu, and to my relief Jack did the same. And then I finally had a chance to relax, if only a little. Until my car was ready to go, there was nothing I could do but sit here anyway. If I stayed so tense for too long, I was going to seriously miss the in-house masseuse Jordan's company had hired a few months ago.

Jack slipped away as soon as the waitress left to put in our orders, but he came back just a couple of minutes later about as clean as he could get without having a change of clothes. If I had thought anything of mine would actually suit him, I would have shared, but living with Jordan the last couple of years had changed my wardrobe enough that even a vagrant like Jack would probably choose mud over a lacy blouse.

"So," Jack said when our food arrived. "I couldn't help but notice all that stuff in your car." Of course he couldn't. He had organized half of it when he repacked my truck. "Road trip?" he guessed.

"Uh, I'm moving. Sort of." That really depended on what I found when I hit the coast. "I'm going to California to meet some family I haven't met before."

I once again thought about that letter sitting on my dashboard, the one with the name I was afraid of. I'd gotten it more than a year ago, and I had just been ignoring it. But desperate times called for desperate choices, and it was finally time to reach out to the family I hadn't known I had until a few years ago.

I was frazzled enough, and going down this bunny hole would only make things worse, so I turned the conversation onto Jack: "What about you?" I asked. "Where are you headed?" Was he headed anywhere, or was he just walking aimlessly and hoping to figure out whatever he was looking for when he came upon it?

It took him a long time to answer, as if he had to think about it for a moment. "San Francisco, actually," he said and stretched one arm across the back of the faded red vinyl seat. "I tried Nashville, but I think the West Coast music scene fits my style better." So he was a homeless musician wandering across the country. Did he plan to walk the whole way? That thought was horrifying. "My family is from California," he continued, though he frowned at the idea and seemed to dim a little. "Thought I would get back to my roots."

"I wish my family *wasn't* in San Francisco," I sighed, and then I cringed when Jack raised a dark eyebrow in interest. I probably shouldn't have told a stranger exactly where I was going, but it was more than that.

San Francisco left a bad taste in my mouth, since any good memories I had of that city were tainted now. I had lived there for almost four years and was left with nothing but pain and disappointment, which was a shame, really. It was a great city, and I hoped I could replace all that darkness when I connected with my family.

I flashed Jack a smile then dug into my cheeseburger without meeting his eyes.

We pretty much ate in silence after that, which was fine by me. I had spent the last week by myself, packing up my car and closing bank accounts and saying goodbye to our Golden Doodle, Roxy.

I was getting used to the solitude.

Like me, Jack devoured his food. Given how skinny he was, I had to wonder how often he even got good meals like this. Not that this meal was good. If he was actually planning to walk to California, it was going to take him a long time, and I really didn't think he had enough meat on his bones to make the journey. But he didn't seem all that worried about it, and he just inhaled his little lunch with the gusto of a ten-year-old who had his favorite food in front of him.

"Well," he said once he'd finished, and then he downed the rest of his coffee. "Thank you for the food, but I should probably be on my way. I want to get as far as I can before it gets dark."

And suddenly a wave of guilt pushed me down into my seat. Bringing him back to the city with me had taken away twenty of the miles he'd already walked, and now he would have to walk even farther. I doubted a little cheeseburger would make up the difference.

"Good luck with everything," he said, and then he headed for the door with his guitar slung over his shoulder.

"Wait!"

I struggled out of the booth, fumbling for my wallet so I could pay for our food before the waitress thought we were dining and dashing. She took her time giving me my change—I definitely couldn't afford to let her keep it—so by the time I got out of the diner, Jack was already at the edge of the parking lot.

"Jack!" I called. The rain was still coming down pretty heavily, but he must have heard me because he paused and looked back. I slid to a stop next to him, embarrassingly out of breath after such a short run, and I coughed as I tried to breathe again. "Um, don't walk."

He glanced at the road ahead of him then cocked one eyebrow. "Huh?"

Well of course he was confused when I said something ridiculous like, "Don't walk." What was I, a street sign? "I mean, let me give you a ride. At least part of the way."

Man, the guy had expressive eyebrows. They shot way up on his forehead as he turned to face me. "That's really nice of you, but I'll be fine."

A clap of thunder shook the air around us, and I felt sick to my stomach at the thought of letting him walk through a storm like this. What were the odds of him getting struck by lightning on the Kansas plains? Way too high, probably. "Jack."

"I would say your name if I knew it," he replied.

Oops. "Amelia Blake. Let me give you a ride. Please. It's the least I can do."

Glancing at the road again, Jack took a while to think it over. Was it really such a terrible thought to sit in a car with me? We were getting soaked again, and the longer we stood here, the later—darker—it was going to get.

"Come on," I said.

"You sure I'm not some serial killer?"

No, I wasn't sure, and now I was suddenly imagining him strangling me with a guitar string as we cruised along I-29. "You would be a little more eager to come with me if your goal was to kill me," I said, sounding a lot braver than I felt. "Besides, what are the odds of us both being serial killers?"

He grinned, laughing a little to himself as he hiked his guitar a little more securely up his shoulder. "Well, a ride is almost as good as free food. But you can kick me to the curb any time you like."

"Deal." I took a step toward my car where it waited at the shop across the street, hinting that he should do the same. When he just stood there grinning at me like he knew something I didn't, I frowned a little. "Are you coming or not? It's freezing out here."

"Yeah, I'm coming," he said, and for a guy who had tried so hard to refuse my offer, he seemed thrilled about the idea.

Ten minutes later, we'd managed to rearrange things on the back seat so he could fit his guitar on top of my stuff, and we were back on the road beneath cloudy but dry skies.

Jack kept glancing at me, as if expecting me to kick him out now that it wasn't raining, but I fully intended to drive him at least to the other side of Nebraska. Or, at least, however long I could go before I fell asleep. I had started driving at four that morning, and it had been an incredibly long day on top of the week I'd had.

But if we had to drive in silence for much longer, I was going to fall asleep and get us both killed. As much as I was getting used to the silence, that didn't mean I liked it. "So," I said after a while, "how long have you been playing the guitar?"

Jack turned to face me, and though I kept my eyes on the road, I could still feel his gaze on me. Boy, did he know how to stare someone down. At least he was smiling when I glanced at him out of the corner of my eye, so it wasn't one of those creepy stares I imagined a serial killer would have.

Don't forget about charming guys like Ted Bundy, I thought then cringed. That wasn't helping. I gripped the steering wheel a little tighter.

"A couple of years," Jack said after a moment. "I bought the guitar when I was in high school, thinking it would help me get girls, but eventually I realized I had to be able to play it if I wanted that to work. The look itself isn't enough to sell the concept anymore."

Without looking at him too closely, I tried to figure out how old he was. Definitely younger than me, but his slender frame might have made him look younger than he really was. But I figured I couldn't just ask him, so I kept my question to myself and asked instead, "What kind of music do you play? Who's your favorite artist to cover?"

"I mostly play my own stuff," he replied. "I like the freedom it gives me."

From there, our conversation turned to the kinds of music we liked listening to—he surprised me by having similar taste to me instead of liking more of the heavier and harder music, which his black-clothed and messy-haired appearance implied—then to what movies we enjoyed, though neither of us had seen one in a while. We talked about how I liked road trips but Jack didn't, and Jack had never had pets before. I even threw in a bit of conversation about marketing and public relations, and Jack managed to hold his own, even though he didn't have experience in that area.

Time passed quickly and easily because Jack could talk about pretty much anything, and before I knew it, the sun was gone and the road was empty except for us.

That was when I started getting tired.

Being married to Jordan had settled me into a rather strict routine, and despite all the chaos of the last week, I hadn't managed to break out of it. Nine o'clock hit, and I was ready for bed. I'd been pushing through the sleepiness for the last couple of hours, but now that it was dark, my body fought extra hard to get me to sleep.

I had been afraid of this part. The drive from my parents' place in Ohio to California was thirty-six hours, and I'd known I couldn't make it in two days without making some stops and sleeping. But sleeping meant needing to find a motel, which meant money. Money I definitely didn't have now that I'd had to buy myself a new tire. And then there was Jack. I highly doubted he could afford a room either, and I couldn't bring myself to force him to sleep in the car. Besides, despite how easy he was to talk to, I didn't like the idea of sleeping in such close quarters with a stranger I'd picked up off the street.

"You're drifting," Jack said suddenly.

I jerked the wheel and pulled the car back into my lane with a squeak, my heart skipping into overdrive. "Sorry!" I gasped. He probably thought I was a terrible driver and would definitely want to be let out so he could find a different ride or maybe even just go back to walking.

But, though I couldn't see well in the dark, it looked like Jack was still smiling. "Pull over," he said.

"I'm fine."

"I said pull over, Amelia. You're exhausted."

He wasn't wrong, and my foot lifted from the gas pedal without my permission until we crawled to a halt on the side of the road.

"I just need a quick nap," I told him as I pulled the keys out of the ignition. "Then I'll be good to go."

His smile grew even bigger, and he held one hand out with his palm up. "How about you give me the keys, and I'll keep driving while you nap?"

I stared at him. "What?"

"I don't mind," he said. "I'm not tired anyway, so we might as well cover some distance, right? I can't imagine you want to stay stuck in this car for longer than you need to."

I still couldn't quite figure out what he was telling me, which meant I was more tired than I thought. He wanted to drive? "I couldn't let you do that," I said.

Jack's smile shifted into a crooked one that made him look like he was trying not to laugh at me. "Is that because you don't trust me or because you feel bad for making me drive?" he asked.

As I blinked, trying to figure out who this guy was, I felt my resolve slowly slipping. If he wanted to do something to me, he probably would have done it already, since we'd been alone on the road for a couple of hours now. He could have asked me to pull over so he could use the bathroom, and then as soon as the car was stopped he could have grabbed me and done whatever he planned to do.

I was pretty sure there was nothing sinister about Jack, which was a small comfort, and yet I still wasn't sure if I could really let him drive. After he fixed my tire and kept me entertained pretty much all night, I really didn't want to take advantage of him any more than I already had.

And yet my eyes were drooping, my vision going blurry, and I had a feeling that even if I tried to argue, he would likely drag me out of my seat and switch spots with me anyway. It would probably do me better to just agree.

"There's nothing special about this car," I mumbled as I dropped the keys into his waiting palm. "And the speed control is broken. Sorry." I'd meant to get it fixed before I left, but… Money.

"I think you mean cruise control." Jack grinned then slipped out of the car to take my place.

When we were both situated, the car seemed to hum rather than whine under his touch, which was a little annoying, but the rumble of the old engine was somewhat soothing. As Jack pulled back onto the highway and accelerated up to speed, I sank deep into my seat and rested my head against the cool window.

"Wake me up in a couple of hours," I told him, since there was no way I could make him drive any longer than that. After all, this was my car, and my trip, and my exhausting day. He was just along for the ride.

I woke to sunlight streaming into my face, and it took me a second to figure out why that was a problem. How long had I been asleep?

One glance at my watch made me sit up in surprise. "Seven o'clock?" I gasped. That meant I'd been asleep for almost eight hours, which was both impressive and alarming. Jack was supposed to wake me long before now, and I had the sudden sinking feeling that maybe he'd left me asleep on purpose so he could take me somewhere else, somewhere he could easily kill me like he planned all along.

A sudden tapping on my window made me scream, and I flinched away from the glass only to find Jack laughing at me on the other side.

"Relax," he said, his voice muffled. Then he gestured for me to get out of the car.

Only when I looked around and realized we were at a gas station did I stop panicking. There were two other cars at the pumps, so Jack probably wasn't going to attack me when I got out of the car.

"Where are we?" I asked, squinting at the towering mountains behind which the sun was just peeking out.

"Salt Lake City," Jack said and stuffed his hands into his black jean pockets. "It was as far as we could get without getting gas. I'm impressed with the mileage this thing gets, though," he added and tapped one of the tires with his boot.

I stretched my neck and shoulders, still trying to wake up despite the scare he'd given me. "Why did you let me sleep so long?"

"Because you were tired," he replied. "But now that you're awake, you can fill up the tank, and I can take my turn to sleep. Assuming you still want to give me a ride. No pressure. At this point there'll be plenty of people driving to California, so I won't have to walk far to find another ride."

"Right," I said, though that didn't really tell him anything useful. I needed to get my bearings and wake up fully. "I'll go pay for some gas," I said, and I hoped I could leave it at that until I'd gone in and washed the night from my face.

Digging into my pocket for my wallet, I counted what I had left and gulped a little. The cash combined with the little in my bank account was barely enough to get me the rest of the way to San Francisco, but once I got there… That problem would have to wait until it arrived, because I was quickly discovering there was only so much I could handle at once. The flat tire had been the evidence of my threshold.

I paid for as much gas as I could stomach then waved out the door at Jack, telling him he could start pumping. It was a risky move, leaving him alone with the car, but I badly needed a trip to the little girl's room and probably some breakfast, depending on how cheaply I could find it.

I took my time in the bathroom, combing my hair with my fingers and washing my face with soap that smelled like cotton candy. I thought about changing my clothes again, but I only had so many clean things left, and I figured I should save them for when I met my family. Assuming I could even find them and they let me in the house…

It had been long enough since I got that letter that there was a high chance their extension of welcome had expired.

"Deal with that bridge when you get to it," I muttered into the mirror, frowning at the state of my face. I was pretty sure I had never looked quite this haggard, and I really hoped it was just from all the stress of the last week. Not because I was thirty and only getting older.

By the time I had gotten myself cleaned up and at least mildly refreshed, I figured Jack had either run off with my car or fallen asleep, and I just resigned myself to accept whichever was true. Honestly, Salt Lake City seemed like a decent place to make a home for myself if I ended up stranded here, and the mountains were beautiful. There were worse places I could end up.

But once I bought a couple of sausage sandwiches that looked only mildly questionable, I stepped back outside to find Jack leaning over the engine, the hood popped up and his hands streaked with black. He was checking the oil—or something like that—and glanced over when I approached.

"It was making a squeaking noise coming down the canyon," he said. "The alternator belt needed the tension adjusted, but it should be good to go now." Once he closed the hood, he brushed his dirty hands on his mud-streaked shirt, and then he frowned when he met my gaze. "What?"

"How did you know how to do that?" I asked. He certainly didn't look like the kind of guy who would know anything about cars.

Ducking his head, he coughed then muttered, "My dad taught me when I was a kid. It's been a while, so I'm no expert, but…"

I had a feeling he didn't want to talk about it, so I changed the subject. "You're still here."

He glanced over at me and quirked that crooked smile again, which was a lot better than him avoiding eye contact. "I'm not sure how to take that surprised tone," he said. "Is that a good thing or a bad thing? Like I said, I can find another ride if I need to."

I didn't know why I was so happy he was still here, but I was. Maybe because I knew the journey, however little I had left, wouldn't be quite as lonely as it had started. Besides, if something else went wrong with my car, it would be nice to know I had someone with me who could fix it.

"How about you wash your hands then get in the car," I said. "We still have a long way to go."

He grinned and gave me a little salute. "Aye aye, captain," he said and hurried inside. He was back a few minutes later and climbed into the passenger seat. "Thanks," he added when I handed him a sandwich then turned the ignition. "I really didn't want to find another ride. You're a whole lot nicer than most of the truckers I've met."

I laughed, and I pulled back onto the freeway feeling pretty good about my choice. At least for now, not everything was completely horrible.

CHAPTER THREE

Jack woke up somewhere around Truckee with a yawn and a stretch that ended with his fist right in front of my face before he realized how close he was to me. He quickly shifted back to his side of the car, and his apologetic smirk made me laugh a little. I was glad he was awake, since I hadn't wanted to wake him up by listening to music, and the endless Nevada desert had gotten incredibly boring. But when he glanced over at me, there was a weirdness between us as if we hadn't already spent a good twenty-four hours together.

"Where are we?" he asked after a moment.

"A few hours away from San Francisco," I said. "How'd you sleep?"

He blinked and rubbed his eyes, looking out the window at the passing landscape. "You didn't drop me off in Nevada," he said.

"Huh?"

He flashed a smile and sat up a little straighter. "Oh, I just expected you to get rid of me long before now."

"Why would I do that?"

"Because you don't know me and you picked me up off the side of the road. Do you need to switch places again? I'm happy to—"

"Don't worry about it," I said, and I meant it. Now that he was awake and we were actually *in* California, I could make the rest of the drive easily. I could see the light at the end of this particular tunnel, which had given me a boost of energy. "Just promise you won't fall asleep again, or I'll die of boredom."

"Happily," he replied.

We were both quiet for a moment, watching the trees fly by, and I figured then was as good a time as any to say what had been running through my head all day. "I owe you one," I said and glanced his way.

He lifted one of those expressive eyebrows then shifted a little so he was facing me a bit. "Oh? Why? You already paid me back for changing the tire."

I shrugged. "I don't know if I would have made it this far without you."

"But I haven't—"

"I'm terrified." *There. I said it.*

Biting his lip, Jack took a moment to study my face—which I kept facing directly forward—and then he asked, "To see your family?"

"Yeah." I glanced at the letter that was still sitting so innocently on the dash.

"Where exactly are they? San Fran proper, or one of the suburbs?"

I honestly didn't know, and my eyes strayed to the letter again because I desperately hoped the address it had come from was still valid. I would have hated to show up at some stranger's house claiming to be a long-lost sister only to find out my family had moved clear across the world six months ago. Why hadn't I just responded when I got the letter in the first place?

Jack must have seen my gaze, because he reached forward and grabbed the letter, scanning the address on the envelope with interest. "Lissa Montgomery," he read. "Whoa, is that where she lives? Does this mean you're related to rich people?"

I had no idea if it meant that, but I was more curious to know why Jack said "rich people" like it left a bad taste in his mouth. "I guess I'll find out when I get there," I said. "I didn't even know I was related to these people until a few years ago. Apparently my dad—my birth dad—was a bit of a…"

"Sower of wild oats?" Jack guessed, nothing but sympathy in his voice.

I sighed. "Yeah. And honestly, when my mom told me about it, I wasn't sure I could believe her. She and my dad—the one who raised me—are so happy together, and I couldn't even imagine she had a wilder past than I'd thought before. But then this letter showed up from my half-sister a year ago, and…"

"And it all became real," Jack finished for me. "So if you got the letter a year ago, why did you wait until now to go meet them? What changed?"

He was insightful for a skinny little homeless musician, I'd give him that. Shrugging, I figured it would just be easier if I spit out my whole life story. I wasn't ashamed of my life, but it wasn't the happiest or the most thrilling tale. I just didn't want him to keep asking questions that could potentially get harder than I wanted to answer. We still had a few hours before we hit San Francisco, and I didn't want those few hours to be completely awkward.

"So I went to UC Davis," I said and glanced at him to judge his reaction to my starting point. He was quiet and looked mildly interested, so I kept going. "Got a four-year degree like everyone else, and I figured I would be the next great ad-making person."

"Ad-making person?" he asked, a bit of laughter in the question. "You mean a marketer?"

My cheeks blossomed with heat. "Clearly words are not my strong suit," I replied. "I'm more of an emotional, visual kind of person. Anyway, I moved to San Francisco and got a job with one of the bajillion tech companies, and that was where I met Steve."

I gripped the steering wheel just a little bit tighter, since Steve Evans was the whole reason I had bad memories of San Francisco. I wasn't sure why this whole thing was relevant to Jack's initial question, but now that I was talking, I couldn't seem to stop. Apparently I should have talked about my life with more people than just Jordan and my mom.

"He was only a few years older than me," I said, "and pretty much the dreamiest guy I'd ever met. He was always off traveling the world and going on crazy adventures. Every guy wanted to be him, and every girl wanted to be *with* him, and for some reason he picked me. We started dating, he proposed a few years later, and everything was good."

"Until it wasn't," said Jack.

I glanced at him again, and though he was smiling as usual, there was more than enough sympathy in his expression to make me feel just a bit better. "Until it wasn't," I repeated. "Steve got in a motorcycle accident on his way home, and it left him almost completely blind. I tried to help him adjust and get back in the swing of things after he recovered, but he had pretty much given up on life. He shut me out, and I had to leave."

To my complete annoyance, tears welled up in my eyes, and I blinked them away before Jack noticed. It had been so long since I left Steve that it was frankly a little ridiculous to still be crying over him. *Years.* And there was still a part of me that missed him.

"Where'd you go then?" Jack asked. Thankfully, he ignored my sniffling if he noticed it. "Clearly you haven't been in California for a bit, so your story probably isn't over."

I shook my head. "I moved in with my parents again in Ohio, until I could get my footing and find a new job somewhere far away from San Francisco. I was grocery shopping a couple of weeks after I moved when I met Jordan."

"Is he the one who belongs to that?" Jack pointed at my hands on the steering wheel.

My eyes went wide when I realized I was wearing my wedding ring. I hadn't thought to take it off, not even after our court date when the divorce was finalized. Swallowing, I slipped the ring off my finger and tossed it into the center cubby thing before I started freaking out. *You're okay with the divorce*, I reminded myself. *It was for the best.*

"Yep," I croaked. "That was Jordan."

"Did Jordan get hit with a case of blindness too?"

I looked at Jack because I couldn't tell from his tone of voice what kind of question that was, and when I found him grinning at me and bouncing his eyebrows, I couldn't help but laugh. "Are you serious? You're going with a joke about me being pretty?"

"Only because you are, so it works."

"Wow." And yet, even though I knew he was joking, I found myself blushing. Jordan used to do that to me all the time because he thought it was funny how easily he could make me blush, and I really hoped Jack didn't discover the same thing. Otherwise, this was going to be a long three-hour drive.

Jack joined in my laughter, and then he said, "Sorry. I couldn't help it. But now I really want to know what happened with Jordan."

It was amazing how laughing could make me feel so much lighter and relaxed, and I silently thanked Jack for keeping my little story from getting too dramatic. Heaven knew I didn't need any more drama in my life. "Well," I said, "I married him."

"I figured that part out," he replied.

"And we just got divorced."

"Ouch."

I nodded.

"When?"

I sighed. "Tuesday. Then on Thursday, I lost my job. And Saturday, my parents moved to Denmark."

"And Monday, you picked up a strange guy who chooses really bad times to make jokes," Jack finished for me. "You've had quite the week."

"Tell me about it."

He shifted in his seat again, this time so he was pretty much facing me directly. "Okay, so I think I've got it all figured out. You lost just about everything but this delightful little Honda of yours, so now you're driving off to meet some unknown sister who, hopefully, is going to welcome you with open arms. Right?"

I gripped the steering wheel again. "That pretty much sums it up. And thanks for making me worry again that she might not let me in. It's probably been too long since she reached out, and it's not like she has any real reason to trust me. We might be related, but that doesn't mean a whole lot."

Oh boy. What if she didn't let me in? Her letter sounded friendly enough, but like I'd told Jack, words were not my forte. Maybe she had only sent the letter because she wanted to make it clear we might have been related but were definitely not family. Maybe she had sent it because she felt obligated. Maybe she had sent it because she was trying to get to my birth father's money or something, though I had no idea if he even had money, since I'd been too stunned by the whole thing to ever look him up. Maybe—

"Hey, Amelia?" Jack said.

I glanced at him. "What?"

"Relax."

I wanted to, but there were so many unknowns in this future of mine. I hated that feeling.

"Everything's going to be fine," Jack said.

"How do you know?"

His smile was warm, and he reached over and put his hand over mine, gently loosening my grip so I wasn't strangling the wheel anymore. "Because it always is."

Easy for you to say. But the longer I sat there with his hand on mine, the more I couldn't stand by my silent comment. Jack was literally homeless. He had been *walking* to California from Nashville, and as far as I could tell, the only things he owned were the clothes on his back and that guitar. If anyone had a right to say things weren't fine, it was him.

So how could he possibly think everything was okay?

Either he was so optimistic that nothing could darken his day, or he was crazy. Maybe he was a bit of both.

Letting out my breath slowly and intentionally, I let my muscles relax as I drove. If a man like Jack could look on the bright side of things, so could I. "Thanks," I said and gave him a quick smile. "I'm just freaking out a little, you know? But you're right. Everything will be fine."

"If she's even a remotely decent person," he replied, "your sister will be happy to see you. Family…" He frowned a little, which was an odd look for a man who seemed to constantly smile. "Family has to stick together."

Well there was a whole lot to unpack in that comment, but I had no idea where to start. He said his family was from California, but were they still there? He said he wanted to get back to his roots, but so far he hadn't been all too happy when talking about family. Something was going on there, and I wanted to know what it was. But how was a girl supposed to start that conversation?

Jack kept talking before I figured out an answer to that question: "Out of curiosity, do you have any idea what happened to Steve? Is he still in San Francisco?"

"Honestly, I have no idea." I'd tried to find him on social media a couple of times, just to check up on him, but I realized that since he was blind he probably wouldn't be on the internet very much. I had scanned the obituaries once or twice and searched for his name, which horrified me every time I thought about it, but if he was still alive, he was probably still wasting away while his miserable life passed him by. "I hope he's okay," I whispered. "I probably shouldn't have left him in the first place, but he was being so…"

"Blind?" Jack said.

I laughed a little and brushed a tear from my cheek. I seriously needed to stop crying over that man. "Yeah. He couldn't see what was right in front of him, in every sense of the phrase."

"Maybe you can look him up," he suggested. "Just to make sure he's doing alright."

"Maybe," I said, though the thought made me a little queasy. If he was fine, then great. If he wasn't… I wasn't driving to San Francisco to try to take care of an ex-fiancé, and I had to remember that. There was a high chance I would want to help him if he needed me, and that would bring more misery than I could handle.

"I'll deal with that bridge when I get to it," I whispered to myself, and we slipped into a heavy silence as the coast grew steadily nearer.

San Francisco was a lot brighter than I remembered it. Even though it was later in the evening, the city seemed to reflect every bit of sunlight in my face, and it was both super annoying and wonderfully familiar. I could have sworn San Francisco was always overcast and gloomy, but that was probably just me projecting my bad memories onto the poor city that really hadn't done anything wrong.

As we drove across the Bay Bridge, Jack was glued to the window and seemed fascinated by all of it. Even when we got inside the city, he was completely silent as he took in the buildings and the trolleys

and the endless hills that I had always kind of hated. I had much pre-
ferred Chicago simply because it was relatively flat.

"Have you ever been here?" I asked Jack, smiling a little as he
craned his neck to get a glimpse of Chinatown as we passed.

"Nah," he said into the window. "I've always been an Easterner."

"Is this your first time in a big city?" Based on the way he seemed
fascinated by the sheer number of people walking the streets, I worried
what would happen when he set off on his own.

Snorting a laugh, he glanced at me then returned to looking out the
window. "Well, I grew up in Manhattan, so…"

"Oh."

He was from New York? He didn't look like he was from New
York. I'd only been there a couple of times—with Steve, unfortunately,
to visit his mom before she moved to Florida—but I'd thought I had
a pretty good idea of what New Yorkers were like. Jack seemed too
cheery and, well, nice. Nobody I'd met in Manhattan acted the way
Jack did.

"Is that where your family lives now?" I asked.

"You know what," Jack said as we came to a stop light, and he
unlatched his seatbelt. "This looks like a pretty good corner. You can
just drop me off right here."

My stomach seemed to do a somersault. "Wait, what?"

But he was already getting out of the car and opening the back door
to grab his guitar. "Thank you so much for the ride," he said through
the open door. "I had fun. Good luck with your family, and maybe I'll
see you around the city." He shut the door before I could say anything,
and the car behind me honked to tell me the light had turned green.

I had no choice but to keep moving, and though I was tempted to
take a few turns and come back to the corner, I told myself there wasn't
any point. I hadn't come to San Francisco for Jack any more than I'd
come for Steve, and I had to stay on task before it got too late. I
definitely didn't have enough money to afford a hotel room in the city,
so if I couldn't sleep on my half-sister's couch, I would have to drive
farther south and find somewhere cheaper. I was still exhausted, and
if I was going to have to make that drive, it would be better to make it
sooner than later.

Though my thoughts still lingered on Jack, I plugged the address on the envelope of Lissa's letter into my phone, silently thanking Jordan for forgetting to cancel my data plan before he'd been charged for this month, and then I took several deep breaths, psyching myself up for this next part.

"You can do this," I said out loud as I drove up a rather steep hill. "It's not like you're expecting anything from her, except maybe a couch for the night, and if she's not there, you'll just drive down to San Jose and find a motel. And then…" My stomach twisted into a knot.

And then I would have to figure out what was going to happen next. I had gotten myself this far, and I didn't have the energy—or the money—to go backward. I just had to move forward, no matter what happened next.

Lissa's townhome was, quite frankly, the prettiest thing I'd ever seen in this city. I'd thought the house I shared with Steve was nice, but this was in a whole different league. It was more downtown than I would have expected, but that only made its facade that much more beautiful. I couldn't have named any of the features, but the golden hues of the paneling and the warm lights glowing from the curtained windows made me feel like I was coming home.

"Please be my sister and not a random millionaire bachelor looking for his third wife," I prayed out loud as I parked. I had already fallen in love with the house, and I feared it would break me entirely if I couldn't at the very least take a step inside.

My hands were shaking as I stepped up to the front door, and I knew I was an absolute mess. But now that I was standing there, I was too afraid to go back to my car and quickly change into my last pair of clean clothes. If Lissa still lived here, and she really was family, hopefully that meant she wouldn't care what I looked like.

"Knock," I said out loud, but I stood frozen. "Come on, Amelia, all you have to do is knock."

I should have written back before I came. I should have looked up her phone number and called to let her know I was coming into town. What was I thinking, showing up out of the blue like this? Clearly, I wasn't thinking at all.

"For goodness' sake, just knock!" I almost shouted then rapped three times before I could run.

My knock was answered by a single dog bark.

That alone made me feel just a little bit better. If Lissa was a dog person, that meant we had at least one thing in common.

I might have stood there waiting for twenty seconds or an hour—I had no idea. But when the door finally opened, bathing me in light, I felt like I was ready to pass out in my panic.

I saw the retriever first, the prettiest dog I had ever seen. His golden fur looked like it was made from angel hair and sunbeams and was probably the softest thing in the world. He smiled up at me from between the legs of the woman who stood at the door, and as much as I wanted to just spend the rest of my life smiling back at such a gorgeous dog, I forced myself to look up—literally up because she was probably six inches taller than me—into the face of a woman who could only be my half-sister, Lissa.

Mom had described my father to me once, when she was trying to convince me that he actually existed and she wasn't just trying to prank me. She said he was tall and blonde and more handsome than anyone she'd ever seen. Even more so than her husband, apparently, though she made me swear to never tell Dad. My father had eyes that were bluer than Hawaiian oceans and a smile that was worth a million bucks. He pretty much glowed.

Lissa was his spitting image, and the fact that she was several months pregnant seemed to make her glow even brighter than seemed humanly possible. She was absolutely beautiful, and suddenly I regretted not finding a shower or at the very least changing my clothes. Would it really have been that difficult?

"Can I help you?" she asked, and even her voice was beautiful.

I swallowed. "Um, are you Lissa Montgomery?"

She only half smiled as she took me in, and the rest of her expression was wary. "It's Lissa Evans now," she said, "but yes."

I was suddenly dizzy. Evans wasn't exactly a rare name, and there was no possible way she could be related to my ex-fiancé, but it was hard not to draw crazy conclusions. "Um." I took a shaky breath. "I'm so sorry to bother you, and this is really, um, well, really rude of me to just drop by unannounced, but I'm—"

"Amelia?" said a deep voice from inside the house, and the world seemed to stop spinning as I stood there on the porch of the one person I least wanted to see.

Because there was my ex, Steve Evans, looking a million times better than I'd ever seen him and sliding his hand into Lissa's as he squinted at me with eyes that couldn't see.

CHAPTER FOUR

If I weren't sitting on the most comfortable couch I'd ever sat on and hugging the fluffiest pillow and petting the sweetest dog, I would have been screaming. I honestly couldn't have said how I'd gotten to this moment, but I vaguely remembered Lissa taking my arm and pulling me inside, then Steve tripping over a rug and sitting down in an armchair for safety, then me sinking onto the couch in the ridiculously nice living room while the two of them had a whispered conversation I didn't even try to overhear.

And now I was here, very slowly coming back to reality and realizing that no, this wasn't a dream, and yes, that was the same Steve Evans that I had almost married. And my half-sister, bless her heart, was doing her very best to keep calm as she sat in between the two of us. Her smile wasn't remotely real, but that didn't stop her from using it, and she had offered me more food and water than I could have consumed in a lifetime if I weren't too shocked to accept it.

Now that I could think again, I wasn't feeling any better about the situation. Steve looked *so good*. He'd always been happy and healthy before the accident, but this was a new level. This was a man who had everything he could possibly want and was thriving. He was thriving even though he was *blind*. And what was I doing? I was most definitely getting dirt on his fancy couch because I had spent the last day and a half traveling across the country in a mud-soaked car.

It had been over a week since I last washed my hair, and that fact was becoming more and more apparent the longer I sat here.

"So, Amelia," Lissa said, and her voice was strained as she tried to sound calm and happy. "What brings you back to California?" She glanced at Steve when he looked in her direction and furrowed his eyebrows, and then she rolled her eyes. "Okay, fine," she said half an octave lower. "This is all sorts of weird. I know."

"What are you doing here, Ames?" Steve asked.

I squished the pillow in my arms a little tighter. Why did he sound so angry? "Well," I squeaked. I coughed and tried again. "Lissa sent me a letter."

"That was over a year ago," he replied roughly. "You just show up here out of the blue?"

"I didn't know *you* were going to be here," I snapped back.

Steve scowled.

"Okay," Lissa said, holding out one hand in front of me and grabbing Steve's with the other. "Let's just all calm down, okay? There's nothing wrong with Amelia stopping by for a visit."

"That's not why she's here," Steve growled.

Lissa looked at me as if hoping for some explanation, but I was just as confused as she was. She must have read that in my face, because she turned back to her husband and said, "What do you mean?"

Steve turned his gaze to me, and even though it was unfocused, I could still feel it digging into me. He'd used that look on me before, whenever he thought I was hiding something from him, and it had completely ruined his surprise birthday party one year because it had pressured me into telling him everything. "What happened?" he asked.

"Steve?" Lissa asked, and she looked ready to drag him into the other room and get mad at him for being rude.

I would have hated to be the cause of marital distress, so I answered Steve's question before he could answer Lissa's. "Jordan left me," I said, and I barely managed to whisper it. That could have been because Steve was just as strong and intimidating as ever, but it was most likely because of my tears that came out of nowhere.

Next thing I knew, I was being engulfed in Lissa's arms in the sort of hug I had always imagined a sister would give. One that said it didn't matter if the whole world was against me because she would always be on my side. And without her even saying a word, I was suddenly telling Lissa everything.

By the time I'd finished my tale of woe, Lissa had slid to a more respectable distance but still kept her arm around me, the dog had his head resting on my knees, and Steve was sitting so low in his chair that I worried he was going to slide out and onto the floor. He still looked angry, but it was a different sort of anger now. It was the kind that made me wonder what he would do if he could see and if Jordan was in the room with us. Was it wrong to imagine my two exes battling it out over me?

Probably.

"You must be exhausted," Lissa said, and she stroked my hair only to pull her hand away with a clump of mud between her fingers.

"Sorry," I said and sniffed, and for some reason I wished Jack were here so he could laugh about the mud with me. However much of a mess I had been when he found me trying to change my tire, I was pretty sure this moment on Lissa's couch was even worse. "It's been a long few days."

Glancing at her watch, Lissa looked over at Steve, who had sat there silently staring at the floor during my whole story, and then she seemed to make a decision. "How about you go upstairs and take a shower?" she suggested, taking my hand and helping me to my feet. "I'm knee-deep in maternity clothes right now, but I'm sure I can find some of my regular clothes that'll fit you."

Steve suddenly snorted, and his whole countenance changed. "You do remember when Brennon wore Seth's pants, right?" he asked his wife. "This'll be worse."

I figured he was talking about his best friend, Brennon Ashworth, but I had no idea who Seth was. Still, I could figure out what he meant. Lissa was a lot taller than me and more athletically built; I would drown in her clothes.

"I have a few things out in the car," I said. And I sounded just as small as I felt. This little family reunion wasn't going how I imagined it at all, which was saying something because I'd spent the last several days running through every scenario I could think of. Not a single one of those, however, had included Steve. He'd thrown off the whole equation.

"I have a better idea," Steve said. He was suddenly so much warmer, and I could feel Lissa relaxing beside me. He probably had no idea how anxious he was making her by being so hard-edged before. Pulling out his phone, he tapped the screen and said, "Call Goliath," then lifted it to his ear.

"Why didn't I think of that?" Lissa said and hooked her arm through mine. "Of course you should meet Seth!"

"More importantly," Steve added, "his wife is a little closer to Amelia's size. Hey Sasquatch," he said into the phone, "tell your better half to grab some clothes she doesn't want anymore and get over here." He grinned as he listened to the person on the other end. "Because I said so. Fine. Because Lissa said so."

He rolled his eyes, but Lissa was trying not to laugh, so I figured this was normal behavior.

"How about this?" Steve said after a moment. "I've got *both* of your little sisters sitting in my living room, and one of them is in desperate need of something to wear that isn't covered in mud. Yeah, that's what I thought." He hung up then grinned at the pair of us. "Seth'll be here in twenty minutes. Plenty of time for you to take that shower."

"And I'll bring those clothes up when Catherine gets here," Lissa added, guiding me out of the room and up the gorgeous staircase.

Only when we reached the bathroom did something click in my mind. "Wait," I said, turning to her. "Who's Seth? Is he…?"

Lissa smiled. "I guess I forgot to mention him in that letter I sent, huh? He's my half-brother. *Our* half-brother. The one and only Seth Hastings."

I could have been imagining it, but I was pretty sure I'd heard that name before. "Isn't that the name of that soldier a few years ago who took down a whole terrorist group on his own?" I asked.

Grabbing a towel from a closet in the hallway, Lissa handed it to me and replied, "Well, he had a little help."

I nearly dropped the towel. *It's true?* "We're related to Captain America?"

Lissa laughed as she pushed the bathroom door open for me. "Oh, Seth would *love* it if he heard you called him that. But Steve might never talk to you again, so you might want to choose your words carefully." She gestured to the shower. "Okay, so the knob on the shower is a little finicky, so just turn it all the way to hot then back to whatever temperature you want. I'll be right downstairs, so just call down if you need anything."

She shut the door before I could reply, and I glanced at myself in the giant mirror as I tried to figure out how I had suddenly stepped into a whole different dimension. Steve aside, in all my scenarios I had never imagined there would be more to this family of mine than Lissa. Never mind the likes of Seth Hastings, who was the sort of person I read about in magazines at the dentist. Was I actually related to a real-life superhero?

I had planned for Lissa. Maybe her parents, maybe a husband and some kids. I certainly hadn't planned for Steve, definitely not Steve expecting a baby, and Seth was a surprise. But with Seth came a wife, and that wife would have family of her own. I was barely holding myself together, and I really wasn't sure how long that was going to last. Lissa was so nice, and Steve seemed to be calming down and returning to something closer to the man I knew before the accident. Their house was incredible and comfortable and welcoming, not to mention they had the sweetest dog on the planet.

As far as families went, this one seemed pretty darn spectacular.

I stood there in the bathroom and stared at my weary face in the mirror, wondering how long it would be before I woke up and realized all of this was just a dream and I would eventually have to leave it all behind like I had everything else.

"Okay, that looks so much better on you than it did on me." Catherine Hastings said those words almost the instant I crept back into the living room after a long and rejuvenating shower, and I only had to take one look at her to convince myself it was a complete and utter lie. If I'd thought Lissa was pretty, it was nothing compared to the young woman who had offered up a portion of her wardrobe. Everything about her, from her dark hair to her makeup to the way she stood with the confidence of a queen, was perfect.

Then there was Seth, who was impossible to miss in the small room, since he took up half of it. Where Steve was intimidating, Seth was downright terrifying. Both his stature and his presence were huge, and it made perfect sense why he would be credited for taking down a terrorist group when all he had probably done was snarl a little to send them scurrying back to their holes. And if I hadn't known my father was somewhere in his fifties, I might have thought Seth was him, since he fit almost exactly the description my mom had given me, though he was probably a whole lot stronger than his dad. He had that sandy blonde hair, like Lissa's, and his eyes were such a vivid blue that they almost didn't look real.

Honestly, nothing about any of these people seemed real, even Steve. They were far too perfect, and I was starting to think I wasn't really related to them at all. My mom must have been wrong. Or delusional. Or…

"It's nice to see you looking clean," Steve said, breaking the silence that had followed Catherine's comment. He stepped forward, bumping into Seth's arm.

Seth surprised me by shoving Steve back onto the couch where he'd been sitting. "You can't see at all," he growled then stalked toward me with his hand outstretched.

I nearly ran back upstairs, since this giant of a man was sending me into a full-blown panic just by existing in such a cold-spirited state. But then Steve started to laugh, and Catherine grabbed her husband's arm before he got close enough to touch me.

"Seth," she said gently, while Steve got back to his feet and moved to Seth's other side so the giant was hedged up by the two of them. "You have your soldier face on."

"You're going to scare her away with that hideous mug of yours," Steve added.

Seth's fingers curled into fists, and he looked ready to shove Steve onto the couch again. But he glanced at me and took a deep breath, holding it for a few seconds before letting it go. All of my tension seemed to go at the same time his breath did, and for a moment I couldn't figure out why. But then I looked at Seth again and realized he was suddenly nowhere near as fearsome as he'd been a moment ago. He looked almost sheepish as he slid his hands into his pockets and hunched his shoulders to make himself a little smaller.

"Sorry," he said, and his voice was soft. Safe. "You can blame Evans for putting me in a bad mood."

"You're always in a bad mood," Steve replied, reaching his hand behind him.

Lissa grabbed it and joined him, creating a line of the four of them that made me feel like they were appraising me for auction.

"I'm Seth," Seth said, and when he held out his hand to me this time, it didn't look like he was about to grab me and throw me to the ground. His fingers were warm when I grasped them, and his smile was even more so. "I'm the Hastings Mongrel Number One, and Blondie over there is Number Two."

"So I'm Number Three?" I asked hesitantly.

Seth shrugged one shoulder. "So far, but there's always a chance you could get booted. Dad is still trying to round up potential candidates, but he'll be the first to admit he can't remember all his good times."

Seth made it sound like we were participation trophies, not children, and I didn't understand how he could be so calm about it. I glanced at Lissa, hoping for something more reassuring, and she gave me a warm smile.

"Don't worry about it too much," she said. "Dad has actually gotten pretty decent over the last couple of years."

"Which is really unfair, if you think about it," Seth replied. "I had to deal with the awful Gordon for thirty years, and you got the good stuff."

"Says the man who got a BMW for his sixteenth birthday and never had to take out student loans," Lissa shot back.

"Well—"

"Yeah, yeah, we all had rough childhoods," Catherine cut in. "Can we save this fight for another time? Mostly because we all know I'll win, but also I think we're starting to overwhelm her."

Her who? Oh, her me. I swallowed and tried to put on a smile. "It's just been a long drive," I said, even though Catherine was completely right. Seth and Lissa were acting exactly like siblings should act, and Catherine and Steve were just as comfortable within the family that I was pretty sure strangers who saw these four would be able to tell in an instant this was a tight-knit, well-loving family.

"So, Amelia," Catherine said, and with her words everyone apparently heard some kind of cue and settled into seats, leaving me to take the armchair where Steve had been sitting earlier. "Lissa was telling me a little bit about what brought you here"—I glanced at Lissa and wondered just how much 'a little bit' was—"so what's next for you? Are you thinking of staying in San Francisco?"

I was too tired to come up with an answer that wasn't the blunt truth: "I hadn't thought it through this far," I said. "I wasn't even sure if Lissa still lived here, and I don't really know anyone else in the city."

Steve slowly reached for Lissa's hand again, which she'd rested on her pregnant belly, and though he was looking down at the ground, I could feel his focus on me. It was hard not to wonder what would have happened if I had stayed instead of running away. Would he have eventually pulled himself out of his depression, or was it Lissa who saved him? Would we still have gotten married? Would that have been me carrying his baby instead of my sister?

I swallowed those thoughts and looked away from the pair of them, focusing instead on Seth and Catherine, who both seemed to have caught something in my gaze and were doing their best not to look at Steve. This family was close enough that they probably knew all about our history, and I suddenly wanted to hide.

"Well," Catherine said, and she was clearly fighting for something to say that would continue the conversation before things got awkward.

"I'm going to call Ashworth," Seth said, pulling his phone from his pocket. "He might know where to find some good job openings, just in case."

"Indie has a community board in the shop," Catherine added. "She'd probably have some leads too. Maybe even for apartments. Lissa, can you call Lanna and ask her if—"

"Already on it," Lissa said, her phone at her ear, and soon all three of them were talking to these unknown people who were making me feel guilty because I didn't even know them and they were helping me.

Then there was Steve.

He may not have been able to see me, but he could have fooled me. He was looking right at me, his dark eyes penetrating deep beneath my defenses like they always used to. He drew a little closer to Lissa and frowned, and when his gaze shifted down to her stomach, I wanted to run because whether or not he was wondering the same things I was, I didn't want to come anywhere near messing things up for him or Lissa. He was happy, and he was exactly where he needed to be.

Our time together was long over.

Before I could get to my feet and sneak away, Lissa finished her phone call and left Steve to come up to my side. "You hungry?" she asked, even though she'd already asked that many times tonight. Without even waiting for a response, she took my hand and gently tugged me out of the room.

I opened my mouth to apologize and tell her I was leaving, but she beat me to it and said: "I know this is a lot to take in. And Seth can be intimidating even on the best of days. But he's the best brother in the world, and if you leave, he'll just track you down."

I didn't doubt her, and I folded my arms tight, wishing I had just stayed back in… Where? My childhood home in Ohio was sold and gone. I didn't have anywhere in Chicago but Jordan's large house. And I'd never lived anywhere else but here in San Francisco.

I had nothing.

"Look," Lissa said, and she leaned close. "Our family is all sorts of messed up. I know that. And it can take a long time to get used to all of this. But we're really glad you came and found us."

Were they? Seth seemed to think being the child of Gordon Hastings was a curse, and Lissa wasn't nearly as friendly toward me as she'd been at the beginning. Before she remembered my connection to her husband.

Sighing, Lissa took a step back so we were no longer shoulder to shoulder. "I don't want things to be weird between us," she said, as if reading my thoughts. "With Steve, I mean. You took care of him as much as you could, and I will always be grateful for that because other- wise I might never have met him. I just…" She took a deep breath and touched a hand to her belly, and I was pretty sure she wasn't even aware she was doing it. "You didn't come here for him, did you?"

Had she been wanting to ask that question all night? Probably. And when I glanced into the living room, where Steve was sitting and staring at the floor while Seth and Catherine continued their phone conversa- tions, I wondered if he could hear us all the way out here. He'd learned to rely on his hearing a lot more after the accident, and that had probably only improved over time.

Did I want him to hear what I had to say? I didn't know. But I knew I had to say it. "Honestly," I said, "if I had known Steve was here, I never would have come at all."

Those words made me feel terrible, no matter how true they were, but Lissa brightened and wrapped her hand around mine as if every- thing were fine now. "Come on," she said cheerfully and pulled me back into the living room, even though I wanted to be anywhere but there. "I got you a place to stay, and I wouldn't be surprised if those two have already found you a job."

"Cool," I said, though it was anything but. All I'd wanted was to meet a half-sister and take a moment to breathe. And while I'd accom- plished that, I wasn't sure I had the strength to take everything else that apparently came with it.

CHAPTER FIVE

The next three days flew by in a whirlwind of job applications and apartment hunts and a toddler screaming for my attention because apparently I was so much more fun than any of the billion family members he had to play with. I'd been sleeping in a guest room at Catherine's cousin's house, which was the fanciest house I'd ever seen and put Lissa and Steve's little place to shame. Lanna and Adam Munroe were gracious hosts who were way too happy to make me dinner and offer old clothes to wear and speak words of encouragement every other sentence, and their youngest son, Harry, had decided we were best friends, which meant I got very little alone time when I was at the mansion.

They were wonderful, but it was way too overwhelming, so I was more than glad when I finally found an apartment that wasn't crazy expensive, since I was still looking for a job.

I had figured the job would have to be the first thing to come, since I couldn't pay a first month's rent with no income, but on the morning after I arrived in San Francisco, I had checked my bank account to see what I had left and was alarmed to see an obscene amount of money in there. I was so sure that it was a mistake that I brought it up with Lissa, but she smiled and said Seth had gotten in contact with our dad the night before, and Gordon Hastings had been quick to show his support.

Honestly, I wouldn't have even considered touching the money if I didn't need it to put a deposit down on a place to live. The very moment I made enough to return it, I would be sure to pay Gordon back and let him know that I had not come to California for his charity. No, I had come to find family and start over again. And I didn't need him in order to do that.

Catherine came with me to sign the lease on my little apartment, and I was glad she was willing to leave work to help me out. She worked for the FBI, she told me, and it was nice to get a break sometimes, since the longer she was there the more stressful things seemed to get.

"I love what I do," she told me as we walked down the street in the summer sunshine, "but now I understand why Seth was eager to leave the military and start working for Adam. My job doesn't make life any easier."

My terrifying super-soldier brother was a bodyguard now, protecting Catherine's cousin-in-law, Adam Munroe, and apparently they made a great pair. Adam was called "The King of Art" because he was California's top art dealer, and Seth was almost just as business savvy and helped him make some incredible acquisitions and sales. I had seen some of the paintings they'd collected, since they hung in Adam and Lanna's house where I was staying, and they really knew what they were doing.

I hooked my arm through Catherine's and took a deep breath. "Thanks for coming," I told her yet again. "I've never actually had to find an apartment by myself, and it's more intimidating than I expected."

Pulling me close, she smiled her breathtaking smile and replied, "Anything for family, right? I'm just glad you'll be fairly close to Seth and me!"

I was glad my new apartment was nowhere near Steve's house.

We were only a block away from the apartment building when something caught my ear. Music? Pausing, I searched for the source. In the several years I had lived in this city before, I'd never heard music, and I wondered where it was coming from. It wasn't any of the cars driving past, nor did it seem to be coming from any of the nearby office buildings.

"What is that?" I wondered out loud and veered up the wrong street, dragging Catherine with me. The guitar music seemed to fill the air with magic, bringing a strange sense of life to the otherwise dull city street, and though the voice that sang along with it was soft, it was deep and velvety and amazing.

"Must be a street performer," Catherine said, and thankfully she seemed willing to take this little detour with me. We didn't have to be at the apartment for another fifteen minutes, anyway, and I wanted to see who was able to play so well that I wasn't the only person drawn in this direction.

It seemed San Francisco had its own Pied Piper.

The crowd was decently large around the musician, who was hidden from my view, but the closer I got, the more I wanted to see who was playing. So even though Catherine slipped out of my hold when I started pushing my way through people, I just kept moving forward until I made it to the front and got a good look at the guy.

"Jack!" I said in surprise.

He must have heard me, because he grinned at the sound of his name, but he kept his eyes on his guitar as he stroked the strings and sang a song that was so hauntingly beautiful that it had transfixed the crowd, who watched in silence. I barely even understood the words he was singing because I was more focused on the melody and the way he seemed to put his whole soul into the song, like it was lifegiving in a way nothing else could be.

He was amazing.

When his fingers plucked the last few notes, he stood motionless for a second, as if letting the song fully leave him, and then he looked up and met my eye at the same time the crowd broke into applause. A moment later, when they realized he was done playing, the crowd started to disperse, and Jack still smiled at me even though several people dropped money into the open guitar case at his feet.

"Hi," I said when most of the crowd was gone.

"Hey," he replied. "Looks like you found your fam. Is that your sister?"

I glanced back at Catherine, who had decided to keep her distance even though most of the people were gone. "Sister-in-law, actually. Turns out I have a brother too."

Jack was eyeing Catherine carefully, which I'd come to learn was pretty standard when it came to her. She'd spent her young adult life working to get attention, and even though she no longer actively sought it, she still managed to turn heads wherever she went. "Rich people?" he guessed and flashed his crooked smile.

"Yeah, but they're the nice kind." Almost *too* nice, and I was glad I was finally getting my own place to live so I could stop preying on Lanna and Adam's charity. "Your guitar is beautiful," I said next, before we slipped into an awkward silence.

Glancing down at it, Jack nodded. "I probably paid more for it than it's worth, but it's served me well so far."

It really was a gorgeous instrument, and I had a feeling it was worth more than he was giving it credit. I was infinitely glad I hadn't let him walk all the way here to California, because there was a high chance it could have gotten hurt on the long journey.

"You play really well. You're probably better than playing on street corners."

He shrugged, his ever-present smile just as warm as always. "Maybe," he said, "but I have to start somewhere. I'll get there eventually, and this'll be enough to buy me a bed for the night." He tapped his toe against the guitar case and made the coins inside jingle a bit. "Maybe even get some dinner, if I play long enough. This seems to be a good corner. Looks like I'm up!"

He flashed me a grin then turned to a few people who were walking up the street, and when he started to play, he pulled them to a stop with just a few measures of music because he was just so good.

I could have stood there all day and listened to him play, but I reluctantly wandered back to Catherine, though not without throwing Jack one more glance. I hoped he could do well here. At least make more than a few bucks in change.

"So who was that?" Catherine asked as we started back down the street.

I could hear the extra questions in her voice, and I tried not to let her read too much on my face. "I gave him a ride from Kansas," I said, though I was tempted to keep quiet so I could hear the last little bits of his song before we got too far away. "He's a nice guy."

"Normally I would get mad at you for picking up a hitchhiker, and maybe don't tell Seth about it, but he does seem like a nice guy. And a really good guitar player."

Really good didn't exactly cover it, but I just smiled and followed her into my new apartment building. It was nice to know Jack had a fighting chance, and both of us would hopefully find a new start in this city that had pulled us across the country.

CHAPTER SIX

The day after I signed the lease for my apartment and moved in with my few belongings, I managed to get myself an interview with a company in need of a graphic designer, and it went better than I could have hoped. I said all the right things and asked all the right questions, and the three people who met with me all expressed their enthusiasm for me joining their team. The company was in a building not too far from my apartment, so I would be able to walk to work if I left early enough, therefore saving on gas and parking, and the pay was pretty decent. They were a smaller company, but they assured me they were planning to grow a lot over the next few years and hoped I could help them do it.

They offered me the job on the spot.

I told them I would think about it.

I left with the weirdest feeling in my stomach, and I really didn't know why I didn't just accept the offer and finally start making some money so I could stop freeloading. It was a perfect job for me, one I was actually qualified for, and everyone in the company was friendly and welcoming, something I pretty much craved when it came to jobs. But even though logically it made sense to say yes, something had stopped me.

I wished I knew what it was.

Since I didn't have anywhere I needed to be, and my little apartment was pretty cold and bare, I took to wandering the streets. The sun was bright and warm, and San Francisco had slowly been growing on me again. Except for those rare moments I had been around Steve, life here was pretty good. Comfortable. I really liked getting to know Seth and Lissa better, and I was starting to feel like myself again.

"Why don't you want this job?" I asked out loud and was glad no one was near enough to hear me talking to myself as I walked. "Have you lost your mind, Amelia?" I probably had. Maybe everything with Jordan and Steve and my parents and all of it had just been too much and had broken down my ability to think rationally.

Though I tended to be more driven by emotion if I wasn't careful, I liked to think I was pretty logical. But there was just something about that job that didn't feel quite right. I couldn't put any words to it, but I wasn't sure if I was meant to work with them, no matter how great they were.

"Next thing you know you'll start checking your horoscope every morning before you leave the house," I muttered and sat down on a bus stop bench so I could try to think things through. I didn't believe in a higher power, really, nor in the idea of fate or destiny. Everything I had in my life had just come from circumstance or my own choices, and it was ridiculous to think there could be something pulling the strings.

And yet…

I sighed and got back up, deciding I had best go home and start researching other jobs. If I was really going to listen to my gut or what-ever this feeling was, I would need another option. There were still a few companies who hadn't gotten back to me after I sent in my resumé, and I had mostly been focusing on the general marketing side of things. There had to be some advertising-specific jobs out there I could try for.

I heard the guitar only a block later and turned without thinking, following the sound and surprised to find myself hoping it was Jack. I really didn't know the guy, and I couldn't exactly call him my friend at this point, but I was still eager to see him again. It was probably just because of his skill on that guitar, but still. His music called me up a hill to the edge of Lafayette Park.

And there he was, still wearing the same black t-shirt and jeans that he'd been wearing since the day I met him. Jack had an even bigger crowd around him than the last time I'd seen him, and since he stood on a little hill, everyone could see him better.

Smart, I thought and moved in closer. He would do better to get some more clothes, though, since I could see bits of mud on the cuffs of his pants still, which meant he hadn't been able to wash them well, if at all. "And you need a haircut," I muttered with a frown. It was falling over his eyes as he bent over his guitar, and his icy blues were worth seeing.

The crowd applauded as he finished his song, and he barely acknowledged them, just glancing around and offering a little half-smile that wasn't nearly up to par with what I knew he could do. And when the clapping stopped, he jumped right back into playing.

"Come on, man," I muttered with a grimace. "At least say thank you."

The idea struck me at the same time he glanced up and caught my eye, and though he smiled when he recognized me, I couldn't bring myself to smile back. Jack had so much potential, and his music was worth sharing. But he clearly had no idea how to make his music worth money, and he couldn't just play for spare change the rest of his life. He needed someone who could help him meet his full potential, someone who could help his image and his crowd sense, maybe even get him some gigs in actual buildings instead of parks benches and street corners.

I waited until he finished his song, and then I walked up to him with a determination I didn't realize I would have when it came to something like this. I wasn't usually this strong-willed or spontaneous, but if I was going to start following my gut, I might as well do it whole-heartedly.

"Hi," he said when I reached him.

"I want to be your manager," I replied.

He'd been about to start playing again, but his fingers froze over the strings. "What?" he asked, looking up at me. Yeah, he definitely needed to use those piercing eyes to his advantage. It felt like he could see right through me in the best possible way.

"Your manager," I repeated. "You know, tell you what to wear and how to do your hair and when to play and stop and all that."

He glanced at the dispersing crowd, looking slightly disappointed that his audience was leaving but still managing to smile when he returned his focus to me. "You want to tell me what to do?"

I really couldn't decide what he thought about that idea, but I nodded anyway. "Look, I need a job, and you need someone to help you get more than…" I glanced into his case and quickly counted. "Sixteen dollars or so. You're better than that."

"You said that last time," he said, his smile growing.

It was probably time for me to plead my case before he decided to stop talking to me, and I took a deep breath to clear my thoughts. "I may not be good with words all the time, but I know how to make a man look good. I spent two years making the head of that tech company here in San Francisco look the part of billionaire CEO, because when I started at that company, he thought it was a good idea to wear turtle-necks and chew tobacco at public events."

"And you think I don't know how to look like a starving musician?" Jack asked with a slight laugh.

I looked him over. "That's the problem. You *do* know how to look that part, so that's all you're ever going to be. Unless you want to be playing on street corners for the rest of your life, you're going to need some help."

"Maybe this is why Nashville wasn't kind to me," he said and pulled his guitar off his shoulders to set it in the case. "So you think you can turn me into some fancy, famous performer by giving me a makeover?" He gestured for me to sit on a bench behind him then sat next to me, curling one leg up beneath him so he could face me. "What's in it for you?"

I shrugged. "Honestly, probably not a lot unless you start playing some high-paying gigs."

His smile twisted into the crooked one he used when he was extra amused. "You confuse me, Ms. Blake. Why would you want to help me?"

Because your music could save the world. "Because I think you're worth investing some time into. And I don't have a job at the moment, so I have plenty of time to spare."

I could live off of my father's money for just a little bit longer, until Jack started making some actual money and I could take part of the cut. I would have to look into how to create a contract, but for now it didn't really matter. We were both dirt poor, so there wasn't a whole lot either of us could lose.

"Come on," I said to Jack, since he seemed to be taking a really long time to think it over. It wasn't like he was doing anything else with his time here in the city. "This is the first thing I've come across in months that actually sounds like fun, and at least this way you'll know you'll always have at least one person in your audience."

He narrowed his eyes a little. "You really want to do this, don't you?"

If I had to start begging, I would, but this wasn't all about me. "You could be doing so much more, Jack. The world needs to hear your music."

"Okay," he replied and brushed his black hair out of his face.
I blinked. "What?"
And Jack grinned, looking out over the bay just beyond the city as he tried not to laugh. "You can be my manager," he clarified. "Until you get yourself a real job. I wouldn't mind sharing my music with more people, and if anyone can make me look better, I'm sure you can."

I ducked down to reach into my purse, mostly to grab my phone to take some notes but also to hide the blush that spread across my cheeks. Why was it so hard to keep myself from doing that? He hadn't even said anything particularly flattering.

"So the first thing we need to do is figure out who you are," I said.

Jack frowned as I straightened back up, and it was strange again to see him without his signature smile. "Meaning?" he asked, and his lips pressed into a tight line.

I rolled my eyes. "Meaning I can't just walk onto a stage and say, 'Here's Jack!' What's your last name?"

He took a lot longer to answer than he should have. "Let's go with Thorn."

That clearly wasn't his real name, but at least it had a nice ring to it. Maybe his actual name was something like Zebrowski, which was a lovely name but not exactly stage-worthy for the California scene. "Jackson Thorn," I said thoughtfully. "I can work with that."

"Good."

"And then there's this." I gestured vaguely at him.

He glanced down at his clothes, bringing his smile back. "What, you don't like what I'm wearing?"

"At this point I'm a little afraid your clothes are going to disintegrate the next time you put them in a washing machine," I said. "Besides, it's a little too punk rock for the kind of music you play."

Grinning now, he reached for his guitar and hoisted it onto his lap, and then he started playing a song I recognized from high school but couldn't name, especially because it sounded so different on an acoustic guitar that if I hadn't just said the words *punk rock*, I might have thought it was more along the lines of a classic rock love ballad.

"I could be punk," he said and winked at me.

I laughed and grabbed the neck of the guitar before he started playing anything else. I needed to concentrate. "I'm still going to argue that you're not, which means we…" I groaned inwardly and thought about how much I was going to have to pay Gordon back when I finally started getting my own money. "We're going shopping," I said, trying to say it with gusto so Jack would think I was excited about the idea. "And getting you a haircut," I added as his hair fell into his eyes again. The hairstyle was a decade old and not doing him any favors.

"Whatever you say, boss," he replied, and he grinned at me with a smile as warm as the sun.

Within a few days of my agreement with Jack, I was starting to get a little desperate. I hadn't been back in the city long enough to know the more popular eateries and music venues, and my internet searching hadn't done me a lot of good. Even if I found places where I could book Jack, no one was interested in a completely unknown, especially one whose manager was just as inexperienced.

I had told Jack to stay easy to find, since he didn't have a phone, but as yet I hadn't had a reason to seek him out. I didn't want to have to tell him that I was already a terrible manager and he was probably better off without me. At least for now he could keep playing those street corners, and maybe something would turn up before long.

"I hope," I muttered before knocking on Seth's door. I would have gone to Lissa for help, since she would be less protective about me working with a vagrant I had known for a week and a half, but she was busy with the restaurant she and Steve ran, and I was still trying to avoid Steve as much as I could. Besides, I figured if anyone knew the ins and outs of this city, Seth and Catherine would. They seemed to live for the social scene.

"Amelia!" Catherine greeted when she opened the door. "Come on in! How did your interview go?"

It was the best interview I've ever had, so I turned it down. "It didn't work out," I said with a shrug. I sat next to her on the couch and tried not to look as desperate as I felt. If this didn't work, I was really going to have to knuckle down and find myself a job, and that would require knowing what I wanted to look for. That was becoming harder and harder as the days went on.

Catherine gave me a sympathetic smile then patted my hand. "That's okay," she said. "You'll find something soon."

"Actually…" I gulped as Seth walked into the room. He may have been my brother, but the guy was seriously frightening until he remembered to smile a bit. "I think I might have already found something," I said, "but I need your help."

"Something as in a job?" Seth asked and plopped into an armchair. "Did you find a marketing gig?"

"Sort of?" This was the scary part. In order to get help from them, I had to explain the situation, and that could go a number of different ways when it came to Seth. I could only imagine how he would be if he thought I was putting myself in danger by working with Jack.

"So I have this friend," I said, watching Seth carefully. "We drove to California together."

I caught Catherine's look of warning, and unfortunately so did Seth.

"Friend?" he asked, sitting up straight. "And how long have you known this *friend*?"

Was it too late to change my mind? Probably. And unfortunately, I knew better than to try to lie. "Technically, we met on the road, but—"

"A hitchhiker?" Seth's voice was lower than normal, and the room seemed to chill with those words. "Amelia, are you out of your mind?"

Did he really think I was so incapable of taking care of myself? "I'm not stupid, Seth," I said. "I knew he wasn't dangerous."

"How?" he growled back. "How did you know? How do you know he won't do something now?"

"Not everyone is out for blood," Catherine tried.

Seth waved her off and scooted forward so he was face-to-face with me, a whole lot scarier than I liked him. "Keep talking," he ordered.

I swallowed. "He's a musician," I squeaked. "And he's amazing, but he needs help with the whole promotion part of things. That's where I come in."

"So this isn't even an actual job," Seth replied. "That's great."

For crying out loud, it wasn't like I was signing my life over to some stranger. "Seth, it's not a big deal."

"What's his name?"

"That's not impo—"

"Tell me his name, Amelia."

"Jack."

"Jack what?"

I had to laugh a little. "I don't know," I said and silently dared him to think I was lying about that part. "And I don't care. I'm not telling you about him so you can do a background check or have him followed or whatever it is you think you need to do. I'm telling you about him because I need your help finding him places to play."

"And why would I do that?" Seth growled.

"Seth!" Catherine said, and for the first time since I'd met her, she actually sounded angry. Even Seth was surprised, and his whole aggressive act shifted into sudden chagrin when he caught sight of her expression. Catherine took a slow breath, which was probably smart because she looked ready to shout or maybe be sick to her stomach, and then she said, "Stop being an idiot, okay? Amelia—*your sister*—needs your help. When are you going to learn that you can't control the people around you just because you want them to be safe? You can't plan for everything."

Seth's shoulders slumped, and he rubbed his hands over his face before turning back to me. He was only a few years older than me, but he looked like he'd already lived through enough for a couple of lifetimes. "I'm sorry, Amelia," he said, and it sounded like he actually meant it. "Too many bad things have happened to the people I care about, and the older I get, the more I realize there's only so much I can do." He looked at Catherine, who smiled back at him with a look that held a lot of meaning in it, though I had no idea what she was saying to her husband as she hugged her middle where she sat. "Life still knocks me off my feet, even when I think I'm ready for it."

"Oh, boo hoo," replied a man behind us, making all three of us jump.

Seth made it to his feet alarmingly fast before he got a good look at the guy standing in the open doorway, and then he sank back into his chair with a groan. "What is wrong with you, Davenport?"

"Door was unlocked," the other guy said with a smirk. "That's really dangerous, you know."

I hadn't met Catherine's cousin, Matthew Davenport, yet, but I instantly liked him because apparently he wasn't at all intimidated by my brother. I would have to ask him how he managed it, but for now I was just glad he had lightened the tension in the room. That, and the little girl he held in his arms was the cutest baby I had ever seen, and she smiled at me with several little teeth, her green eyes bright and happy beneath brown curls.

"I could have killed you, Matt," said Seth breathlessly, apparently still on edge from being surprised. I wouldn't think a guy like him could be so tense and anxious when he seemed so untouchable.

Catherine was on her feet in the next second, and Matthew happily handed his baby over to her as he laughed and said, "I would love to see you try. Artie just woke up from her nap, so she should be a handful for you tonight, just the way I like it."

"You're never a handful, are you, Artemis?" Catherine cooed as she hugged the baby.

Someone else came in through the door behind Matthew, a younger woman with jet black hair and the same eyes as little Artemis. She smiled as she took us all in. "She keeps threatening to start walking," she said. "Hey, Seth. Catherine, thanks for babysitting."

"Oh, anytime!" she replied. "You're the only ones who let me do it because Adam is too much in love with his own children to want to leave the house without them."

"So I see we've adopted another stray," Matthew said, and to my surprise, his eyes landed on me. "You must be the elusive Amelia we've been hearing about." Stepping forward, he smiled and shook my hand. He looked very much like his sister, Lanna, though his hair was darker like Catherine's, where Lanna was blonde. Overall, he had the face of someone who could brighten any room, and his smile was light and easy. A lot like Jack's. I had a feeling they would get along. "I'm Matthew," he said, "and this is my wife, Indie. That little ball of terror my cousin is fawning over is Artemis."

Indie rolled her eyes and stepped forward so she could pull me in for a hug that was surprisingly gentle and comforting. "Don't worry," she told me. "Lissa had that same look the first time she met the family. You'll get used to us eventually."

I wasn't so sure about that, especially when it seemed every other day there was someone new for me to meet. "I hope so," I managed to say.

Smiling even wider, she glanced behind her as Matthew and Seth started to get into an argument about whether or not Matthew could have gotten far enough into the house to touch Seth before he noticed him.

"Here's the important things you have to know," Indie said. "Adam and Lanna are the calm ones, kind of the mom and dad of the bunch. Catherine and Molly are the ones who know everything, and if you want to get something done, go to Colin and Beck. Brennon and Lissa can make anyone feel like they're the most important person in the world, and Seth is the protector, though you probably knew that one already. And Matthew is basically the glue that holds everyone together, but don't tell him that because his ego is big enough already."

I noticed she didn't include Steve in her list, and I wondered if that was because he didn't have a role or because she knew who she was talking to. "Where do you fit in?" I asked her.

She shrugged a little. "I'm still working on that part," she replied, and I instantly felt like I could find a dear friend in Indie. I'd only just met her, but she seemed to understand exactly how I felt.

"You, my darling," said Matthew as he slid his arm around Indie, "are the one who keeps the rest of us sane." He gently kissed the top of her head then said, "But you and my ego are going to miss our movie, so…"

With her face pink, Indie smiled at me again. "So it's time for us to get going. It was nice to meet you, Amelia. If you need anything, let me know. I've got this city on lockdown, and you'd be surprised by the things you can learn in a coffee shop."

"In other words," said Matthew, "Indie gets told more things than bartenders do, and that's saying something. She can get you information about anything, from a hitman to where to find a slam poetry night. Don't you dare start walking without us," he added and pointed at his daughter, who smiled back at him with a bit of mischief in her eyes, though she probably had no idea what he said.

An idea popped into my head, and even though they were heading out the door, I said, "What about a place where a new musician can play?"

Indie brightened as she looked back. "I've got a friend who has an open mic night every week in her bakery. I'll give you a call."

And though the door closed on our conversation, it felt like a very large door had just opened wide for me. Sure, an open mic night wasn't exactly a paid show, but I knew that as soon as people started hearing Jack's music, it wouldn't take long for the world to realize how great he really was. Tonight wasn't a waste of time after all.

"Now," Seth said and lifted the baby out of Catherine's arms. For a man as huge as he was, he was surprisingly gentle as he set Artemis on the floor in front of him and gave her a tender smile. "How about we teach you how to walk and show your daddy that you like us a lot more than you like him?"

CHAPTER SEVEN

Jack looked great. When I found him at Lafayette Park again a couple of days later, I almost didn't recognize him because I had left him at the barber's after taking him shopping, and I hadn't seen him since. His hair was still pretty long on top, but the sides were shorter, and his natural waves had been cut so he could push it back and to the side in more of a controlled mess than it had been before. It showed off his face, particularly those eyes of his.

I was especially glad he had let me pick some lighter colors of clothes for him, too, since he had almost exclusively searched through the black items while we were at the store. Now that he was dressed in a light gray tee and a pair of blue skinny jeans, his black hair stood out more and somehow made his eyes even more striking. Plus, he didn't look as much like a vagrant anymore. He was approachable. He was still incredibly skinny, but I hoped once he started making money and getting more regular meals, he would fill in a little bit and look less like a fifteen-year-old and more like the kind of guy who could spend an hour singing on a stage without falling over.

The crowd around him, I noticed, had changed a bit in demographics since the last time. There were fewer old Chinese men and more women, many of whom had their phones out and were giggling to each other as they snapped photos of the rather oblivious guitarist. He wasn't singing today, but that didn't mean he had any fewer fans listening to him play.

I moved through the crowd slowly, trying to just take this moment to listen before I distracted him and stopped him from strumming the strings.

But when I reached the front, he surprised me when he said, "You like what you see, Ms. Blake?" without even looking up.

I grinned. "I do, actually."

The corner of his mouth quirked up. "I should hope so. This was, after all, all your fault."

"You make it sound like it was a bad thing," I replied.

He finished the last notes of his song and let the notes ring for a moment before he grasped the neck of the guitar and looked up as he pulled the strap over his shoulder. "So does this mean you've found me my path to fame and fortune?"

The crowd clapped, though they seemed a little surprised that the song had ended, as if they'd actually been mesmerized by it.

"It means I've found a start," I said. "Tomorrow night."

He nearly dropped his guitar, barely managing to catch it before it landed on the cement at his feet. "Tomorrow?"

I raised an eyebrow, as surprised by his reaction as I was by how much money was sitting in his guitar case now that I was close enough to look inside. He'd certainly been doing well for himself over the last few days. "Wait, are you nervous? You've been playing every day, no problem."

"Parks aren't stages," he mumbled, and clearly he didn't like the idea of his nerves any more than I did. "I just… Give me a second to process. Hey, thanks again for what you told me," he said to a man who walked past. They exchanged nods, and then he turned back to me. "I figured I'd have a couple more weeks before this point."

"Did you really have such little faith in me?" I asked, slightly offended and more than a little curious about what the man had told him. It was none of my business, of course, but based on the way Jack expressed his gratitude, it was worth a good deal to my new client.

Jack smiled, watching the man turn a corner and disappear. "Nah," he said, "you're not the problem. And before you jump into praising my skills and all that, I know you're right. Playing in the big leagues isn't any different from playing out here. I'll be fine."

Well that was easy. "Oh. Cool. So you'll play?"

"If you tell me to."

That felt like a strange way for him to say it, but I nodded. "I mean, that's sorta my job, right?"

Then he laughed, and I felt myself relax. I hadn't even noticed how tense I had been the last few minutes. "I don't actually know what a manager does," he admitted, "so you could pretty much make it all up, and I'd probably believe you. You're not going to cheat and swindle me, are you?" And before I could even answer, he laughed again. "I may not know you all that well yet, but you definitely don't seem like the cheating type."

"I'm definitely not," I replied. "At least, I'm not if you're not." Seth was overbearing and at times ridiculous, but if somehow Jack wasn't as good as I thought he was, at least I would have someone like my brother backing me up. Though perhaps I should give Jack fair warning…

As he put his guitar into his case, Jack glanced out over the disappointed crowd as they left. Apparently he'd forgotten they were there, because he pulled his eyebrows together and looked monumentally confused. "I've gotten out of the habit of cheating people," he said, still a bit distracted.

"Well that's good to hear." I felt strange standing there, and I had a feeling he did too. Our conversation felt forced, not like it had been in the car, and I wasn't sure why there was a difference. Was it simply because this had turned into a business relationship instead of a tentative friendship?

"Well," I said, though I really didn't have anything to follow it with.

He flashed a brief smile. "I guess I'll see you tomorrow. Where am I going, and when should I be there?"

I told him the address of Indie's friend's bakery. "Be there before six, and make sure you're wearing something nice."

That comment brought out a better smile, one closer to what I was used to. As he was the happiest person I knew, anything but a wide smile just felt wrong. "Hmm," he said as he slipped his guitar case onto his back. "I have about a twenty percent chance of getting that wrong after our little shopping trip, so I'm not going to wear my black t-shirt."

Grinning, I shook my head. I had bought him exactly four shirts. "That would be wise. Anything else I bought you will work just fine. And, uh…" My cheeks burned a bit as my last comment came out: "Do your hair like that. It looks good."

His eyes seemed to twinkle as he met my gaze again, and though he walked backward toward Clay Street, he kept his full focus on me. "Anything for you, Ms. Blake."

Indie and I got to the bakery around 5:45 on open mic night, and I was immensely glad she had agreed to come when I took in the sheer number of people inside. I hadn't planned on asking her to join me, but all morning I had been freaking out a little bit, so I called her and begged her to come help me relax.

"What if he doesn't come?" I asked her, bouncing my legs as we sat at one of the little tables inside. "What if he can't find it? He doesn't have a phone, so I—"

"Calm down," Indie replied and put her hand over mine. "Granted, I don't know the guy, but he doesn't seem like the sort to stand you up. He's probably smart enough to find a way to get here, so he'll be here."

"I really hope you're right," I muttered. If she wasn't, and Jack turned out to be less of a standup guy than I wanted to think he was, that would mean this little venture of mine was a dead end. I'd managed to get this far without job hunting again, and I was dreading the idea even more now. Now that I'd had over a week of jobless freedom, I was seriously enjoying it.

The lack of money outside of what Gordon had wired to me, on the other hand…

"So how did you meet this guy again?" Indie asked as she scanned the quickly filling bakery.

I wondered if she would judge me like Seth, or if she would be more like Catherine and be wary but confident that I knew what I was doing. I hoped it was the latter, because I really liked Indie. "Well," I said, "he helped me change a flat tire as I was driving out here, so I gave him a ride."

"That's nice of you," Indie said, and she seemed to be fighting a laugh for some reason. When she caught my silent question, she grinned and shook her head. "Trust me, I am the last person who's going to judge you on how you met the guy. I met my first husband when I tried to steal his wallet then broke into his shop the next day."

Matthew wasn't her first husband? But she was so young—younger than me, at least. Besides, the two of them were hopelessly in love, which I'd realized when I stopped by their house to pick her up and Matthew spent almost ten minutes saying goodbye to his wife. I wondered what had happened to get Indie to this point in her life, and I felt a stronger kinship with her now that I knew she hadn't had a perfect life either.

"So," Indie said, oblivious to my thoughts, "most of the people who play at this thing are decently good, but they consider performing more of a hobby than a career. Jack shouldn't have any problems getting noticed if he's any good, and a lot of the people who come to these things can probably suggest other places he can play."

I nodded, my eyes straying to the door. It was almost six, and if Jack didn't show up… "Thanks for helping me out," I said. "I'd run out of ideas, and I was about ready to give up."

Smiling, she clasped my hand and gave it a squeeze. "Are you kidding? You're giving me a good reason to get away from the Davenports for a bit. I love them all, but they're a bit too much to handle for long periods of time. While Beck is gone running her summer camp, I feel like I'm the only normal one around. You're a breath of fresh air, Amelia."

Beck was one of the ones I hadn't met yet, and I was starting to have a hard time keeping track of everyone. Instead of a sister, I'd come to California to discover a whole tribe. A big, wealthy, overwhelming tribe of people far better than me. Knowing Indie was one of them had made things easier. She was blissfully normal.

"I can see what you mean." I managed a small smile. "Lissa's not too bad, but Seth is…"

"Seth is Seth," she agreed. "I—"

"Jack!" I said and jumped to my feet, maybe a little too quickly. He'd just appeared in the doorway, guitar slung over his shoulder and a worn leather jacket over a light blue t-shirt. I had no idea where the jacket had come from, but I didn't care. He looked amazing.

Though he smiled when he spotted me, it was the kind of smile a person had when they were anything but happy. I'd seen him wary and nervous, but I'd never seen him quite this frustrated or dejected, and my heart twisted a bit in my chest as he slowly navigated his way through the crowd to get to us. Something was wrong.

"Jack?" I asked when he finally dodged the last table. "What's wrong?"

Touching my arm briefly, he looked around the room instead of at me. "Just some bad news," he said. "But I'm fine." I might not have believed him if he didn't give me a more convincing smile before turning his attention to Indie. "Hi," he said. "I'm Jack."

"Indie," she replied and shook his hand. "Amelia's been telling me all about you."

"Good things, I hope."

"Maybe."

Jack grinned, and I was glad the two of them seemed to be getting along. More so, I was glad he didn't seem *too* bothered by whatever had happened today. He was still happy Jack.

"You're going up fourth," I said and grabbed another chair so he could join our table. "Do you need to warm up or anything?"

Shrugging, he sat down and scanned the crowd again. "I don't usually, but I've also never played for this many people before." *Please don't get cold feet on me.* But Jack looked back at me and grinned again. "Don't worry, Ms. Blake. I'll play my little heart out and make sure you get all the big bucks someday soon."

I really wished he wouldn't call me that, but I wasn't sure how to say that without sounding like I was whining. It wasn't the greatest, being reminded of my life with Jordan, but at least I didn't have as many bad feelings as I did with Steve. Besides, Jordan was clear over in Chicago, far enough away for me to try to forget about him.

"They usually let you play a couple of songs," Indie said. "Sometimes more, if the crowd likes you."

"Sounds like I have to make them like me," he replied and sent me a wink. Yeah, they were definitely going to like him. How could they not? Everything about the guy was likeable.

As Indie's friend stepped up to the stage and began welcoming everyone who came to support the local musicians who would be playing, we settled in to listen. The first artist was a man in his sixties who did a pretty decent cover of "Stairway to Heaven" on a beat-up guitar. The crowd applauded politely when he finished, but I could see a lot of people chatting with their friends and only sort of paying attention. I tried not to get worried about that fact and kept an eye on Jack, but his back was toward me so I had no idea what he might have been feeling as he watched the next musician, a teenage girl, hop up onstage and start playing a song I was pretty sure was by Miley Cyrus. She got a bit more support from the audience, but not nearly as much as she deserved.

Next up was a woman somewhere in her thirties, and she managed to play her banjo in a way that made me forget it was a banjo, which was saying something. Her voice was a bit breathy, but it worked with the original song she played, and the crowd seemed to thoroughly enjoy it, begging her for another. Weirdly, that made me more nervous than people not paying attention—which was still happening, I noticed with a frown. The woman was talented, and memorable, and Jack would have to do really well to get any notice after she played a third song to please the eager audience.

Finally, Indie's friend announced Jackson Thorn, and he flashed me a brief smile before he made his way up to the stage and got himself situated. He was nervous, and that made me nervous. There would be other places to play, but I really hoped tonight would give him a good place to start a fan base, if only a small one. But he had to play well if he wanted to be remembered.

"Hi," he said into the mic, and then he started to play.

I was really going to have to teach him how to have a better stage presence if he ever wanted to make a name for himself. But my annoyance died almost the moment his song started, because no matter how nervous the guy was, that didn't stop him from being able to play. And when he started to sing?

As much as I wanted to just sit and watch him, I scanned the audience and was both amazed and delighted to see that nearly every conversation had stopped. Whatever magic spell Jack used in his music had worked, and everyone in the crowded bakery had paused to listen to the man who clearly knew how to pour his soul into a song. One man had even stopped with a cookie halfway to his mouth and was gazing open-mouthed at the stage as if he'd never heard anything like it.

It was probably true.

I couldn't even pinpoint what it was about Jack's songs that made them so special, but they were unlike anything I'd ever heard.

When Jack started up his fourth song to appease the transfixed audience, I felt a hand grab mine, and I turned to Indie, who was beaming at me.

"I think you found a good one," she said.

Boy, did I know it.

I felt bad for the three people who had signed up to play after Jack, but thankfully the crowd was polite enough to at least pretend to listen as they sang their songs. Jack was stuck up near the stage, though, and people were practically lining up to talk to him. That was a good thing, for sure, but I wished I could be standing up there next to him so I could get info about other places he could play. I didn't want to try to force myself through the crowd, so I stayed where I was and watched Jack smile and chat with everyone who came up to him.

He wasn't great on the stage, but at least the guy knew how to talk to strangers.

"Excuse me?" someone said and tapped my shoulder, and I turned to a young woman who looked somewhere in her twenties. "You're here with Jackson Thorn, right?"

I smiled and sat up eagerly. Hopefully this was someone who could help me find Jack a real gig. "Yes," I said. "I'm Amelia."

She looked me over. "Are you his girlfriend?"

"What?" I said, and then I realized what she'd asked. "Oh, no, I'm his manager. I—"

"Oo, is he single then?"

I didn't know why her question bothered me so much. Why would she be talking to me about that when she would do better to go over and ask Jack himself? Besides, she was making it harder for anyone to come talk to me about scheduling him to play. "I think so," I said and got to my feet, though I wasn't sure why.

The girl grinned and scurried away, shoving her way through the line of people until she made it all the way to Jack's side.

And when she introduced herself, Jack's smile grew wide.

"Well she was kind of awful," Indie said as I sank back into my seat. She was watching the two of them talk like I was, and she seemed to have a similar feeling toward the girl as I did. "She looks like she's trying to throw herself all over him."

"Lucky Jack," I muttered.

For the next twenty minutes, Jack smiled and the girl laughed as if they weren't surrounded by a bunch of other people who wanted to chat with him, and I kept telling myself that I could give them a few more minutes before I had to interrupt and discuss Jack's next options. It was ridiculously hard to keep myself in my seat.

Suddenly Jack was talking to Indie's friend, and then he was pulling his guitar out again and going back onto the stage amid enthusiastic applause.

"Wow," Indie said, her eyebrows high. "I've never seen anyone get a second turn like this. Your Jackson Thorn is making history, Amelia."

I certainly hoped so, or this little job of mine was going to cost me more than it earned.

Somewhere in the middle of Jack's second song, someone tapped on my shoulder, and I turned to greet a middle-aged man who didn't waste any time with small talk. "You're this guy's manager?" he said, glancing at the makeshift stage.

"Yeah," I replied, trying not to get my hopes up.

"Is he going to be playing at the wharf next weekend?" he asked.

I had no idea what he was talking about, but I said, "Yes."

"Awesome! My son would *love* his music, and this might actually convince him to come with me."

I watched him head out of the bakery, and then I grabbed Indie's arm. "What was he talking about?" I asked, suddenly in a mild panic.

Laughing, Indie shrugged. "I have no idea, but I'm sure Jessie will know. I'll ask her, so don't freak out just yet." She slipped away to find the bakery owner, and I cringed as I sat there by myself. I probably shouldn't have done that, and if I couldn't actually find a way to get

Jack to play at whichever wharf that man was talking about, I was going to have a seriously annoyed kid on my hands for making him go to a show he clearly didn't want to go to.

"I wasn't that bad, was I?"

I jumped and looked up at Jack just as he slid into Indie's empty chair. He was smiling, but I was pretty sure his question was serious. "Oh, you were great," I said, though I didn't sound as convincing as I should have. "Really."

"So this little panicked face you have is your way of saying good job? You're a strange one, Blake."

Huh. So in the course of one open mic night we'd gone from Ms. Blake to just Blake. Was it really so hard to say my first name, the one that actually belonged to me? He had used it before, so what changed?

"I might have found you another place to play," I said, though given the increasing length of Indie's conversation with her friend, I was worried that wasn't actually true.

Jack raised an eyebrow. "And that's bad because…?"

Well, if I was going to be Jack's manager, it was probably a good idea to stay as honest with him as possible, especially if I wanted him to be the same way. Running my hands through my hair, I gritted my teeth and gave him a nervous smile. "Because I don't actually know if I can get you on the list. Or where it is. Or when it is."

He studied me for a moment, and then he started to laugh, loud enough that he drew several heads in our direction and sent a rush of heat into my face. "Sounds like you're as good at being a manager as I am at talking on a stage," he said. "That's right, I saw your face, and I know I'm terrible."

"But at least you can play," I breathed.

"I'm glad you think so," he replied, his grin warming the room as he watched me. There was something different about the way he looked at me. Unlike most people, he seemed to be able to see right through the walls I usually put up, but that didn't feel like a bad thing. He saw more than what other people saw, and in a strange way, it made me feel more alive. How did he do that?

"Good news!" Indie said and put her hands on my shoulders. "Jessie is friends with the guy who's in charge of that festival down on Fisherman's Wharf, and she already texted him and got Jack on the list. I gave her your number, Amelia, so she can send you all the details. Jack, you sounded great up there!"

I couldn't help myself, and I jumped up and pulled Indie into a tight hug. "I owe you one," I said. "Anytime you need a babysitter, I'm there."

"Don't say that to Matthew or he'll definitely take advantage of it. In his words, he badly needs more conversations that aren't just babble."

"Personally, I'm a fan of babble," Jack said, though he was focused on a couple of girls who had started singing karaoke on the stage.

I rolled my eyes at him, but I couldn't stop smiling. A little music festival on the wharf, especially with other artists playing, was nothing big, but it was something. And something was a whole lot better than nothing, so I was going to take what I could get and do my darndest to help Jack find his place in the world. I may not have known him well, but I was pretty sure he deserved to have everything he could possibly want.

CHAPTER EIGHT

"That's a lot of people," Jack said with a frown, gripping the strap of his guitar case so tightly that his knuckles were white.

He wasn't wrong. Jessie had told me the Fisherman's Music Festival was a new event, and there was a chance not a lot of people would attend, so I had expected a couple dozen people to show up on the wharf. Instead, it felt like the whole city had shown up, and there wasn't even space in front of the tiny temporary stage for anyone else to view the concerts, so people were milling about the wharf itself, where they could at least hear the performances if not see them. There had to be at least a hundred.

"It's not that many," I said, though my voice squeaked a bit, and Jack lifted an eyebrow as he glanced over at me. I was just glad we'd made it on time, since finding parking had been a nightmare. We'd had to park so far away that it almost would have taken us less time to just walk from my apartment. "You're on in ten minutes." I searched for the best way to get up to the stage without having to push through that monstrous crowd. "You sure you're up for this?"

"Sure," he replied. At least it wasn't a no, though his answer didn't exactly spark confidence.

"Let's try this way." I led the way into the mess of people at the edge, hoping we could move fast enough to get up there before Jack had to be on the stage.

Somehow we made it to the barrier that kept the audience from reaching the stage, and I breathed just a little easier. "He's on the list," I told the big guy guarding the stairs and gestured to the guitar case on Jack's back. "Jackson Thorn."

The guard must have memorized the list because he nodded and pulled the temporary fence aside to let Jack pass. To my dismay, he didn't let me through and glared at me when I tried to follow.

"It's fine," I said just as Jack was about to argue with the man. "I want to be down here to watch anyway. Wait." I reached out, and Jack stepped a little closer so I could smooth out the front of his t-shirt— pale green this time. Then I brushed his hair back a little more so it wouldn't fall into his face, since his eyes were such a great feature that he needed to use them to his advantage. There were already plenty of women eyeing the young guitarist even though they should have been watching the folk band who were just finishing up.

"How do I look?" Jack asked and grinned at me.

A little too good, I thought to myself, even though that was the point. There were going to be plenty of women like that one at the open mic night, all of them fawning over this guy who was too good for them. "You'll do great up there," I told him without answering the question.

He looked at the crowd and frowned again, which made me nervous. Jack frowned so rarely that it had to mean he was more worried than he pretended to be. "Yeah, I think so," he said, and then he hurried after the stage tech who was gesturing for him to follow.

"Please be able to work your magic." I hoped Jack stopped being nervous as soon as he started playing. I liked to think he lost track of what was happening when he started to play and just got caught up in the music, but if I was wrong…

Before I knew it, the folk band was running off the stage to applause, and Jack was stepping into place in front of a microphone, his blue eyes scanning the crowd. I'd spent all morning with him going over things he could say so he could actually connect with the crowd, but he seemed to have forgotten any of the lines I suggested and just stood there looking out over the hundred people who had shown up to the festival. This was a lot different from an open mic night in a little bakery, and I suddenly wished I had known more about the festival before I agreed to have Jack play. It probably would have been a good idea to start smaller and work our way up more slowly.

But then Jack looked down at me and caught my eye, and his smile was so warm that it convinced me all of his nerves were gone. "How's everyone doing?" he said into the microphone, his clear voice cutting through the buzz of chatter. "What a beautiful day today, huh? I'm Jackson Thorn, and I hope you guys like what I have to share. If not, I'm pretty sure there's a fruit stand just a ways that direction with a whole lot of ripe tomatoes just waiting to be thrown."

Several people laughed, Jack grinned at me again, and then he started to play.

This time I was smart, and I lifted my phone so I could record the whole thing. Never mind starting small; the internet most definitely needed to discover Jackson Thorn.

That night, Lissa and I went over to Matthew and Indie's house to hang out with Indie and her daughter while Matthew and Steve had a "guys' night," whatever that meant. Apparently, Steve and Matthew were good friends, and neither Lissa nor Indie thought it was a good idea to know too much about what the pair of them did in their free time. I had no idea how, but they were perfectly happy to stay ignorant.

"It makes it easy to keep Seth in the dark," Lissa explained as she drove us to Indie's. "As you might have noticed, Seth thinks Steve is an idiot, and Steve does what he can to keep it that way. Matthew likes to play along, so they could be doing any number of stupid things, and I'd rather not be the one to clue Seth in on it. At least Steve got the archery out of his system last summer," she added as she pulled into the driveway. "Oh, looks like Lanna's here too."

"Adam heard about guys' night and wanted to have his own," Lanna told us when we got inside. "So he's got the kids, which means I get to finally have some time with my favorite niece." She was sprawled on the floor with Artemis and reading a book, and she looked perfectly content with her husband's decision.

"You're only going to get to call her that for a couple more months," Lissa replied and patted her belly. "Clearly my little girl is going to be so much cuter."

"Clearly you've never looked at Matthew properly," Indie shot back. "He's as cute as they come, so Artie definitely has the advantage."

"How did I get cursed with two boys?" Lanna asked Artemis in baby talk, but I was pretty sure she wasn't serious. When I'd been staying at their house back when I first arrived in San Francisco, both Lanna and her husband were obviously completely in love with their children, and outside of Harry's ridiculous energy and need to do everything with me, her boys had been absolute angels.

I felt just a little out of place, since I didn't have any kids to talk about, but I didn't mind. Mostly. I'd wanted kids, but Jordan hadn't been ready for that, and now I was glad I'd listened to him. If we'd had a baby, it would have made the divorce a lot more complicated. And what would I have done then? I could take risks with Jack when it was just me I had to worry about, but if I'd had a kid to look out for? I would have taken that marketing job in a heartbeat, and I probably would have been miserable.

"Is Benny excited to be starting first grade?" Indie asked Lanna, and the three of them began talking about Lanna's oldest and which school he was going to and which subjects he was best at so far.

I sat in my spot quietly and pulled out my phone, curious to see if anyone had watched my video yet. I had had to make a new account, since mine was full of corporate training videos from my Chicago job, and I wasn't sure I had done the best job of editing the video, since I didn't have a computer to work on it and had to use my phone. But I hoped at least a few people had taken the time to search for Jackson Thorn and found the video I put up after today's show.

I squeaked when I saw the view count, and the other ladies looked at me in alarm. "Three thousand views," I gasped and handed my phone over to Indie, since I wasn't sure how to even say what crazy emotions were coursing through me. There was no way I was seeing that right.

"Oh wow," Indie said and started scrolling through the comments. "People love this guy."

"Who?" Lanna asked.

"The hitchhiker?" Lissa guessed.

"Jack," I said, and a whole lot of tension slipped from my shoulders. The video was doing even better than I'd hoped.

"A whole lot of people want to know where he's playing next," Indie said, still reading the comments.

I sighed, knowing I was supposed to have an answer for them. "So do I," I mumbled. "I'm working on it."

Lanna sat up so she could look at the screen as well, and she squinted at the freeze frame of his face. I hadn't been close enough to get a really good shot, something I was definitely mourning as I considered the sheer number of views the video could have gotten if people had really been able to see him. "He looks familiar," she said. "Is he from around here?"

"New York," I replied. "But he said something about family here."

"Well," Lanna said, "I don't know any Thorns. Maybe he just has one of those faces. What does he sound like?"

Indie hit play, and Jack's incredible music caught even baby Artie's attention. The audio in my recording was pretty terrible, but luckily Jack's voice was clear and strong enough that he still sounded pretty good. Eventually I would have to get some decent recording equipment, but that was something for a lot farther down the road.

"Wow," said Lissa after a moment. "Amelia, he's really good."

"Talking to the choir," I said. "If any of you know any paying gigs, maybe I can show his talent a little better, but…" I highly doubted any of them would be able to help me from here on out, though I would forever be indebted to Indie for getting Jack into that open mic night.

To my surprise, it was Lanna who said, "I know of something." When all of us looked at her, she raised an eyebrow. "What? Just because they're rich, it doesn't mean they don't have good taste."

She'd lost me, though Indie and Lissa looked thoughtful about the idea, whatever it was. "Uh…"

Smiling, Lanna lay back down next to Artemis then explained, "I have a little side business I've been doing for a few years, and I have a whole bunch of small businesses and freelancers who book events and jobs through me, since I have good access to most of the best-paying customers in the city."

I still wasn't following, and I must have looked confused because Lissa added, "She knows all the rich people, so whenever they need to hire caterers or decorators or whatever, they'll come to Lanna, since she's a little more reliable than the internet."

"And this way, my clients don't have to face the wrath of the elites, since if something goes wrong, I'm the one who takes the fall. This Jackson Thorn of yours isn't quite the type the elites usually book for their parties, but it seems like his music speaks louder than his appearance."

And what's wrong with his appearance?

This time it was Indie who caught my expression, and she patted my hand. "It's nothing against Jack or the clothes you bought him," she said.

Lanna's eyes went wide. "Oh! No, Amelia, sorry, that's not what I meant at all. I just mean, well…"

"Rich people are snobs and think everyone should look like peacocks," Lissa said.

"Yeah," Lanna agreed. "That. Though it might not be a bad idea to let Catherine have him for an hour or so."

"As long as she doesn't change his hair," I said without thinking, and then my face burned with heat as I waited for them to start teasing me about saying something so ridiculous.

But Indie said, "She definitely won't change his hair," and the three of them grew silent as they continued to watch the video.

I probably should have known better, since these women were some of the kindest people I'd ever met, but it still caught me off guard that they were never as critical as I expected them to be. If I'd said something like my hair comment around Jordan, he would have made note of it for days afterward. He had never been good at letting things go.

Since the ladies seemed pretty preoccupied watching Jack play, I slid down to the floor to take up the book Artemis was flipping through. She looked at me, and though it was hard to know what she was thinking, she seemed happy enough to have me join her, and I smiled. I may have gotten more family than I bargained for when I came to California, but they were pretty great, even if they were overwhelming.

At some point, the doorbell rang, and Indie glanced at her phone as it pulled up a video of the person at the front door. "Oh!" she said, loud enough to make the rest of us jump. "It's Molly!"

"Brennon's back?" Lanna asked eagerly as Indie hurried to go open the door. "Benny will be thrilled!"

I vaguely remembered Molly being the name of Steve's friend Brennon's wife, and I hoped they were talking about the same Brennon. I was dying to see him and more than eager to see what kind of person he'd ended up with. Brennon and Steve had been roommates in college and stayed friends after they graduated, so I saw a lot of him while I was dating Steve. He was one of the nicest people I had ever known, but I was pretty sure he had had something in his past that kept him from truly opening up to people and letting them in. Hearing someone had finally broken through his walls made me happier than I would have suspected, since it had been a few years since I saw him last.

Apparently Molly was a photojournalist, and the two of them had been in Switzerland for several weeks as she followed a story.

It was Catherine's voice that reached us first, preceding her down the stairs to where we were all gathered. "Seth was feeling left out, so he and Brennon went to join Adam's guys' night. I'm pretty sure they're trying to make it a competition to see whose is better. Oh, hey, Amelia!" she said when she got to the TV room. "Nice to see you, as always. And you finally get to meet Molly!"

Molly Ashworth was pretty much the opposite of what I expected. Brennon worked in finance, so I figured his wife would be strait-laced and put together, just like he always was. But Molly had the most incredibly curly blonde hair that seemed to spill onto her shoulders with a life of its own, and she wore what looked like those clothes you keep in your drawers for when you push laundry day a little too far. She practically bounced with energy as she came up to me with a wide, genuine grin.

"You're Steve's Amelia?" she asked then winced. "Sorry, probably not the best way to word that. What I meant was you're the one Brennon talks about all the time? I'm glad I actually get to meet you!"

I cocked my head. "Brennon talks about me?"

Snorting a laugh, she plopped herself down right next to me. "Brennon talks about *everything*. I know," she added when she saw the shock on my face. "Apparently he used to be such a quiet guy, which kinda blows my mind because I've never known that Brennon. He's always been Can't-Shut-Him-Up Bean to me."

"Bean?" I asked, wondering if I should laugh or be worried Brennon had married someone who didn't seem suited to him at all. I couldn't even imagine him being a chatterbox, and his quiet nature had always been one of the reasons I liked him. He'd always made me feel like I was worth listening to, which I hadn't encountered very often.

I wished Brennon were here tonight. He would have made me a lot more comfortable, since he was always predictable. I never wondered how I should act around him like I did with most people.

Grinning, Molly reached down and grabbed Artemis so she could pull the baby onto her lap. "When we were kids he was always ridiculously skinny. Bean pole. And he absolutely hated it when I called him that, so of course it stuck. Anyway, he's had fifteen years to make up for on the talking front, so it's been a whirlwind year. Geez, Artie, you need to stop growing. You're huge!"

So she had known Brennon since they were kids? That made a little more sense. But I still couldn't imagine my quiet friend jiving well with someone like Molly. I must have missed quite the story when they got together last year.

"Well," said Indie, "since we're all here, I think that means we absolutely need ice cream."

"If Beck finds out we had a girls' night without her and Macy, we're done for," Molly said, "but yes, we definitely need ice cream." She hopped up to help Indie grab it, handing Artemis over to me.

I looked at Lissa and was a little afraid to ask the question that had popped into my head. I'd heard Beck's name a couple of times, but I had no idea how she actually fit in with the family. Were there any others I didn't know about?

Catching my gaze, Lissa grinned. "Beck's husband, Colin, is good friends with Brennon. We kind of adopted her into the family last summer, since Lanna's dad is her lawyer."

"That doesn't make any sense," I muttered.

"I know," she replied, "but that's how this family works. We just keep growing. You should be able to meet Beck and her family in a couple of weeks, when her summer camp is over. I think you'd like her."

I hoped so, because I had just about reached my limit on overly friendly family members.

After a few minutes, Indie and Molly returned with bowls loaded with ice cream, and though I was tempted to join in on the conversations that broke out, I was more drawn to my phone, where the number of views and comments on Jack's video just kept climbing. If this was any indication of the future, things were looking pretty good for my easy-going friend, and I couldn't wait to tell him.

CHAPTER NINE

"You know," I said when I met Jack in Lafayette Park the next afternoon, "it would be a whole lot easier to get in touch with you if you had a phone."

For the first time, he didn't have his guitar out, and he was just lounging on a bench, basking in the sunlight. He smiled at me as I sat down next to him. "I can't even afford my own clothes," he said. "What makes you think I can afford a phone?"

"They have those pay-by-the-minute ones, you know."

"I kind of like making you hunt me down," he replied lightly. "Does this mean you found me another gig?"

"I found three, actually, and these ones actually pay."

That got him to sit up, his eyebrows high. "Oh, we're moving to the big leagues already? I'm impressed, Blake."

I rolled my eyes. "I'm not completely inexperienced," I said, even though I really couldn't say I was experienced either. "You need to stop sounding so surprised."

"I never doubted you. Besides, even if you couldn't find me paying jobs, things would work out."

I still had no idea how a guy like Jack—someone who literally had nothing—could be so optimistic and carefree, and I wished he would share his secret. Even with Lanna helping out and getting me in contact with some of San Francisco's wealthy who needed a musician for their parties, I still worried I wouldn't be able to get Jack where he needed to go. Especially on my own.

"You know what you need?" Jack asked.

Actual training in music management? "What do I need, Jack?"

"You need to relax a little. Soak up the sun. Stop and smell the roses."

I was living off borrowed money from a father I'd never even met, since despite Lissa's insistence that I at least call him, I hadn't worked up the courage to contact him. And even if Jack played shows that earned him some money, that didn't necessarily mean I would get much of anything. We'd agreed I would get ten percent of every gig he played, but these three parties combined from Lanna wouldn't even get me a fraction of my monthly rent. As great as an idea this whole manager thing sounded at the beginning, I wasn't sure how long I could viably make it last.

"I wish I could," I muttered, though I did tilt my head back a little to get some sun in my face. It felt pretty good. "What have you been doing all day?" It was a question I'd been wanting to ask for a while, since he couldn't very well play in the park for hours on end. What did a guy like Jack do with his free time? *Stop and smell the roses?*

He chuckled a little. "Wandered the city a bit. Talked to people. Learned some things. Overall, it's been more productive than most." He sounded pretty content, and I envied that.

"Is that why you're sitting here doing nothing now?" I asked and turned to look at him.

Jack did the same, his eyes fixed on me and his expression fairly neutral. "You think this is nothing?" He didn't sound angry, but neither was he amused. I was pretty sure he was just curious.

"Isn't it?" I couldn't even remember the last time I hadn't had something on my to-do list. Even now, when my list was literally only about Jack, an anxious knot was forming in my stomach. The longer I sat here, the less time I had to prep for these upcoming parties. If Jordan saw me now, he would tell me I knew better and to get to work. That work ethic of his was one of the things I'd first admired about him when I met him, and over the course of our relationship, he had taught me to value my time.

Letting out a sigh, Jack shrugged a little and returned his face to the sunshine. "It depends on how you look at it, I suppose," he said. "I like to think I am doing my best to not take life for granted. You never know how much you'll get, so it's a good idea to make the most of it."

The knot in my stomach seemed to double in size. "You're not dying, are you?" I asked warily. It would explain his positivity if he was.

Laughing, he shook his head. "Relax, Blake. I'm fine. When's my next gig?"

"Friday night."

"So that leaves you four and a half days before you have to start fixing my hair for me and telling me what to wear," he said. "Sounds like you can admire some flowers to me. Do nothing for a change."

I fully planned to spend the next four days researching how to make it big as an independent musician, as well as look for other venues and figure out a more distinct style for Jack, since a t-shirt and jeans wasn't exactly an outfit that would make him stand out.

But I smiled and said, "Maybe," because he seemed set on the idea of me taking a break. I was pretty sure he didn't believe me, so I decided to change the subject. "You didn't want to play today?" I asked.

He glanced at his guitar, which he'd shoved underneath the bench, and shrugged. "I have a new song idea rolling around in my head, and I want to ruminate on it a bit without letting older stuff influence it. This one feels unique, and I want to make sure it gets the attention it deserves."

"How do you come up with songs?" I asked. With my past jobs, I'd always gotten ideas by browsing the internet and taking the bus around the city, but mostly I tended to rehash things that already existed and just put my own little spin on it. I was eager to know how Jack created such emotionally charged music. And on top of that were his lyrics, which I honestly hadn't paid much attention to—words were not my thing—but there had been plenty of comments on the video I uploaded about how Jack seemed to speak directly to his audience with his poetry.

Closing his eyes, he leaned a little farther back on the bench and smiled up at the bright summer sky. "Most of the ideas just kind of come to me," he said. "Or they come from things that happen to me or people I meet. I don't really know how to explain it, but it's like I can be walking down the street and suddenly there it is, right in front of me, and I have to hold onto it before it disappears. And then some-times certain songs won't go away and keep popping up until I accept they're here to stay. Those ones are usually my best songs because it's like they know I'm the only one who can make them real."

"You talk about your songs like they're alive," I said, but I didn't mean it in a bad way. I was fascinated by the idea, and I wished I could put things into words as well as he did. Even just talking about his music, he had a sense of poetry about him.

He laughed a little. "Maybe they are."

"I think I get it now."

He looked at me, one black eyebrow slightly above the other. "Get what?"

"Why you would give up everything to chase your dreams."

Then he tensed, which was not the reaction I was expecting from what I said, and he slowly sat back up, looking almost like a completely different person. "Who said I gave anything up?" he asked, and his voice had gotten low. Rough.

This was not the happy-go-lucky Jack I knew, and my first instinct was to run. Without knowing why he had shifted so suddenly, I didn't want to be anywhere near him. It was too much like after Steve's accident, when I couldn't figure out what he wanted from me so I couldn't help him. It would be so much easier if I ran, and I was just about to push myself up to my feet when Jack grabbed my hand.

"Sorry," he said, and his expression said he meant it. "I wasn't trying to… I know what you meant. Please don't run away."

How could he possibly know that that was what I was going to do when I hadn't even moved? I didn't even know what to say, so I just sat there and looked at his hand wrapped around mine. His fingers were rough from his guitar strings, and his skin looked like it had been put through the wringer more than once.

"How long have you been on the road?" I asked quietly, and I looked up when he didn't answer.

There wasn't any trace of his smile, and his icy blue eyes were sad as he gazed back at me. "Amelia, I keep my past a secret for a reason."

"I get that," I replied, and I badly wished I could do the same thing sometimes. "But I know pretty much nothing about you, Jack. I don't even know if Jack is your real name. If we're going to work together…"

Nodding, he slowly pulled his hand away and tucked it between his legs. "You're probably right," he said and frowned at the dirt beneath his feet.

His shoes were falling apart, I realized, and I hadn't even thought to buy him some new ones when I took him shopping. I added that to my mental to-do list for the week then returned my focus to his face.

"If I tell you some things," he said, "will you promise not to ask questions?"

That seemed a little too vague of a promise, and I pursed my lips, thinking it over.

He smiled. "I mean questions about my past," he amended. "It's better for everyone if I'm just a twenty-six-year-old guy from Manhattan who showed up one day playing his guitar."

Ah, so he was twenty-six. That was good to know. "I guess that sounds fair," I said, though I wished he would trust me enough to tell me more than the basics.

Satisfied, he thought for a moment. "My name really is Jackson. I took to the road about a year ago, and I *did* leave everything behind, though that's kind of a given for someone who sets out on foot, and I haven't looked back. The only things I own are my guitar"—he tapped the case with his heel—"and a stubbornness I inherited from my mom. I can't tell you why I came to San Francisco, but I will say I might have finally found what I was looking for. Or I'm close. Anything else doesn't matter, because I'm not the same person I used to be."

I shouldn't have agreed to his terms, because now I wanted to know everything, particularly the bit about San Francisco. But something told me he wouldn't tell me that. "I do have one little question," I said, wincing when he frowned again. But this question was important if I was going to spend all my energy trying to get him to his maximum potential. "Do you promise to be honest with me? You don't have to tell me about your past, but I do have to know I can trust you."

To my utter relief, Jack's answering smile was warm and wide, exactly how it should be. "I can easily promise that," he said and took my hand again. "I have never wanted to lie to you, Blake."

"Well good. Then we should be able to work together just fine."

We sat there for a moment in silence, just enjoying the early August sunshine, and I felt like things were looking pretty good for the first time since Jordan stopped by my office to tell me we were getting a divorce.

It wasn't like things had ever gotten truly terrible, though making the drive to California from Ohio while barely being able to afford gas had been mildly terrifying, but I finally felt like I had a direction to go. With these parties for Jack to play at, he would get more and more exposure, and I would hopefully be able to start building a contact list and create my own shows in the bigger music venues in the city. If I could get a big enough online following for him, once I managed to get some decent recording equipment of course, I might even be able to set up a small tour for him, which would lead to bigger shows around the country. And from there…

"Did you know you get this little scowl on your face when you're thinking?" Jack said suddenly, making me jump. He laughed a little and clasped his hands behind his head as he leaned back. "And I won't pretend to not be self-centered enough to think you're thinking about me, so now I have to know if my ego is going to remain intact."

I grinned back at him. "I was thinking about you," I admitted, "but in a pretty broad sense. I'm making a plan for the future."

"Plans don't always go how you want them to," he warned.

"I know that." I really knew that. I'd planned to spend my life living an adventure with Steve, and then the accident had turned him into a closed-off man with no desire to live his own life, let alone share it with me. I'd planned to build a family and a home with Jordan, to stay in that suburban dream house we had and grow old together. And he'd decided we weren't compatible. I knew very well there was a high chance I would never be able to help Jack get famous. But…

"I'm willing to take the risk," I said. "Are you?" And I held out my hand, wondering just how deep his optimism ran.

Jack smiled and looked out over the city for a moment, and I wondered what was going through his head. But then he grasped my fingers and shook my hand, his expression warm and eager. "If you're taking this journey with me, Blake," he said, "then I like the sound of my odds."

I had spent enough time with my new family over the last several weeks that I was pretty sure I had a decent idea of what it was like to live the wealthy life. They all had the nicest cars, the prettiest homes, the best clothes, and they never worried about other people's opinions because they could afford to be whatever they wanted to be. Ergo, they could be as kind and friendly as they wanted without considering how people might take advantage of them or criticize the way they used their fortunes.

Clearly the Davenports were a rare breed, because by the time I showed up to Jack's fifth show, the third of the parties Lanna had helped me book, I was definitely starting to figure out that most of the elites were all exactly the same, and they were terrible.

It wasn't just the way they looked at Jack and me like we were dressed in the worst possible way and were clearly far beneath them. Technically, if I really accepted the fact that I was a Hastings, I was one of them, so it didn't really matter what they thought of me. Jack definitely didn't care, and he'd shown up to this particular party wearing that worn leather jacket again. It was a good look for him, but it made him stand out when everyone else was wearing designer.

More than the way we stuck out like odd thumbs, what got to me most was the way the elites demanded the impossible most of the time. "He has to play for two hours straight, no breaks longer than a few seconds," the first host had told me, and it had taken a whole lot of arguing to convince him that something like that just wasn't possible. Then he proceeded to tell me that if I took any photos, he had to approve them first, and I had to delete anything that wasn't a "true depiction of his hosting prowess," whatever that meant.

The second client had insisted that Jack stay hidden behind a curtained partition of the house so he wouldn't "be an eyesore" and his music could "come out of nowhere" like the house itself could play it, and though Jack hadn't minded the arrangement, I'd been tempted to refuse to follow through with the gig. In the end, the host had agreed to let him play in the corner if he didn't interact with any of her guests, and I had spent the night shooing away anyone who came too close.

This particular host, however, took one look at Jack and shook her head with a lot more conviction than the others I'd already dealt with. "No," she said. "I don't care if he comes recommended by the Queen of Art herself. I am not going to let some vagabond play for my husband's birthday."

Said husband was standing right behind her, and though he was talking to one of the early arriving guests, I could have sworn he glanced at his wife and rolled his eyes a bit.

"Mrs. Foster," I said, "I'm not really sure what the problem is." I knew exactly what the problem was, but I wanted her to realize it was a ridiculous issue she was taking. Yes, Jack had worn the leather jacket, but he looked incredible. Besides, the whole reason he was here was to play his music, not serve as part of the decoration.

Mrs. Foster's nostrils flared as she took another good look at Jack, who was pretending he had no idea what she was saying about him because he was entirely focused on the elaborate koi pond next to him.

"Ms. Blake," she said, and then she turned that examining gaze to me. Clearly she didn't like what she saw, and I tried not to take offense to that. Thank goodness Catherine had thought to lend me some of her clothes again, so I at least looked like I could fit in, even if I didn't have the sour personality for it.

"I live my life to a high standard," she continued. "My husband is turning fifty tonight, and there is nothing in the world that could convince me to allow something less than perfect to slide by."

Then I suppose you aren't going to accept those wilting flowers over there? I wanted to ask. But that wouldn't help the situation. "You did sign a contract," I said instead. "If you don't want Jack to play, then he doesn't have to play, but that doesn't change the fact that you owe him a hundred dollars for showing up tonight."

She scoffed a laugh. "You really think I am going to pay someone who looks like he crawled out of a gutter? You're out of your mind,

Ms. Blake, and I assure you I will be making my thoughts on your business ethic clear to those in my inner circle. You and your gutter dweller can leave."

"It's a sewer actually," Jack said suddenly, cutting off my own retort and putting his hand on my shoulder. "More shelter than a gutter. But a lot of people make that mistake, so don't feel too bad. After all, you can't differentiate between real pearls and fake ones, so I understand your confusion."

Mrs. Foster's hand shot to the very expensive-looking necklace at her neck, and she turned a lot paler than I expected. Wait, was Jack actually right about the pearls? "I promise," she practically snarled at me, "your little Jackson Thorn is never going to play in this city again if I have any say in the matter."

"You're Jackson Thorn?" Mr. Foster said behind her, since apparently he'd finally decided it was time to join the conversation. "I've been wanting to meet you for over a week now, but no one knows how to get in contact with you."

"I'm working on a website," I said quickly and stepped a little in front of Jack, just in case. "And I'd be happy to give you my email."

Mr. Foster smiled warmly, the complete opposite of his wife as he grasped my hand. "You must be the woman who keeps his head on straight," he said.

"Amelia Blake," I replied. "And happy birthday, Mr. Foster."

His face turned a bright red, and though Mrs. Foster threw her hands in the air in exasperation, he completely ignored her. "Thank you," he said. "And please, call me John. Now that you've managed to bring the one guy I've been trying to find, I think we've crossed beyond formalities. And you." He grasped Jack's hand next, a little more enthusiastically than he'd done with me. "I've heard your name more times in the last two weeks than I can count, and I'm wondering if you'd be interested in doing a charity show in the next couple of months."

Jack's eyebrows shot high onto his forehead, complete surprise in his eyes. "Oh. I didn't realize that was a thing out here. What kind of charity?"

"The best kind," said someone else. "John! Happy birthday!" A young woman somewhere in her twenties threw her arms around Mr. Foster's shoulders in a hug that was so enthusiastic it nearly knocked him off his feet.

"Thank you, Miss Al—uh, Mrs. Donovan. It's nice to see you back in the city."

"And clearly I've been gone too long if you've gone back to using last names," she replied. "We just got back this afternoon, but there was no way I was going to miss your party tonight." She was dressed in jeans and an old tie dye t-shirt, which was getting her concerned looks from some of the nearby guests, but she clearly didn't mind the stares, nor the fact that she had random little braids in her hair and looked like she'd come straight from a summer camp.

I wasn't at all sure about my suspicion, but I chanced a guess: "Beck Donovan?" The one family member I hadn't met yet.

She grinned at me and held out her hand. "The one and only. And I've been catching up on three months of family texts for the last few hours, so I'm pretty positive you're the mysterious Hastings sibling."

"Hastings?" Mrs. Foster asked, though it was more of a squeak than a word. "As in Seth and Catherine?" Goodness, she was even more pale than before, which meant she was probably just as terrified of my half-brother as the rest of the world.

I looked at her and wondered if I should use the name to my advantage, but then I glanced at Jack and saw him staring down at his feet with an odd look on his face. It wasn't anger as much as it was wariness, but there was something else to it. Disappointment? And I couldn't really understand why.

I was so confused by his expression that instead of exploiting my relations, I shrugged and said, "Yeah, but that's only a technicality. Seth and I don't really get along all that well."

"Oh," Beck said, perking up a little more, which was impressive, given the amount of energy she already had. "Is Jack going to play tonight? Everyone's been talking about him, and I've been dying to hear him."

Jack looked up and only managed a small smile. "That depends on if my sewer-dwelling sensibilities are to Mrs. Foster's liking," he said quietly. "Though it's John's birthday, so it should probably be up to him."

Mr. Foster chortled and put his arm around Jack's shoulders, which was difficult with his guitar sitting there as well. "Of course you're playing tonight! Did Mckenna pay you yet?" he asked me.

I shook my head. "There's a couple days' grace period in the contract," I said, but he was already pulling out his wallet and stuffing a hundred-dollar bill into Jack's hand. "You can set up over there, and the speakers and everything should be ready to go. Beck, I have several things I would love to discuss with you before you leave tonight, if you don't mind."

"I never mind," she replied with a grin, and she seemed absolutely fond of the man as he wandered off to greet other friends who had come to celebrate with him. Clearly he was nothing like his wife.

"I'll go get ready then," Jack muttered, and he gently touched my elbow as he passed me to set up on the little temporary stage that had been put up in the yard.

Beck was quick to pull my attention away from my mood-stricken musician as she wrapped me up in a sudden hug. "Indie was telling me about how hard it's been for you to get situated with the family," she said, as if we'd been talking for hours and were finally ready to get to the heart-to-heart stuff. "How're you holding up?"

"Fine," I said, though I wasn't sure I meant it. "But they are a lot to handle." But that wasn't true either. "They're wonderful, really, but this whole lifestyle doesn't really feel like me." Well, if I was going to say something like that, I might as well add, "Being in this city reminds me a lot of what my life was like when I was…"

Beck smiled. "Dating Steve?"

Wow, did the whole family just sit down every day and discuss the gruesome details of everyone they knew?

Laughing a little, Beck linked her arm with mine and directed me toward the food-laden table not too far away. "The Davenports like to take interest in anyone who needs their help," she said. "It's a little ridiculous sometimes, but they haven't actually been telling me all about you, if that's what you're thinking. It was Colin who made the connection, actually, though he's pretty sure you won't remember him." Then she touched the shoulder of someone who was munching on a carrot as he perused the other food items, and when he turned to us, I suddenly felt a little dizzy.

"Wait, you married Colin *Donovan*?" I sputtered. How had I never made the connection with his name?

And Colin grinned, setting his mostly empty plate on the table as he took me in. "It really is you," he said, as if he hadn't believed it was possible. "Everyone was talking about Amelia Blake, and I never thought they could have actually meant you. How've you been, Ames?"

Colin Donovan looked exactly as I remembered him from our days at Blackpoint Tech, though he was a bit tanner than I'd ever seen him, as if he'd spent several weeks in the sun. We hadn't worked in the same department, but he and Steve had been decently good friends before Colin started his own company, so I had often ended up tagging along whenever they went out for lunch or drinks after work or whatever. He'd been one of my favorite people in that job, outside of Steve, and seeing him was both a happy moment and a painful one. He was yet another reminder of the life I'd lost with Steve.

"I'm good," I said when I realized he'd asked me a question. "You?"

And then I glanced at Beck again, because I had met Colin's wife. More than once. And Beck wasn't her. Colin had been ridiculously in love with Jada, enough that I sometimes wanted to ask them if they were in a different reality from mine, and I really couldn't imagine him ever leaving her. Or the opposite.

Colin's smile faded a little, but when Beck took his hand, he brightened again, as if just having her near enough to touch gave him everything he could ever need in life. "Life's had its ups and downs," he said. "I lost Jada a few years back to a car accident."

My heart sank. "Oh no," I whispered, and I couldn't stop tears from welling up in my eyes. "I'm so sorry, Colin."

He shrugged. "It happens. I wish it didn't, but it's not like I could have done anything to prevent it. But now I have Beck"—his smile changed into something I'd never seen before—"and I can honestly say I can't imagine my life any other way."

"Love you too," she said quietly and rested her head against his shoulder. "So you worked at Blackpoint with Colin?" she asked me.

"And Steve," Colin added, frowning at me a little. "How're you handling that little bit of coincidence?"

I really didn't know how to answer that question, and luckily I didn't have to. In the next moment, a cough sounded over the speakers, drawing our attention to the stage.

"Looks like I lost a bet," Jack said, looking out over the waiting crowd. "I was convinced no one actually liked John Foster and I'd be playing to an empty crowd, but I'm happy to say you've all proven me wrong."

The guests all laughed, and I could see John Foster beaming over by his still-irritated wife.

"I've heard," Jack continued, "that I'm a bit hard to find, so in case I'm actually good at what I do, I've been told I need to direct all your attention to that lovely woman right over there." And he pointed at me.

My face burned with heat, and I was half tempted to pretend I hadn't even noticed. But there were too many eyes on me, and I could see Jack grinning at me as if he knew exactly what his little announcement was going to do to me. I fought against a glare and waved a little.

"Any questions about my schedule can be directed to Amelia Blake," Jack said. "If you ask me, I can honestly say I have no idea if I'm free next Tuesday, so you should probably go straight to the source. On that note…" He lifted his guitar and started to play, bringing the crowd's attention back to him completely.

"I like him," Beck said almost immediately. "I don't know what Seth is talking about."

"I've found it easier to never trust Seth's opinion of people," Colin replied. "I mean, the guy thinks Steve is an idiot, and that's ridiculous. Steve's one of the smartest guys I know."

Can we please stop talking about Steve? And Seth, for that matter? It was hard enough to focus on Jack's career. I didn't want to have to worry about the weird dynamics of my newfound family as well.

As always, Jack played a perfect show. He kept the crowd completely captivated, so much so that even Queen Foster herself couldn't seem to look away from him as he played.

Colin pulled his new wife into his arms and held her close, his smile small but completely content as the pair of them watched the show. They seemed happy, and I envied them for it. Beck seemed like the sort of person who wasn't afraid to go for what she wanted, and I had never met anyone steadier than Colin Donovan. What would it be like to find someone who completed me, like these two clearly did for each other?

When Jack finished, the party guests swarmed him, and I knew it would be a while before he returned to my side. That was perfectly okay, since I happened to get swarmed as well, person after person wanting to hire Jack to play at their next event.

Finally, after what felt like hours, the last person left my side, leaving me alone by the garden gate with a splitting headache but a whole lot of promise for Jack's future, which I hoped was worth the endless conversations. I doubted most of these contacts would lead to anything, but at least I had more leads than I had before the evening started. That was something.

"Out of curiosity," Jack suddenly said in my ear, and he paused when I jumped and nearly stumbled back into the hedge behind me, waiting until I was steady again. "When were you going to tell me about that website?"

"Oh." I wondered why he looked weird, and it took me a second to realize he was scowling. Of all the expressions I'd seen on the man's face, I'd never seen a scowl. "I was going to tell you about it."

He raised an eyebrow.

"When it actually looked like a website," I continued, and when he still didn't say anything, I shrugged. "The notes app on my phone can only do me so much good, so I figured I would use my very limited coding skills to design a way for people to book you for gigs. Nothing special."

His expression softened, and he nodded a little. "Yeah, okay, that makes sense."

What was wrong with setting up a website to showcase his talent? I didn't want to bring back that scowl if I asked. "I'll let you look it over before it goes live, if you want."

"I trust you," he replied and turned to look at the few guests who remained at the party. Mrs. Foster had been reluctantly pleased by the results of Jack's playing and had spent the night accepting praise over her choice of entertainment. It hadn't quite softened her earlier blows, however, since she had refused to acknowledge the fact, and she couldn't seem to avoid sending glares my way any time she looked over.

"You wanna get out of here?" Jack said and touched his hand to my elbow.

I looked at him in surprise. "What?"

He laughed a little. "I mean do you want to go get ice cream or something? My treat, since now I'm filthy rich." The man had all of a hundred bucks in his pocket, but his grin was a little hard to resist. It was after ten o'clock, and he had to have been as tired as me, probably more so. But the thought of doing something that wasn't work sounded incredible.

"Yeah," I said.

He grinned. "Good."

The Bay was beautiful at night. We walked along Fisherman's Wharf with overpriced milkshakes from the Ghirardelli shop, and neither of us said much as we looked out over the water. I wondered if Jack was thinking about anything in particular, but it was hard to tell. He looked neither happy nor unhappy, though I would have thought he would be thrilled about playing such a successful show. Jack was so chill all the time that I really had no idea what he thought about anything.

That should have bothered me, because if I couldn't read his mood I couldn't adapt to it, but it didn't. I liked how Jack just took life in stride, never concerned by things he couldn't control. I wished I could do the same.

"So," he said after a long while, and he gestured to a bench and slipped his guitar off his shoulders. "I'll be honest with you; I had a reason for coming out here aside from wanting ice cream."

I'd figured as much, so I smiled. I had my suspicions he didn't do well with crowds, so it wasn't hard to believe he wanted some time away from people. "And what reason was that?" I asked.

"You looked way too stressed, and you needed a break."

I almost dropped my shake. "Wait, what?"

Grinning, he shrugged and played with his straw. "You might think that because I only see you once or twice a week so you can make me money, I don't know how hard you've been working. But I do. You're designing websites, and booking gigs, and mapping out how long it'll take us to get somewhere, and the only reason I've even been able to play anywhere outside of street corners and parks is because you're spending all your free time on me. And all I've been able to give you is some ice cream and a few bucks." His smile turned apologetic.

"I knew exactly what I was getting into," I argued. *Sort of.* "It's not like I'm hating what I'm doing."

"Yeah, but are you loving it?"

I frowned. "Why does that matter?"

As he raised his dark eyebrows at me, he didn't have to say anything for me to understand that apparently it did matter, which was surprising. As long as I was doing my job, he shouldn't have cared how I felt about it. Besides, I'd told the truth. I didn't hate the work, as stressful as it could be.

"I like finding you places to play," I said. "I like making you look better. And if I wasn't doing this, I honestly don't know what I would be doing with my time, so it shouldn't—"

"What's your dream, Amelia?" He turned to me when he asked the question, folding one leg up onto the bench and staring me down with his icy blue gaze.

I cocked my head. "My dream?"

"Yeah. If you could do anything, what would it be?"

What kind of a stupid question was that? That couldn't possibly be something anyone had an answer to. "I don't know. Does anyone know that?"

"I do."

"What would you do?"

"I'm doing it."

"Oh."

"Come on, Blake. Anything in the world. What would it be?"

I had already had this conversation with myself since turning down that perfect job, and I was no closer to finding an answer than I'd been then. "Do I really have to answer that?" I asked quietly. *How about we sit in silence instead of digging into the fact I've never had a dream?* At least not like he had.

"Look," he said, grabbing my hand. "I may not know tons about you, but I'm pretty sure your plan when you got to San Francisco was not to become a manager for a sort-of-good guitarist. So unless you want me to feel like I've derailed all your best-laid plans, at least tell me something. One thing you've always wanted to do."

I wanted to tell him that he had absolutely no reason to feel guilty, but I knew he wouldn't accept that as an answer, and I figured he would make me give him a real answer before he let me head home. So I sipped at my shake and thought about it.

"No," he said forcefully, catching me off guard. "Don't think, Amelia. Just talk. One thing. If you could do anything right this minute, what would it be?"

"Play your guitar," I blurted out, though I had no idea where that had come from.

And Jack grinned, grabbing his guitar without a word.

What am I doing? My fingers shaking, I grasped the instrument like it was a priceless porcelain doll that had already been dropped once.

Jack rolled his eyes. "You're not going to break it, Blake. Calm down. Just hold it on your lap." He positioned it for me then laughed when he saw my face. "I'm starting to think you don't actually want to do this."

"I want to," I insisted and took a deep breath. I was being ridiculous. *Get a hold of yourself, Amelia.* "Sorry, I just… I know how much this guitar means to you, and—"

"There are other guitars out there. Now, I'll teach you some of the easier chords." He hesitated for a second, and then he scooted close. "Uh, I don't know how best to do this, so…"

To my alarm, he wrapped his left arm around my shoulders and tapped my fingers where they rested on the strings. "Put this one on this string here. This one here. And this one…"

I could feel every little muscle in his arms, which surprised me because he was so skinny, but that didn't stop my face from burning. Or maybe that was because his face was right next to mine, closer than he'd ever been. If my face hadn't already been on fire, I might have felt the warmth of his cheek.

"Okay," he said, "so just push those strings down and strum."

I ran my thumb down the strings and was surprised to hear something almost musical come out. "Oh!"

I couldn't see him, with him this close, but I was positive I felt him smile. "Now try this one." He positioned my fingers again, and a different but equally beautiful chord came out.

He showed me one more chord, and then he ran through all three again to help me remember how they go. "I'll tell you when to switch," he said, and then he started to pick the strings, his left arm still wrapped around my shoulders.

Somehow he managed to play something magnificent, even if I messed up the chords several times. And while it wasn't anything close to what he could produce on his own, I still felt like there was a magic to the music as he seemed to caress the strings, like he was coaxing the melody out of the instrument rather than creating it.

It wasn't long before my fingers hurt too much to keep pushing the strings, and our little duet came to an end. I figured Jack would shift back to his side of the bench, but, as always, he paused where he was as if frozen, letting the silence following the song fill the air around us for a moment. When he finally did move, it wasn't far, and he just pulled his arm back over to his own side so we sat shoulder to shoulder.

"So," he said softly, almost with reverence. "What's next?"

I still couldn't believe I had helped make such a beautiful song, so I was a little disoriented. "Hmm?"

"You played my guitar, so what's next on your list?"

I didn't have a list. It had been hard enough to get to the whole guitar playing idea, and I couldn't figure out why he didn't understand that. I wasn't like him. I wasn't calm, and carefree, and endlessly optimistic. I couldn't just trust that things would work out when experience had taught me that it often didn't. I wished I could be like him and have my dreams all laid out in front of me.

But I wasn't.

"I don't know," I said and looked into his face, wishing I could get some of his wisdom just by sitting next to him like this. Honestly, how did a twenty-six-year-old have the whole world figured out when I felt like I was only starting to scratch the surface at thirty? Handing his guitar back to him, I tried not to look too grumpy as I turned my gaze back to the bay and waited for him to keep pushing.

Thankfully, he didn't. He slipped the guitar back into its case, and he settled into the bench. I refused to look at him and get even an idea of what he was thinking about, because sometimes Jack was just a little too knowing. I may have been older than him, but he'd clearly lived a fuller life and therefore knew more than I did.

"You should get to bed," he said after a while and held out his hand to me to help me up. "I'll walk you home."

At his words, I suddenly felt exhausted, and I nodded. It would have been a whole lot easier to call a car, maybe even call Seth or Catherine to come pick us up, but it was late enough that I didn't want to bother anyone. I had two perfectly good feet, didn't I?

By the time we reached my apartment, I felt like I could have fallen asleep standing up, and I was barely able to acknowledge Jack as he told me goodnight at the main door before continuing on his way. I paused, however, with my hand on the door, a thought jumping into my head so quickly that I was amazed I'd never thought about it before. It was strong enough that it woke me up just a little bit, and I turned and called, "Jack?"

He looked back. "What's up?"

"Where have you been staying all this time?" We'd been in San Francisco for almost a month, and I was horrified that I'd never wondered that before. He could afford an apartment even less than I could, and I got the sudden image of him actually living down in a sewer like he'd told Mrs. Foster.

Flashing a brief smile, he shrugged. "There's a hostel on the other side of town that's not too bad. Lots of interesting people there, and sometimes you can trade things with people."

He'd been staying in a grungy hostel for a month? Suddenly I was imagining a bunch of druggies sharing a twin bed with him. (I had no idea how hostels worked, but I figured they weren't the greatest of accommodations.) Shuddering a little, I spoke before I could talk myself out of it: "You wanna sleep on my couch tonight? So you don't have to walk all that way."

Jack grinned. "I'm fine."

But I wasn't. Not now that I knew he really didn't have a place to call home. My apartment wasn't nice by any means, but at least it was mine. "Jack. It's nearly midnight."

"Which is exactly why you should go to bed and stop worrying about me," he replied.

"I'm serious."

"So am I."

"I'm never going to be able to sleep now that I know about the hostel."

He huffed a little in annoyance, but I could tell I was wearing him down. If there was one thing I had inherited from the Hastings side of my family, it was stubbornness. "You're really not going to give up on this, are you?" he asked, his smile growing.

I shook my head. "How long are you going to make me stand out here?"

With a massive sigh, he spun on his heel and came back to my side, grabbing the door to let me in first. "You are a lot feistier than you look, Blake," he muttered as we took the stairs up to the fourth floor.

"Steve used to tell me that all the time," I said, and then I cringed, pausing at my door as I tried not to think too hard about the things Steve used to tell me. There was no point in going down that road.

"Your ex-fiancé?" Jack asked.

"And my new brother-in-law," I replied bitterly.

"Whoa."

"Yeah."

Unlocking the door, I pushed it open and trudged inside, exhausted again. It had been a long day, and I was ready for it to end. Tomorrow would bring follow-up emails with all the contacts I'd made and more venue research and maybe even looking into a proper camera at least so I could put up another video of Jack playing, but for now I just wanted to sleep.

"When did you move in, Blake?" Jack asked behind me. He was looking around at the front room, which had nothing but a couch I'd gotten for ten bucks from an online yard sale.

"A few weeks ago," I replied, and I could imagine what he was thinking. Yes, my apartment was a little sparse, but I was rarely here anyway, so I didn't mind it.

Jack gently leaned his guitar against the side of the couch. "Where's all your furniture?" he asked next.

Yep, exactly what I thought. "It's hard to afford furniture when technically I can't even afford my rent," I muttered. "But it's fine. At least I have a place for you to sleep." My bedroom door was just beyond the couch, and I hurried inside to grab him one of my blankets. "I don't have a pillow, sorry," I said as I handed it to him.

He took it, but he was still staring at the place my dining room table should be. "You bought me clothes," he said, frowning. "Amelia…"

"I used my dad's money to buy those," I argued. "And I'll pay him back when I can. It's fine. You're still starting out, so of course there's not going to be a lot of income for the first little bit."

"You should be getting half, not ten percent."

I rolled my eyes. "Jack, that's not how this works. I wouldn't be getting anything if you weren't doing the important part. Eventually you're going to get rich and famous, which means I'll be at least one of those, and then I can buy the fanciest apartment stuff in the world."

He almost smiled at the words *apartment stuff*, but it wasn't quite enough to get rid of that frown. "What if I don't get rich and famous?" he asked quietly. "What if life decides to send me on a different path and I can't bring you with me? I don't know if I'm meant for this, Amelia."

Of all the times for him to not be an optimist? Sighing, I slipped back into my bedroom and stopped in the doorway to look back at him. "You'll get there," I assured him, and then I closed my door before he could try to argue. He was supposed to be the one who saw the silver lining, and I was way too tired to do it for both of us.

CHAPTER TEN

"Morning," I mumbled, though it came out more as a moan than a word. Bleary-eyed and stumbling, I made my way into the kitchen and grabbed a bowl and spoon from the drying rack on the counter. I could barely see straight enough to pour cereal into the bowl without missing a few pieces. As they bounced across the countertop, I sighed and watched them disappear from view on the other side of the counter.

I'd get them later.

As soon as I managed—barely—to get milk into the bowl, I wandered over to the couch and sat down. Thankfully, Jack was already munching on his own bowl of cereal, so I could ignore the grin he was fighting and just focus on getting some food in me before I fell asleep again.

"Good morning," he said eventually.

It had been three weeks since the first time he'd slept on the couch, and I'd really gotten used to him being around. It made my life feel a little more normal, knowing there would be someone there to wish me good morning. I'd gotten used to that little bit when I was married to Jordan, and I really enjoyed having it back.

"How are you even awake?" I said, hating that he looked as bright and alive as ever. He'd been up just as late as I had, and he'd had to play a whole show. I'd just sat there in the back, mesmerized by his music as always.

"Thai chi," he said, which meant he'd already been out to Lafayette Park to play for a local group who practiced every morning and had fallen in love with his calming music, just like I had. I had no idea how he did it, since the group usually met around 5:30 in the morning. "But now that you're up, I'm going to take a shower, if that's cool with you."

I had told him many times he could come in and use the bathroom whenever he needed to, even if I was asleep. He had refused just as many times, and I loved him for it.

"Don't spill your food on my bed, Blake," he added as he hopped up and headed for my bedroom.

"That was one time!" I complained, but he'd already shut the bathroom door.

It had been his fault, anyway, since he had been out on my tiny little balcony but had come up behind me without warning. He'd scared me badly enough that my entire sandwich had fallen apart onto the couch when I jumped. Still, I didn't mind his teasing. We'd fallen into an easy routine with each other, and though he spent most of his time during the day playing at the parks or whatever else he did, while I spent mine at the library where the internet was faster than on my phone, I'd gotten used to our little routine.

What I hadn't gotten used to was him calling me Blake, and I really wished he would stop. I was trying to get over Jordan and forget how much I missed my life with him, and it didn't help that Jack kept reminding me that I'd gotten my last name from him. I figured Jack was too used to doing it now, though, so there was little point in trying to change the habit.

Once I had finished my cereal and was finally a little more awake—it took a lot longer than I wished it did—I pulled up my email on my phone and groaned when I saw eighteen unread messages, all from the website. That meant eighteen people who wanted to book Jack for their birthday party or bar mitzvah or fancy dinner, and I would have to weed through them to find the ones that were actually worth it. Most people who contacted me through the site wanted Jack to play for free, which was ridiculous, and many of them tried to get a discount because he was still somewhat unknown, though that part was quickly changing. I'd tried to keep myself from overextending his schedule as best I could, but the only way to get him recognition—and to get both of us money for food and stuff—was to have him play as many shows as he could handle. It was a delicate balance, one I wasn't sure I was maintaining well.

Of course, Jack would never complain.

When Jack came out of the shower, hair dripping and eyes bright, I'd managed to reject four or five of the requests, those who had wanted Jack to play for chump change or free. But I was still pretty tired, and I really didn't want to keep reading through the emails.

Jack settled on the couch next to me as I stuffed my phone in my pocket, hoping the emails would answer themselves if I did that, and he gave me his signature grin. "That bad, huh?"

I shrugged. "You're too popular, Jackson Thorn."

"I highly doubt that, but thanks for making me feel good about myself."

I turned to him, wishing I could have his never-ending cheerfulness. "You don't have a show tonight, so what's the plan for you today?"

He stretched his arms out behind him and shrugged. "Maybe play at the park again and talk to some more people." He'd been doing that a lot, though I had no idea why he was so content to have endless conversations with strangers. It seemed important to him, though, and it was almost like he was searching for something in particular. "Maybe try to work on some new songs," he added then frowned at the blank wall opposite us. "You really need a TV, Blake."

He had said that more than once, so I rolled my eyes. "I don't have time to watch it anyway, so why would I spend the money I don't have?"

I knew exactly what would come next, since he'd done the same thing almost every day for the last two weeks: "At least get yourself a kitchen table," he continued. "Then I can stop finding breadcrumbs underneath me in the middle of the night."

"One time!" I said again, rolling my eyes. "Jack, I can barely afford my rent, so what makes you think I can buy myself a table? It's not like I *really* need it."

"Maybe," he said, "but a good table could turn this place into an actual home. Don't you feel unsettled living like this?"

"Don't you?" I countered. He was living on a couch, after all.

"I chose this life. You didn't."

I couldn't really argue against that, as much as I wanted to. "Well," I said, "if I can figure out how to book you for some shows where people actually pay to hear you play instead of just individuals hiring you, then maybe I'll get myself a table. Maybe."

A thoughtful look on his face, Jack turned to me and said, "Don't hate me for this one. You could always use your dad's money, right?"

After an especially late show last week, I had caved and booked us a car on the internet to take us back to my apartment so we didn't have to walk clear across town. I had stupidly decided we should walk there, since my car was struggling a bit, and I had only realized just how far the event was after it had taken us a lot longer to get there than I'd planned. So I'd said something about the obscene amount of money sitting ignored in my bank account, and Jack hadn't said a word.

Clearly he'd been listening to my tired babbling, though.

"That money is only mine temporarily," I said. "Eventually I'll have to pay him back, so I don't want to use it if I don't have to. As much as I want one, I don't need a table, Jack. I'm fine."

Though I could tell he wanted to keep arguing, he dropped the subject and went back to staring at the wall as if I actually had a TV hanging there. After a couple of minutes, he pulled out a pen and a little notebook from his pocket and scribbled something down.

"New song?" I asked with interest.

He shook his head. "Sort of. I've been working on it for a while. It's being difficult, though."

"What's it about?"

He shook his head again. "Not until it's finished," he said. "So what are *your* plans today, Blake? Please tell me you're doing something other than Jackson Thorn stuff. You're going to start hating me if you spend so much time with me on your mind."

"That's unlikely," I replied then frowned when my comment made him grin. "Don't read into that," I warned him. "I'm not one of your little groupies."

And thank goodness for that. He'd collected half a dozen young women who seemed to be at every party Jack was hired for, and I had no idea how they could know where he would be at all times. It was a little concerning, and I made a mental note to ask Colin if he could check the security of the website I'd built, just in case. He was better at the whole computer thing, and I really liked spending time with his wife, Beck.

After several outings with her and Colin's daughter, Macy, I had quickly figured out why Indie liked her so much. Beck was, at least compared to the rest of my family, blissfully normal, and I felt like I could actually relate to her because she hadn't grown up surrounded by money.

As much as I'd been trying to become a part of the Davenports, I still didn't feel like I was one of them. I was worried I never would. They were just as overwhelming as ever, and I found excuses to stay away from full family gatherings whenever I could. Every time I did that, I felt guilty. My family was the whole reason I'd come out to California.

"So?" Jack pressed. "What's on Amelia Blake's agenda today? No wait, I'm adjusting my question: What non-Jack-related things are you doing today?"

At least I had an answer for him today, though I wouldn't have usually. "I'm going out to lunch with Indie," I told him with a smile. He didn't need to know that we were planning a concert in her coffee shop so she could try to increase her customer base. "But after that, I'll have to finish going through all these show requests, whether you want me to or not."

Thankfully, he smiled and got up, slipping his guitar onto his shoulders. "What time do you think you'll be home?" he asked, since he had adamantly refused to accept the second key to the apartment. Apparently he was perfectly content to be a houseguest, even though it was starting to feel like this was as much his apartment as it was mine.

I ran through my schedule in my head. "Probably around two?"

"Sounds great," he replied, and then he was gone.

After two months of knowing the guy, I would have thought I would understand him more, but there was nothing about Jack that made sense. There was nothing about him that was normal. He was completely unique, and I really loved that about him.

Even if it made it hard to know exactly how he wanted me to be around him.

It probably wasn't a good sign that, at the moment I saw my half-brother sitting with Indie in her shop, I nearly turned around and walked straight back to my apartment.

I loved Seth. I really did. He'd gotten a lot softer around me since I met him, and he was generally a happy guy, even if he usually had the facial expression of a supervillain having a bad day. He was probably one of the most kind-hearted people I knew, and I felt honored that he never once hesitated to call me his sister. But the problem with having a guy like Seth Hastings for an older brother was knowing exactly why he would be sitting in Indie's coffee shop on a random Tuesday morning.

This was about Jack.

Taking a fortifying breath, I counted to ten before I stepped into the shop, hoping I could keep my bitter thoughts to myself this time. The last time Seth had mentioned Jack, we'd gotten into a rather heated argument that had ended with me almost cowering beneath his glare because he'd slipped back into "soldier mode," as Catherine called it. He had immediately apologized, but the resentment still festered a little inside my chest. He wanted me to be a distrustful person, and I just couldn't do that. Especially with Jack.

"Hey, Indie," I said when I stepped inside the shop. "Hi, Seth."

Seth sent me a well-practiced smile then dropped it a moment later when he realized I didn't believe it. "Okay, fine," he muttered and folded his arms.

Indie rolled her eyes as she gestured for me to sit. "Please don't make me feel like I'm some kind of mediator between the two of you. You're the one who wanted to be better about all of this, Seth."

I sat. Reluctantly. "All of this meaning…?"

"I was telling everyone at dinner on Sunday about this concert idea," Indie said. "Everyone liked the idea. Except…"

"It's not like I'm against you hosting a concert, Indie," Seth growled.

I glared at him a little, which thankfully worked to soften his scowl a bit. "You're just against Jack," I guessed.

"Which is ridiculous," Indie replied, and she took my hand in a gesture of solidarity. "I've met him more than once, and he's a really nice guy."

"*You've* met him," Seth said. "I haven't. Neither has Matthew, or Adam, or Steve, and we're just—"

"What?" I interrupted. "You're jealous?"

Indie snorted in laughter, and I was infinitely glad she was here with me. Like her husband, she never seemed intimidated by Seth, and I badly wanted her strength so I could better stand my ground this time.

"Why are you so convinced he's up to something sinister?" I asked Seth. "He's just here to play music, and I'm pretty sure he's not even in it for the money."

"I'm convinced he's hiding something dangerous," Seth replied. "Why else won't he tell you his last name?"

"Because he doesn't want to be dragged down by his past," I said. "It doesn't matter what's in it, because he's a good man now. Shouldn't that be enough?"

Except, I didn't really accept my own response. Not entirely. Yes, Jack had grown to be a part of my life, but there was a lot he didn't tell me. Like whenever I asked him about his day, he often got a look in his eyes that didn't match his general brightness. Like there was a sadness lurking just beneath the surface.

I was infinitely afraid he wasn't happy and I was failing as his manager, but until the day he sent me away, I would keep trying to get him everything he deserved and more.

Seth narrowed his eyes and leaned a little closer, his turquoise eyes cutting into mine and making me wonder if there was more to this man than super strength. Could he read minds too?

"You like him, don't you?" he growled.

This time it was me who snorted out a laugh. Of course I liked Jack, but my brother clearly thought there was more to this relationship than there was. "What?" I asked, my eyes wide. "Are you serious? He's my friend, Seth. That's all he's ever been." I honestly couldn't tell if Seth believed me, but I really didn't care. Jack didn't deserve this from him, and I was not going to stand for it. "Thank you for being worried about me," I told him, "but I don't need you looking into every little thing that could potentially be a threat. I can take care of myself, Seth. And now that you've said your piece, Indie and I have a concert to plan. Thanks for stopping by."

To my amazement, Seth left after studying me a moment, and I stared at the door as he disappeared through it, not entirely sure how I'd managed to make that happen.

"Wow," Indie breathed. "You really are a Hastings when you put your mind to it."

I felt a little dizzy sitting there, so I was glad she was still holding onto my hand, just in case I fainted. "Apparently," I muttered and took a slow, calming breath. "Do you think he's going to hate me?"

She smiled, shaking her head. "Seth is incapable of hating anyone. I know it's hard for you to see it, but he just wants what's best for you, and his strength is one of the few things he thinks he has. I think…" She frowned as she thought for a moment. "I think something's going on with him, because I've never seen him this bad. He's scared, and I've never seen Seth scared."

"So it's not just me?" I asked, surprised by how much better that made me feel to know I wasn't the only one who thought Seth was overreacting with the whole Jack thing. "Catherine's been weird too. But what sort of thing would scare him?"

Indie shrugged, deep in thought. "I can't pretend I'm an expert on the Davenports, but this family has been through a lot. Those two in particular. I have my suspicions, but… I just hope it doesn't take too long for them to remember that they don't have to deal with everything on their own." She gave my hand a squeeze then said, "I really don't think it has anything to do with you, Amelia, and he'll come around about Jack. I promise."

I hoped so, because no matter how frustrated he could make me, I still wanted to keep Seth in my life. After all, we were family, and family was one of the most important things in the world.

"Let's plan this thing before I start to freak out," I said and pulled out a sheet of paper, ready to help Indie create a night to remember.

I got home just after two and found Jack waiting for me in the hallway, which surprised me.

"It started raining," he explained when I gave him a questioning look, though that fact didn't seem to bother him. In fact, he had a wide grin on his face, as if nothing could be better than getting soaking wet. "I'll just play some more tomorrow for the people who didn't get to hear."

I had to admit, he looked really good after getting caught in the storm, with his dark hair dripping into his face and making his eyes even brighter than usual by contrast. It reminded me of the day we met, and I loved how he managed to smile even when things didn't go according to plan.

As I unlocked the door to let him inside, I said, "Maybe we should rethink this whole playing for free thing," because if people wanted to hear him play so badly, they would probably pay to do it. Even if it was only five dollars a ticket, that would still be more money in Jack's pocket.

But Jack apparently had other ideas. "I like playing for free. I know it's not exactly business savvy, but you've probably guessed I don't do this for the money."

"Why *do* you do it?" I wondered out loud. I might have told Seth that he wasn't in it for the money, but that didn't mean I knew the reason why. Maybe if I could understand why he was here, I could be exactly what he needed me to be.

Jack took a while to answer, settling himself on the couch after stowing his guitar in its usual place in the corner. "Money isn't everything," he said finally.

Maybe he was right, and my life had certainly felt different since being forced to keep track of my every penny. But still… "Money helps you stay in control of your life," I argued.

"If I've learned anything being on the road," he replied, "it's that you can't control anything, so it's better to learn to roll with the punches."

I frowned at him, because for how often he told me things would always work out, that sounded a lot more like a pessimist's view than it should have. Maybe my perception was tainted by my interaction with Seth, but I was pretty sure something was bothering Jack, and I wished he would just tell me what it was so I could help.

Before I could say anything, however, there was a knock at the door, and I left him to go see who could possibly be wanting to visit me in the middle of the afternoon.

"Amelia Blake?" asked the guy on the other side. He wore what looked like a delivery outfit, and there were two other guys just behind him with a huge, plastic-wrapped thing on a dolly between them.

"Yeah," I said warily, "but I didn't order anything."

As if he'd expected this, the man plopped a clipboard into my hands and rolled his eyes. "If you're Amelia Blake," he said, "and this is apartment 4D, then I'm supposed to deliver this no later than 2:30, so I'm on the clock. Sign there." He pointed.

I stared at the invoice. It was clearly my name and my address, but I had absolutely no idea where the thing had come from. "Wait," I muttered, looking at the item description. "A table?"

"Table and four chairs," the man confirmed. "If you could just…" He waved his men forward, and I had no choice but to get out of their way as they rolled the table forward and through the door.

I watched as they unwrapped the rather gorgeous table and put it in the empty spot by the kitchen, and a moment later they returned with four equally beautiful chairs. I signed the receipt without thinking when the man pointed again, and then suddenly they were gone, and my apartment had a brand new, most likely expensive dining set sitting there looking all innocent.

I immediately turned to Jack, who had said nothing as he sat there on the couch and watched. "Did you buy me a table?" I asked.

He raised an eyebrow. "Seriously, Blake? I'm sleeping on your couch for a reason; you really think I could afford something like that? It's got to be worth a couple thousand dollars."

I had no idea how he knew that, but I believed him. And though I still had my suspicions, since he had said only that morning how much he wanted me to have a table, he made a good point. The guy had all of five shirts, four of which I'd bought him, and I was pretty convinced the only time he ate real food was when he was with me. He couldn't afford this table any more than I could.

Approaching the set slowly, I touched my finger to the mahogany surface and couldn't help but smile a little. The design really was incredible, and I found myself imagining how nice it would be to be able to sit across from Jack while we ate breakfast instead of next to him. It would make things feel a little more normal.

"Maybe that scary brother of yours?" Jack said.

I glanced back at him and frowned. "How do you know my brother is scary?" I tried not to talk about my family with Jack, partly because I felt like it was wrong to not want to spend time with them, but mostly because I didn't know anything about Jack's family since he never talked about them. I didn't want to broach any touchy subjects.

"Even I've heard of Seth Hastings," Jack replied as he got up so he could come to examine the table with me. "And I saw his wife; pretty sure they're wildly rich."

He wasn't wrong, and I pulled my phone out of my pocket, texting both Seth and Lissa, just in case. If it wasn't one of them—though I couldn't fathom how they would know I didn't have a table—I had no idea where it could have come from.

Lissa texted back first: *No, that wasn't me.*

Seth was quick to follow: *Hang on, you haven't had a kitchen table until now?*

I grimaced, easily picturing his irritated scowl, and I suddenly worried that he would show up here so he could assess the state of my home and promptly fill it with everything it was apparently lacking.

"That's not a good face," Jack said as he glanced down at my phone.

Did you look at the invoice to see who bought it? Lissa texted.

Sure enough, Seth's next text made me groan a little: *Please tell me you at least have a bed in that place.*

"A crappy twin," Jack muttered under his breath, and I made a face at him.

"I like my bed," I said, though I was pretty sure he didn't believe me.

Calm down, I texted before Seth came to any more ridiculous conclusions. *I have everything I need. So neither of you bought it? What about the Davenports?*

Could have been Dad, Seth replied, and Lissa quickly agreed.

Which meant I would probably never know, because I had no intention of ever contacting my father if I could help it.

"Mystery solved?" Jack asked when I just stood there clutching my phone.

"I guess so?" But the longer I looked at the incredible table, the more I knew I wanted to keep it, and that wasn't going to fly. Even if my father had bought it for me, I didn't want his charity any more than I had when I found the money in my bank account. "I'm going to return it," I decided and started searching the company's website so I could get the delivery guys to come back before they got too far.

But Jack snatched my phone out of my hands. "No you're not," he said and looked at me like I'd said something completely crazy.

Though I tried to grab it back, Jack was faster than me. "Hey!"

Grinning, he darted around to the other side of the table to get himself a decent distance from me. "I know you're stubborn," he said, "but I warn you; I'm worse."

"No you're not." Go-with-the-flow Jack was as far from stubborn as they came. "Give me my phone so I can call the company and get this thing out of here."

He shook his head. "I can't do that."

"Why not? It's *my* table."

"Which means you should want to keep it, not get rid of it."

"Jack! I don't want to keep it." I leapt for my phone, but before I could grab it, Jack grabbed me instead, wrapping his arms around me and pinning mine to my sides as he pulled my back against his chest.

"Are you really selfish enough to give it back?"

I froze, not sure what he meant by that. Or maybe it was because he was so close, closer than he'd ever been. I could feel his warm breath on the back of my neck and his heartbeat pounding in my shoulder blade. "What?" The word came out breathless, and I didn't think it was because he held me too tight. Everything about this moment was confusing, and I didn't know why my heart was racing so much as he held me against him.

"That doesn't make any sense," I whispered.

"There's a difference between being proud of your accomplishments and simply being proud," Jack replied. His voice had gotten softer, gentler, as he spoke into my ear and sent a shiver through me. "Sometimes you have to be willing to accept help from people, because maybe they need it as much as you do."

I had to gain some control of the conversation back, even if I had no idea how I'd lost it in the first place. How did one touch make me crumble? "Did you learn all this fancy wisdom from your unsettled life on the streets?" I asked in a sarcastic grumble, hoping it would make things feel more normal.

"Yeah," he replied, and there was nothing sarcastic in his response. "Just keep the table, Amelia. Trust me." And he released me so I could turn around and look at him.

The look on his face—the kind of look that said he knew from experience what he was saying was true—kept me from arguing again. Was this part of his past creeping up? Or was it just Jack, who was probably a whole lot smarter than I realized?

"Fine," I said, though I felt like I was missing something now that he'd let go of me. "I won't return it. Happy?"

He smiled warmly. "Always. Now, I'm pretty sure you spent your fun little lunch talking about me, so how about we go for a walk before you start working again? You need a break."

I glanced out the window, if only to give me a reason to try to catch my breath. It still hadn't caught up to me after Jack grabbed me like he did. "It's still raining," I pointed out, hoping that would be enough to get things back to normal.

But Jack held out his hand toward me. "So? I happen to think rain is a lot more healing than people think. Maybe it'll do you some good."

And though I knew I had too much to do to get ready for this concert, my heart beat out my head this time, and I reached out and took his hand. I very much wanted to spend some more time with this guy and maybe absorb some of his wisdom just by being near him.

Heaven knew I needed it.

CHAPTER ELEVEN

Indie managed to sell out of tickets for her night of music in two days. She couldn't have been more pleased, and I was thrilled to know people *were* willing to pay to see Jack play, which meant my musician's future was definitely looking bright. Jack seemed excited about the show's potential and promised me he wouldn't get nervous.

When the day of the event came around, though, I came out of my bedroom after getting ready and found him pacing the living room after being out all morning. I'd never seen him pace, and that worried me.

"What's wrong?" I asked, trepidation sinking into the pit of my stomach.

Jack glanced at me and tried to look natural when he smiled at me. "You look great."

"Jack."

"Nothing's wrong."

"Uh huh."

"Indie called while you were in the shower," he said, glancing at my phone where it sat on the table. "She said your family is really excited to spend some time with you. Are they all going to be there?"

I nodded, trying not to let my nerves show. "It'll be the first time I've been around all of them at once. They're great, but they can be overwhelming. Is that why you're nervous?"

His expression hardened. "No, of course not. I'm sure your family is great."

"Then what's going on?"

"She also said she had so many people wanting to come to the show that she started selling outdoor seating, and she'll just open up all the windows."

I cocked my head. "Isn't that a good thing? It means you're popular, Jack."

"It means a couple hundred people are going to be there," he replied.

"Again, a good thing." He hadn't played to an audience that big since the festival on the wharf.

"Yeah." And he started to pace again.

"You said you wouldn't get nervous," I reminded him, wondering what drugs could help him relax without impairing his ability to play. This was his first ticketed show, and it needed to go well for both him and Indie.

"I'm not nervous to play," he replied, snapping a little. Then he froze and looked over at me with the expression of someone who had just accidentally offered up some great insult. "I'm sorry, Blake," he muttered, and he truly looked it. "I wish I could explain."

Why can't you? I didn't often mind him keeping secrets, since they usually involved his past, but this felt different. This wasn't a past problem; this was a *now* problem. As much as I wanted to push him for more information, I would much rather have him trust that I would trust him. That was our whole thing; trusting each other. It had been from the beginning, when I'd let a total stranger ride across the country with me. He had always been worth trusting before now, so I swallowed my questions and smiled.

"But you'll play?" I asked.

He nodded. "I'll do anything you ask me to."

A warmth filled my chest at his words because I absolutely believed him. "Are you ready to go?"

But his frown deepened, and though he slid his guitar onto his shoulders, he shook his head, making my stomach flop. "I'm going to have to meet you there. There's something I have to do first."

"What kind of something?" I was already cutting it close, and it was a lot more important for Jack to show up than it was for me.

He bit his lip, and I could practically feel how much it hurt him to say, "You promised not to ask questions."

So this involved his past? But what would he need to do right before his biggest show yet? Why wouldn't he just be honest with me? Why did it hurt so much to think he didn't trust me after all this time? I tried to hold them back, but the tears welled up in my eyes anyway, and I felt completely ridiculous because I had no reason to cry about this.

"Amelia." Jack was suddenly right in front of me, his hands on my cheeks and his thumbs brushing away my tears. "I'm not going to let you down," he said, and when he pressed his lips to my forehead, his touch seemed to filter down through me until I was calm again. I loved how easily he made everything better, just by being himself. "I will be there, and I will be there on time, and I will play the best show I've ever played. I promise."

He bent down a little to better meet my gaze, and his bright blue eyes seemed to search mine, looking for something. "You believe me, right?"

"Of course I believe you," I said, and I meant it. If only I could tell him what I really wanted to say: *I just wish you would trust me like I trust you.*

He kissed my forehead again, and then he was gone, leaving a bright spot of warmth behind.

I took a deep breath, forcing myself to pull it together. What Jack did with his time was none of my business, and he would show up at the coffee shop with plenty of time to spare. I, however, really needed to get going, because all of my family was probably already there. I had hoped Jack would be there with me, but I would just have to face them on my own. The problem with showing up on my own, though, was being thrown into the Hastings/Davenport chaos without any kind of buffer. Indie had promised she would help me through it, but she was also hosting the thing. There was only so much she would be able to do.

As predicted, I was the last one to arrive, which meant I had to do the whole greeting thing all at once instead of staggering things as people came. All twelve adults were already there, as well as their four collective kids, and I'd never seen them all together like this. Lissa had invited me to Sunday dinner every week, and I had politely pretended to be busy every week to avoid being overwhelmed by the family, but this was not, unfortunately, something I could skip out on.

At least Colin and Beck were the closest to the door, which started the evening on a good note. I was familiar enough with Colin and comfortable enough with Beck that it didn't feel like they would start an inquisition about my life over the last few weeks. I noticed their daughter Macy over helping Indie put snacks on trays and made a note to go say hi to the girl, but I still had a whole lot of actual family I had to talk to first.

Beck must have seen my terror as my eyes took in the sheer crowd of people behind her, because she wrapped an arm around my waist and pulled me close. "Just take a deep breath," she whispered to me.

"You have nothing to worry about, Amelia," Colin added.

Matthew Davenport was next in line—they literally formed a line—and shook my hand rather than going for a hug, which I appreciated. I hadn't seen him since that first night I met him, and stories from Indie weren't exactly enough to make me feel like we had any kind of relationship. Plus, he had little Artemis in his arms.

"I was starting to think I'd imagined you," he told me. "Glad to see you really do exist." I didn't deserve his friendliness, since I had purposefully ignored an invitation to little Artie's first birthday party a month ago, at the beginning of September, but I was grateful he was still willing to talk to me.

I laughed nervously at his joke and was glad when Lanna was just behind him. Her, I did hug, because even though I hadn't spent a lot of time with her since moving into my apartment, she was incredibly calming whenever I saw her.

"It's good to see you again," I said and smiled at her husband, who had one kid in each arm.

Harry, the younger one, must have recognized me, because he immediately reached out as if we were still the best of friends, even though it had been a couple of months since I saw him.

Thankfully, Adam quietly said, "Not now, Harrison," and returned my smile before stepping aside. He was a gentle man, at least on the outside, and I could see why Lanna loved him as much as she did.

Next were Seth and Catherine, who both embraced me, though Seth's focus was behind me. "So where's this oh-so-wonderful rock star you're so fond of?" he growled, though he sighed when Catherine smacked his arm. "Sorry. But really, where is he? He's not leaving you in the lurch, is he?"

"He'll be here," I said. *I hope.* Whatever errand he had had to run, it had seemed important, and I silently prayed it didn't keep him away.

"Tonight's going to be great," Catherine assured me.

Next up was Molly Ashworth, and as nice as she was, I was more interested in the man at her side, the one who'd been too busy catching up on work after his extended trip with his wife that I hadn't even had a chance to see him yet.

I punched Brennon in the shoulder before he could get a word in.

"Ow!" he said, his eyes wide but laughter in the word. "What was that for?"

I narrowed my eyes, but I figured my glare wasn't all that effective because I was grinning at the same time. "Brennon Ashworth, what kind of person thinks work is so important that he can't take the time to come and see me at least once?" And then I hugged him, because there was something about seeing my old friend that made the night just a little bit more familiar.

He returned the embrace with enthusiasm. "Man," he said over my shoulder, "if I had known you were going to react like this..." When he pulled back, he took me in and smiled. "You look really good," he said, and then his smile faltered. "Sorry about...you know. Things with Jordan."

And just like that, any happiness I felt was gone. It wasn't Brennon's fault. It only made sense that he would mention my ex, since the last time I had talked to him was to tell him I was getting married. That had been a risky move at the time, when I had no idea if Steve was still his friend or even still around, but after three years of hanging around my boyfriend's best friend, I felt like he was one of my best friends too. And I had missed him.

"I'm excited to meet Jack," Brennon added, and I could tell he was hoping that changing the subject would help things.

Only, someone else replied to his comment before I could: "So am I," Steve said quietly.

Brennon and Molly stepped aside, and a nervous churning filled my stomach as I caught sight of Steve for the first time in weeks. I hugged Lissa when she came up to me, but it was hard not to focus on her husband when it felt like the whole room disappeared except him. How was it still so hard to see him looking so alive and happy?

"I'm sure you'll like Jack," Lissa said, glancing between Steve and me.

"You haven't met him either," Steve replied. His eyes were pointed in my general direction, and I wondered how much he could see tonight. It apparently fluctuated, Lissa had told me once, depending on how tired or stressed he was.

If I were in his position, my vision would be completely dark right now.

"Well, now that everyone's here," Brennon said suddenly, breaking my gaze, "Mol and I have an announcement. Well, it's really just her announcement, since it doesn't really have anything to do with me. I mean, it sort of does, but—"

"You're pregnant," Catherine gasped, and she'd gone surprisingly pale. Not the reaction I would have expected...

Molly laughed and took Brennon's hand as he turned a little pink in the cheeks. "I'm taking a new job," she said. "Here in the city, so I can start to settle down a bit. It was getting too hard to be away from Bren so much, and the San Francisco Chronicle offered me a full-time gig!"

"And also she *is* pregnant," Brennon added with a roll of his eyes.

The whole family jumped into a flurry of congratulations and hugs and every other conversation that could possibly have started after an announcement like that, and I found myself slowly backing away toward the door. I was happy for Brennon, and of course for Molly, and there was so much love in this family that I should have considered myself blessed to be one of them.

But I really didn't feel like I was one of them.

When I reached the door, I bumped into something solid but warm, and a pair of hands clasped my shoulders to keep me from stumbling back.

"So this is the infamous Davenport clan," Jack said softly. "Can I ask why you're running away from them?" He hadn't moved his hands yet, and his fingers were warm against the bare skin of my arms.

I had to fight the urge to lean against him and try to get some kind of strength from him, and though our position immediately reminded me of our argument about the table, specifically the way that he'd held me, I tried to sound calm and unaffected. "I'm not running away," I said.

"I'm not judging you if you are," he replied. "You don't see me hanging around my family members for a reason." So he *did* have family. I wondered if they were back in Manhattan, or if they were somewhere else. "Yours look a whole lot nicer than mine," he continued. "Want to introduce me?"

Not really. "You met Colin and Beck already." I waved a little to the pair of them, who were hugging Molly and Brennon with gusto. "And you know Indie, back behind the counter."

"You don't really understand this whole introducing thing, do you?" Jack asked with a laugh, though it was soft. His hands disappeared, and before I could stop him, he walked straight up to Seth and said loudly, "Hi, I'm Jack."

I nearly fainted right there in the middle of Indiana Brews. With those three words, the whole shop went silent as everyone turned to watch Seth's reaction to finally meeting the man he'd been determined to hate for weeks.

Seth's expression was mostly empty, and he glanced down at the hand Jack offered without any indication of taking it. If it came to a fight—*please don't turn into a fight*—my brother would snap Jack in two with one hand, and Jack had never looked smaller than when he was standing next to Seth, nearly a foot shorter and half his weight.

Though I couldn't see Jack's face, I could hear the sheer confidence in his voice as he said, "Amelia didn't want us to meet because she thought you would do something drastic, but now that we *have* met, I can tell you're much too level-headed for that. You're a lot like her, you know."

Seth pulled his eyebrows together, probably thinking—like I was—that Jack was talking nonsense, since Seth hadn't said a word or even really reacted at all. I glanced at Steve, who was fighting a laugh, and I was pretty sure Matthew would be doing the same thing and hopefully be there to ease the tension in the room.

But to my surprise, Matthew was staring at Jack like he couldn't believe what he was seeing. What was that about?

Ever so slowly, Seth reached out his hand and grasped Jack's, practically drowning his hand. "So you're the one who's been hanging around my sister?" he said, and amazingly he didn't have any growl in his words.

Jack grinned. "Technically, she's the one who keeps finding me. I spend most of my time in the parks and chatting up landscapers, and she just shows up and tells me what to do."

Now Lanna was frowning just like Matthew.

"I hope you listen to her," Seth said.

"Always," Jack replied.

And apparently that was that. They stepped apart, and Catherine greeted Jack as friendly as ever, as did Lissa, Molly, and Brennon. At that point, I felt like I was being rude standing back and letting everyone introduce themselves, so I made my way forward to be a good friend and sister.

Only, the next person up for Jack to meet was Steve.

"Oh," I said in alarm.

Both men looked at me with confused expressions, though Jack recovered faster. "You must be Steve," he said and held his hand out.

I was pretty sure Steve couldn't see anything at all, but somehow he knew to put his hand forward too, and they managed a clumsy handshake. "I've been hearing a lot about you," Steve said. "Beck and Colin say your music is magical."

Jack chuckled a little. "My music is music, same as any other. People get out of it what they want. I'm just lucky enough to help them find what they're looking for."

I smiled. It had been a while since I'd heard Jack talk like that, and I hadn't realized how much I missed it. The last few weeks had been filled mostly with talking shop, and I suddenly wondered how we'd gone so long without talking like we had that first day in the car. Talking to Jack was supposed to be easy, and I was pretty sure I was the reason it hadn't been.

Maybe he was right. Maybe I needed to take a break more often.

"Sounds like you know what you're talking about," Steve said, and he actually managed a pretty decent smile, even though he still seemed determined to try to catch at least a glimpse of him. "Thanks for being a friend to Amelia. My family probably hasn't made it very easy on her."

How did he know that?

There were only a few introductions left, but I wasn't worried anymore. I'd thought it would be hard enough to put Jack and Seth together, but now that I could suddenly breathe more easily, I realized I had been most worried about Steve. Jack knew as well as just about anyone what had happened between the two of us, and yet he hadn't seemed to have let that color his opinion of my brother-in-law.

"This is my sort-of cousin, Matthew Davenport," I said, gently tugging Jack closer to the rest of the family. "And his sister, Lanna. And—"

"What's your last name, Jack?" Matthew asked suddenly. He stood frozen, and I had no idea what his expression meant. It was like… I didn't even know. It was like he was looking at someone he thought he should know but couldn't quite place how or where he'd met him.

Jack frowned a little. "Thorn," he said, though I could hear his hesitation. He glanced at the door, as if he was tempted to run.

"Is that your real last name?" Lanna whispered, and she gripped Adam's arm so tight that I was sure he would have been wincing if he didn't have the exact same expression as the other two. She'd said Jack looked familiar when she saw my video of his show, but this was something a lot deeper than familiarity.

As Jack's frown only grew deeper, I tried to understand why it felt like I was missing something that the four of them knew. Had they all met before? And Jack seemed just as reluctant to answer the question as Lanna and Adam were to stop staring at him, and I was pretty sure Matthew was about to shatter because he was standing so tense and still.

"Hawthorne," Matthew said finally, and his voice broke.

Jack flinched.

"Looks like people are starting to line up outside!" Indie said suddenly, and her excitement was clear as she hurried to the closed door. "Jack, are you ready?"

He looked even more disinclined to be here than he had while pacing my apartment, but he nodded a little as the other three grew even more concerned. "As I'll ever be," he muttered and slid his guitar case off his shoulder.

Was Jack's last name really Hawthorne? And if it was, why did it make Lanna and Matthew look like they'd seen a ghost?

"Hey," Jack said, taking hold of my arm and pulling me a little ways away from the others. "I need to tell you something."

Colin and Brennon opened the door and began taking tickets from the people who streamed inside.

"What?" I asked, wondering if it had something to do with Matthew's reaction but knowing we didn't have time to talk about this. Jack had to get up on the platform Indie had put up for him to sit on so he could get ready to play.

"It's…" Jack shook his head, and he looked completely miserable. I couldn't miss the glance he sent to the corner where Lanna and her husband were standing, and I had never seen him in so much distress. Anguish may have been a better word, though I didn't like how easily it came to mind. "I don't know how to… It's…"

"Jack, you can tell me anything. You know that right?"

He nodded, but whatever this was, it was clearly eating him up inside. He grabbed my hand with both of his and stared at it, as if hoping it might give him the courage to say whatever he needed to say. I hoped so too, because this was not the sort of thing I was going to handle well if he didn't just come right out and say it before I came to the wrong conclusion.

"Amelia, I came to San Francisco because—"

"Welcome to Indiana Brews!" Indie said into the microphone, her face alight with excitement. "Please take your seats, and we'll be starting in just a few minutes."

"Jack?" I said, practically begging him to keep talking, though his eyes were on the stage now. "What's wrong?"

He turned back to me, glanced at Lanna again, and took a long, deep breath that was probably supposed to help him but was agony for me because it was only delaying things. Each second ticked by with every beat of my heart until I wasn't sure I was going to survive unless he opened his mouth again.

"Everyone give a big welcome to Jackson Thorn!"

As the quickly filling room burst into applause and hundreds of eyes turned to us, Jack frowned before he plastered on a surprisingly believable smile and hurried up to the other side of the room, leaving me alone, confused, and absolutely terrified.

Jack played a perfect show. Probably his best one ever. Everyone inside was transfixed, and everyone outside stood as close to the shop as they could to hear every bit of his music. People who were walking past even stopped to listen, and I was pretty sure the crowd outside had doubled by the time Jack's last note hung in the air like a whisper.

I sat at the back when it ended, and instead of chatting with the family, I just watched Jack. The moment he started playing he had relaxed, and now he didn't seem nearly as uneasy as he had before the show started. Though he still threw occasional glances at Matthew and his sister, he seemed perfectly content to wander through the crowd and chat with his avid fans. His smile was wide and warm—and thankfully real—and it looked like he had really gotten the hang of the whole small talk thing.

Adam and Lanna were currently focused on getting some hot chocolate for their older son, Benny, while Harry slept on his father's shoulder, but Matthew…

Matthew had hidden himself in the very corner of the shop at the beginning of the concert, and he hadn't stopped frowning as he sat on the countertop and hugged his knees. While it was true I didn't know him well, Indie had said more than once he was one of the happiest people in the world.

He could have fooled me, and I really didn't like how he was directing that frown right at Jack.

Now that the music had stopped, most of the people had filtered from the shop, or at least gone outside, where it was cooler, and I scanned the remaining crowd just to get an idea of the demographic that Jack attracted most. I didn't remotely understand what was causing the tension between Jack and my family, so I figured I could use the distraction and do some work. It seemed he drew in everyone from teens to senior citizens, which didn't exactly help me target a specific audience as I moved forward but was illuminating nonetheless. The largest group of people, from what I could see, were people around our same age, those in their twenties and thirties who had grown up trying to find magic in a world that was increasingly harder to live in.

Like the young woman who had found a seat by the window at the start of the show and had spent the whole set with her eyes closed and a smile on her face, or the couple who were talking to Jack just a few feet away from me and clearly expressing how much his music meant to them, since Jack looked like emotion was starting to get the better of him, or the man who stepped through the door as if he'd been drawn here and searched the crowd with his icy blue eyes that…

I blinked, convinced I was seeing things wrong.

The man was Jack.

Well, not quite. He was bigger, without the wiry look Jack had gotten from his year of poor food and sleeping in dirty hostels, and his suit definitely looked expensive, unlike Jack's thrift store t-shirt. His hair was fancier and styled well, but it was just as dark. Just as full. And though he had the same thin nose and sharp chin and even the same ears, his disgruntled expression was not one I'd ever seen Jack make.

And when Jack looked up and caught sight of him, he turned deathly pale.

I couldn't move. Neither could Jack, apparently, because though he looked like he wanted to run, he stood rooted to the spot as his look-alike drew nearer, slowly making his way through the milling crowd until they were only a foot apart. With them this close, I was positive they were twins, and yet they couldn't have been more different from each other as they stood there.

"Jace," Jack said finally, his eyebrows pulling low.

Jace narrowed his eyes. "What is wrong with you?"

I'd never seen Jack look so defeated, and he couldn't even seem to find his words as he stuffed his hands into his pockets and looked down at his feet. He mumbled something about music, but it was clear he knew it wasn't the right thing to say.

Then Jace spoke again, and my heart seemed to get stuck in my throat as I listened: "Dad is *dying*, Jack. You need to come home."

CHAPTER TWELVE

Jack ran. It wasn't just slipping outside and hurrying away; he straight up *ran*. Pushed people out of his way and vanished.

And while I expected his brother to chase after him, Jace just stood there in the middle of the shop, his anger dissipating and leaving him looking simply empty as he stared at the floor.

I walked up to him immediately and touched his arm. "Hi," I said, though that was a terrible way to start a conversation after what I'd just heard. "Um." Geez, Jace had a glare almost as bad as Seth's, and for a moment I forgot what I'd been about to say. "I'm Amelia," I forced out. "I'm Jack's manager."

"I'm sorry," he growled back.

Oh. Well. "I wasn't trying to overhear," I lied, "but you said something about your dad dying. Is he...?" *Is he actually dying?* Or had Jace just said that to try to get Jack to go back home?

Jace looked more than a little wary, but after glancing around at the remaining audience, many of whom quickly pretended they hadn't heard the exchange either, he sighed and jerked his head toward the door. "Outside."

The chairs out on the sidewalk had pretty much all been vacated at this point. After looking around, maybe to see if Jack hadn't gotten very far, Jace settled in the closest one and pointed to the chair next to it. Apparently that meant I should sit. "What has he told you?" he asked.

Absolutely nothing. "Not much. I… Well, I didn't actually know he had a family." And that hadn't really bothered me. Not until now.

Jace grunted and rolled his eyes. "He's probably told you all sorts of lies, hasn't he?"

I thought twins were always best friends. That they had an unshakeable bond and stuck together for all time. Clearly I was wrong. And Jace was not nearly as personable as his brother, and I had absolutely no idea how to talk to the guy. Especially when he just sat there and scowled.

Pretend he's Seth, I told myself. I needed to know how to help Jack, so I needed to understand where the problem was. "Will you tell me what's going on?" I asked. "Jack's my friend, and this sounds like a big deal, so I want to help him."

His eyes cold, Jace studied me for a moment, probably trying to decide if he wanted to trust me with something so personal. "Our dad has had cancer for a few years," he said after a moment. "It's been up and down, but last year it came back too aggressive for him to fight, and the doctors gave him a countdown. Jack disappeared a year ago last May." And he sounded miserable about the fact. Okay, maybe he *was* close with his brother, though he could have fooled me. "I haven't talked to him since, and I didn't even know if he was alive until he used his credit card at a furniture store here in California a few days ago."

The table? It didn't matter. Not when Jack had been away from home for almost a year and a half and his own brother hadn't even known if he was alive.

"I knew I couldn't wander around San Francisco and just hope I ran into him," Jace continued, "so I started searching the internet and talking to everyone I know here. I stumbled on that video of him playing at the wharf, and then I heard about this concert tonight, so I flew out."

And Jack had just run away again. "How long does your dad have left?" I asked quietly.

Jace wilted a little, finally looking more like his brother as an expression other than anger softened his features. "I don't know. Not long."

"Why did Jack run in the first place? Why would he leave when your dad was that sick?"

Shrugging, he clasped his hands in his lap and stared down at them. "He left a note," he said. "Something about how he hated who he had become and wanted to remake himself. That was the night Dad told us the cancer was back. He left his phone, didn't take anything with him, and he was just gone."

Poor Jack. "He was scared," I guessed.

"To death," Jack said behind me.

Jace got to his feet, and the pair of them stood there looking at each other so intently that I wondered if maybe they were having a silent conversation. "Can we talk?" he asked after a moment.

Jack looked at me for a second, and then he nodded. "Let's walk," he suggested.

I watched them until they'd rounded a corner and disappeared from view. Jack kept his shoulders hunched, his hands in his pockets, and Jace was completely stiff, but they kept close to each other, practically shoulder to shoulder. And though I so badly wished I could listen in on their conversation, I knew that wasn't something I had a right to hear. I wasn't part of Jack's family any more than I felt a part of mine.

Most of my family were sitting at the coffee shop tables now, talking amongst themselves without a care in the world, it seemed. Macy was curled up in Colin's lap as he chatted with Brennon, and Beck and Molly were talking about how excited they were to spend more time together. Catherine and Seth had cuddled up on a little sofa in one corner and seemed deep in thought as they sat in silence, while Indie talked to Lissa as she and Steve helped wash some dishes in the sink behind the counter. Matthew and Lanna were both getting their kids ready to leave, and they still looked spooked by whatever they'd seen in Jack.

Then there was Adam, who was slowly approaching me with the expression of someone who was about to have a very difficult conversation.

Uh oh.

"Can we talk for a minute?" he asked softly.

Though we hadn't talked much before, I was pretty sure they sent him to be the one to talk to me because I found nothing frightening about the man whose life was devoted first to his family, then to art.

There wasn't a bad bone in his body. "Okay," I said and followed him back outside, desperately trying to figure out what he could possibly say to me. I knew it had something to do with Jack, but beyond that…

As we sat in the same chairs Jace and I had been in a moment before, I felt the night's weariness start to settle on me. I'd never been good with late nights, and tonight had been especially draining, for a whole lot of reasons.

And I knew Adam wasn't going to make it any better. "This is about Jack, right?" I asked when he didn't say anything.

"Yes," he replied. "And no." Reaching into his pocket, he pulled out his phone and unlocked the screen before he held it out to me.

He'd pulled up an article titled "The Hawthorne Dynasty," and the first sentence said something about the Hawthorne family in New York City, whose patriarch had started a highly successful chain of hotels and had basically created an empire. I didn't read much of it because my eyes slipped to the photo just above the start of the article, a photo of a beautiful, smiling family of six. Jack stood right next to the man who was clearly his father, though he didn't look much like the Jack I knew. He was better-fed, better-dressed, and there was a smugness in him that made him look a lot like Jace, who was on the parents' other side. In fact, the two of them actually looked identical aside from the slight crookedness of Jack's proud smile.

Adam pointed to the man between them, who was listed in the caption as Lucas Hawthorne. He was the spitting image of Jack, aged up thirty years. "I don't know if it's coincidence or if there's more to this," he said slowly. Carefully. "But several years ago, I knew a Luke Hawthorne, and…" He took his phone back and switched to a different photo, one of a younger Adam standing next to an old car and beaming proudly. The man on the other side of the car was…

He was darker skinned, a little rounder in the face, but the young man in Adam's photo bore a striking resemblance to the musician I had come to befriend. They had the same crooked smile.

According to the article, Jack was the oldest of Lucas's children, and the only other boy outside of Jace was a teenager apparently named Wesley. And while I couldn't ignore the similarities between Jack and this Luke, I wasn't really sure how to make sense of what Adam was telling me.

"Are you saying they might be related?" I asked.

Adam shrugged. "I'm saying I nearly had a heart attack when Jack walked through that door because he looks and acts so much like my dead friend that I was almost convinced he'd come back to life. Matt and Lanna thought the same thing. I just thought you might want to know, in case…" In case of what, he didn't say. Instead, he got to his feet just as Lanna stepped through the door with both her boys in tow. "Luke meant a lot to our family," he said quietly, so his wife wouldn't hear.

She offered me a small smile as she passed, but it didn't last long, and she and Adam wandered off to their car, leaving me alone to wonder why everything I thought I knew about Jack was probably wrong.

Jack didn't come back to the coffee shop. It got so late that I couldn't wait any longer, so I packed up his guitar and gratefully accepted Seth's offer to drive me home, even though I could see his concern that I was taking charge of the instrument and therefore would probably have the homeless musician coming to my door. I was incredibly glad he didn't know where Jack slept every night.

After I got home, I fought to stay awake and even tried playing Jack's guitar again, but I was too distracted by every little noise out in the hallway that I couldn't remember how to form the chords, so it just sounded like a nightmarish mess of notes. Eventually I had to rest my head on the couch cushion because it was getting too heavy to hold up, and I drifted off.

Around two in the morning, a soft knock on the door woke me up, and I was up on my feet faster than I'd ever been. "Jack?" I whispered before I even got the door open.

There he stood, looking completely exhausted and disheveled and, frankly, a total mess. He looked younger than I'd ever seen him, and any trace of his usual brightness and carefree nature was gone. I was pretty sure he'd been crying, based on the redness around his eyes, and

I had no idea what I could possibly say to him. So I just wrapped him in my arms, gently pulling him into the apartment and leading him to the couch.

Almost the instant he sat down, he dropped his head onto my shoulder and took a shaky breath, and I clasped his hand and wished I knew how to make this better. But who was I kidding? His dad was dying. There was no way I could make that better, so I just held him in silence as he leaned against me like he was too exhausted to cry anymore.

"Where's your brother?" I asked after a while.

"Hotel," was the croaked response.

"When is he leaving?"

"Tomorrow."

And the most important question: "Are you going with him?"

Jack didn't answer, though I really couldn't blame him. Clearly this whole thing with his dad was a hard one to face, and this was the man who had spent the last year and then some pretending his past didn't exist.

"Jack?" I said and squeezed his hand a little tighter. "Why did you run away from home?" That made it sound like he was twelve and had packed up a backpack, only to spend the night in the treehouse in the backyard and come back inside for breakfast the next morning.

Leaning against me a little more heavily, he took another long, shaking breath that didn't seem to do him any good. "Because I didn't want it to be real," he said. "No matter what I did, no matter how many times I told myself everything would turn out okay, I couldn't make myself believe it."

Optimism could only take a man so far when there was a disease that couldn't be cured. In the more than two months that I'd known him, Jack had been the most positive person in the world, and realizing that his dad was going to die must have nearly killed him when he couldn't see a bright side. *Poor Jack.*

"I don't know if I can go home," he said, his voice breaking. "I don't know if I can face my family after what I did. I thought maybe if I… But I can't."

"That's the beautiful thing about family," I said quietly, and my thoughts strayed to my own family and how hard it was to feel like I was one of them. But I kept talking. "They'll always forgive you, because that's what families do."

He laughed a little. "You don't know my family. They're terrible."

I wasn't sure about that. "Jace wasn't that bad," I said. Given the situation, he'd been downright pleasant.

"He was being polite."

"They're still your family, Jack. He's still your dad. You have to go back, before it's too late." And I realized that if Jack went to New York, he would take my life with it. Without Jack, I wouldn't have his career to distract me, and I would be faced yet again with the unknown future of my livelihood.

But I would deal with that tomorrow. Right now, I had to focus on Jack. "There's nothing more important than family," I muttered.

I immediately wished I hadn't said it, and I glanced at the kitchen table sitting over on the other end of the room. Okay, maybe it had been Jack who bought it, but I had a whole bank account full of money from Gordon Hastings, and I hadn't even bothered to say thank you. Whether or not I used it, he still deserved gratitude for being willing to try. Most people upon finding a long-lost child in her thirties would do the bare minimum if anything at all, and yet Lissa had assured me that Gordon wanted nothing more than to prove he wanted me in his life, whether or not he knew me.

Jack was right; refusing that money was completely selfish of me, and I hated knowing I might have made Gordon feel like he would never be able to do enough.

It was high time I met my father.

"What if I go with you?" I said quietly, wishing I sounded more sure of myself.

Jack sat up so he could look at my face, and though his expression was still mainly anguish, there was a bit of hope in those pale eyes of his. "What?"

"My birth dad lives in D.C.," I explained, "which really isn't that far from New York. I should probably go visit him, and maybe this way it'll be easier for you, if you don't have to travel alone. Or with Jace," I added, since I still wasn't sure how well the brothers actually got along.

Without a word, Jack pulled me into a tight embrace and just held me there, saying so many things in that hold, things that probably didn't have words attached to them. It was like his music and the way he managed to say so much with just a few notes on his guitar.

And I found myself enjoying his embrace a lot more than I would have expected.

"Thank you," he whispered finally, and for the first time since meeting him, I felt like I had found something he actually, truly needed.

CHAPTER THIRTEEN

That article about Jack's family had been right. The Hawthorne family was loaded, and two days after Jace's appearance, I found myself sitting in a first class seat on the most luxurious flight I had ever been on. It was a nice gesture, buying me a ticket when I could have gotten myself a seat back in coach, but I wished they hadn't done it.

I had spent the last two months trying to get settled in my new life and find where I fit in, and within the ten minutes it took to board the plane and find my seat, I had been thrown into disarray again and felt completely out of place. I'd never flown first class before, not even with Steve, who strangely had enjoyed being around the "normal folk" even though he could have afforded the comfort of first class or business. Jordan hadn't liked to travel, so it had been over four years since the last time I'd even gotten on a plane.

Jack may not have looked the part in his old jeans and worn leather jacket, but he seemed right at home as he stretched out and waited for takeoff.

Jack was rich. Not just rich—he was *insanely* rich. I'd done a little more research into his family over the last couple of days, when he was in the shower or asleep on the couch, and I'd realized they didn't just own a few hotels scattered along the East Coast. They owned *the* hotels, the kind only the wealthiest people stayed in because they were the only ones who could afford fresh sprigs of lavender on their pillows and a spa on the third floor and an entire staff dedicated to making their lives as easy and comfortable as humanly possible. The Hawthornes weren't exactly Rockefellers, but they were famous enough—rich enough—that they dominated every internet search I'd done.

They put the Davenports' wealth to shame.

It was hard to wrap my brain around that, especially when I looked at Jack. "Money isn't everything," he'd told me, and I had really believed him. But he had grown up surrounded by it, and it was hard not to wonder if he really meant what he said or if that was just another way to pretend his past wasn't real.

Jack was quiet the entire flight, and though I'd brought a book to pass the time, I wasn't really paying attention to what I was reading. I was focused on him, and the fact that he hadn't smiled in two days, and the way he seemed to have lost all of his light. I was thinking about what it was Jack had been trying to tell me right before that last show and how I was too afraid to bring up the subject. I was thinking about his family and what they must have thought when he disappeared. I was thinking about Adam's friend, Luke, and trying to understand why he looked so much like Jack but didn't seem to exist, according to the internet; any search I had done had just brought up Jack's father, Lucas.

Did Jack know about this mysterious look-alike? Adam said he had passed away, and maybe that was why Jack had never talked about him or why he wasn't listed as one of Lucas's children. But unless I brought it up, I wouldn't get any answers to solve this puzzle, and I really didn't want to add to the cloud of misery that already loomed over Jack's head.

When we landed at JFK, he walked through the terminal with the ease of someone who had been in that airport many times. He grabbed the suitcase we were sharing—since he definitely didn't have one— and slipped his guitar onto his shoulders before heading straight for the exit without a word. And when we got outside, he approached a sleek black car that waited just outside the doors and nodded to the well-dressed man who stood at attention.

"Welcome home, sir," the man said, and he sounded so official that I was almost convinced he had mistaken Jack for some fancy politician.

But then Jack nodded once, muttered, "Hi, Max," and handed over our stuff before opening the back door for me.

As soon as I'd settled next to Jack and our suitcase was stowed in the trunk next to the guitar, the driver slid into his seat and pulled away without another word. Jack made the whole thing seem so routine, and yet again I wondered how he could have fooled me so completely. He clearly knew how to live the rich life, and yet he'd been so comfortable on the streets. Which was the real Jack? The one who easily lived in luxury or the one who despised it?

After a while, Jack finally looked in my direction, and he seemed to realize he hadn't said a word to me in over eight hours. "Sorry," he said.

I furrowed my brow. "For what?"

"For dragging you into all this with me."

"I offered to come, Jack," I argued. "I want to be here." Though I was starting to worry the whole trip would be spent in silence…

He narrowed his eyes a little. "But?"

How did he do that? He always seemed to know when there was more to what I wanted to say. I could have lied, but he would have seen through it. "But you're acting weird," I said. "And I don't like it. I know you have a lot to deal with right now, but—"

"No," he said, frowning. "No, you're right. I'm acting like the old Jack."

I saw the driver glance back at us in the mirror, and he almost looked surprised.

But not as surprised as me when Jack took my hand. Not in the way he'd held my hand before, as a means to stay connected until we got somewhere. This time he laced his fingers between mine and sent a wave of heat through me that didn't make a whole lot of sense.

"I'll be better," he whispered, leaning his head close to mine. "I promise. Just don't be afraid to call me out when I'm not, okay? I'm not sure I can do this by myself."

I had no idea how to react to a request like that, but I nodded anyway. I wasn't sure I was capable of calling someone out, unless it was Seth being stupid about Jack. But I would try. If that was what he needed.

As we entered into the traffic of the city, I could feel Jack's eyes on me, though I kept my focus out the window. I wasn't sure why I didn't want to meet his gaze, but it could have been I didn't want him to think I had lied about being his positivity coach, or whatever he might call it. Plus, there was the fact that our hands were still entwined, and I really had no idea what to make of *that*. It was easier to just ignore all of that for now and focus on what was around us.

I'd always loved big cities. Living in Chicago with Jordan and being in San Francisco with Steve had made them feel like home to me, and New York looked just as welcoming. Full of possibility.

"Have you been here before?" Jack asked after a while.

I shrugged. "Steve's mom lived in Brooklyn when we were together, so we visited a couple of times. But we didn't really do any sightseeing."

Somehow, New York City was just as magical as they made it look in movies. Summer was over, but the air looked alive with color and warmth. The people on the sidewalks were as diverse as the storefronts and buildings, and there was so much energy out there that I would have rolled my window down to soak it in if I didn't think that might be a faux pas in a car like this. We passed Central Park, which was so much bigger than I would have guessed, and I could see the Empire State Building not too far away. I almost couldn't believe that I had never tried to convince Steve to just wander the city for a bit when we came instead of staying across the East River.

But I had never been able to convince Steve to do anything. Or anyone, for that matter.

Eventually the car pulled beneath a covered sort of driveway, and if I hadn't been looking in the other direction, I might have seen the building we stopped beneath. I could see inside the front doors, though, and as I followed Jack out of the car, my jaw dropped.

I had seen pictures of this place in my internet searches of Jack's family, and I had been too in awe to ever think I would see it in person. This was Lucas's first—and fanciest—hotel: eighty floors of five-star luxury worth more than a full block of prime downtown San Francisco realty.

"Hawthorne Tower," I whispered in nothing short of awe.

My comment was met with laughter, and I was alarmed to know the driver would be so openly mocking a friend of his boss. But it wasn't Max who was laughing, and I could hardly believe it when I saw Jack grinning at me.

"Welcome to what I used to call home," he said warmly. Happy Jack was back.

"Should I take this up to your room, sir?" the driver asked, holding up the suitcase and the guitar, and then he started moving without waiting for an answer.

"I'll take it, Max," Jack said and grabbed both before Max could get very far.

The driver looked dumbfounded. "Are…are you sure?"

Jack smiled again, which had an equally dramatic effect on the man. "I'm sure. Thank you, though. And thanks for the ride."

We left Max still standing next to the car as if he couldn't even imagine a world where someone said thank you to him. Or maybe he just couldn't imagine that someone being Jack.

Every single staff member we passed in the gold-gilded lobby greeted Jack with either a "Welcome back, sir" or a respectful bow of their head. Even a man who was wiping down a tabletop quickly shuffled around to face us and nod in deference as we passed, as if Jack was more than just the son of their employer and was actual royalty.

Jack either didn't notice or chose to ignore everyone around us, and my money was on the latter. At least he was still smiling a little.

His expression, however, seemed to confuse the silver-haired butler-looking fellow waiting by the glittering elevator doors. "Mr. Hawthorne," he greeted as we came up to him, though it sounded more like a question. If I hadn't been standing right next to Jack, who was acting like all of this was normal, I would have been convinced his British accent was more for show than from his birthplace. "Your family is upstairs waiting for you." He pushed the button with a gloved hand.

Immediately the doors opened for us, as if the elevator had been waiting for Jack as well.

"Thanks, Hamish," Jack said, and he actually took a moment to set his guitar down and pat the man's shoulder. "It's good to see you."

Hamish pretty much gaped at us until he joined us inside, pulled out a keycard, and held it against a panel that lit up the topmost floor. After he pushed the button, the elevator lifted upward in the smoothest motion I'd ever felt, and I barely even noticed we were rising.

"Hamish has been with the family from the beginning," Jack said quietly, and he leaned a little closer to me, though it wasn't like he could get far enough to not be heard. The elevator was large, but not ridiculous. "He's known me since I still had my baby teeth."

I might have imagined it, but Hamish smiled a little as he kept his focus straight ahead.

I was so lost in this world, but I couldn't help but ask the sudden question burning in my mind: "Do you have any good stories about Jack, Hamish?"

He glanced at me, his smile much more obvious than before. "I could think of a few," he said, though I was pretty sure he wasn't inclined to say them in front of Jack.

Jack must have noticed this too, because he chuckled a little and said, "One time I managed to lose most of my clothes. Long story. And I showed up here at the Tower in nothing but my boxers and one sock. Hamish was nice enough to find me some spare clothes while I hid behind the front desk so I didn't have to show up at home looking like I'd been playing strip poker."

Hamish coughed, and I was pretty sure it was to hide a laugh because he muttered, "I do believe you *were* playing strip poker, sir," before he straightened his expression back to total professionalism.

I raised an eyebrow and tried to imagine Jack being the sort of person to do something like that. He was slightly pink in the face as he smiled at the floor, but I was pretty sure he was genuinely pleased that Hamish joined in on the tale, if only a little.

"Here we are, sir," Hamish said as the doors opened, though I hadn't even noticed the elevator come to a stop because its movement was so fluid. I was never going to be able to enjoy any other elevator ride after this. Not that elevators were all that fun to begin with…

The doors opened, not to a hallway like a hotel floor normally would but to the prettiest living room—if I could even call it that—I had ever seen.

The room was all windows. To our left and directly ahead, I could look out over downtown New York City with a view like I'd never seen before. Though there was a hallway to our right that led to several rooms, from what I could tell, I was too focused on this main room to wonder what might be in that direction. It was huge, and a massive sunken living room took up most of it, three couches spread out across the recessed area and facing a large TV that hung over a gas fireplace. And though a free-standing staircase led up to the next floor to the left, I was so caught up by this room that I hardly cared what the rest of the house might look like.

Everything about it screamed wealth and fashion and importance, but not in a gaudy way, though I half expected to find a full-time piano player stroking the keys of the massive grand piano in the corner.

"Cozy, isn't it?" Jack muttered, and I jumped because I'd forgotten he was behind me. He had a mixture of revulsion and unease in his expression, though how he could hate a room like this, I had no idea.

"It's amazing."

"Jack?" a voice said, almost panicked, and I honestly had no idea where the sound came from because, from what I could tell, the room was empty.

But Jack lifted his head and seemed to speak to the ceiling as he said, "Hey, Mom."

She appeared at the top of the staircase, pretty much flying down the elegant steps in her dangerously high heels. She looked exactly like she did in all the pictures, the perfect sort of woman to live in a place like this with her professionally styled hair and designer clothes and the kind of figure only someone with a nutritionist could maintain without severe dedication and time at the gym.

Jack set his guitar on the ground just before she reached him and wrapped his arms around her, and she barely managed to not fall apart as she held him.

"You came home," she whispered, and her tears shone on her face as she leaned against him, her strength likely gone. "You finally came home."

I felt like I shouldn't be there to witness this reunion. This was a mother and son who hadn't seen each other in almost a year and a half, who were probably incredibly close and had missed each other more than they were willing to admit. This was a family in crisis, and I was just in the way.

"Where is everyone?" Jack asked finally. He wiped his eyes with the sleeve of his leather jacket and coughed as if showing emotion was a weakness.

Mrs. Hawthorne waved one of her hands a little, but she was more focused on taking in every inch of her oldest son. "Wes is on the roof, exactly where you'd expect," she muttered. "And Sara is around here somewhere. Oh, Jackson, you're skin and bone. Have you been eating at all?"

He looked a lot better than he had when I'd met him, but he was still incredibly thin, and I hated to think what his mother might have said if she saw him on the road where I'd met him.

"Jace?" Jack asked.

She waved her hand again, this time toward the stairs. "He's upstairs with your father. You should probably…"

Jack's shoulders stiffened, and he lifted his eyes to the ceiling as if he could see through it to the upper level. "How bad is he?" he asked after a long moment of silence.

His mom pressed her hands to her lips and seemed on the verge of tears again.

Putting his hand on her shoulder, Jack stood there for a long while just gazing at his mother. It was the same expression he had when he played his music, like no matter how many words he could have used, none of them could quite express what he wanted to say.

She couldn't hold her tears back, but she didn't seem quite so burdened after whatever she'd seen in his face. "You should go upstairs," she managed to say.

Jack nodded, and then he glanced back at me. He didn't catch his mother's expression of surprise—I was pretty sure she hadn't even noticed me standing here until now—and yet he spoke softly, as if he knew my presence wasn't exactly best for the situation. "This is my friend Amelia Blake," he said. "She has some business in town, so I thought maybe we could put her in one of the rooms downstairs so we don't get in her way."

I was pretty sure that was a nice way of saying so I wouldn't get in *their* way, but I appreciated the gesture all the same. "I don't want to be a bother, Mrs. Hawthorne," I said quickly. "I can find my own—"

"No," she interrupted and stood a little straighter, the way she was expected to, I was sure. "No, it isn't any trouble. I'll talk to someone downstairs and see what we can do for you. Jack."

He nodded, gave me a brief smile, and then he disappeared up the stairs, leaving me alone with his overwhelmed mother.

"Really, Mrs. Hawthorne," I said as soon as he was gone, "I don't want to add anything to—"

"I insist," she replied and held out one perfectly manicured hand. "You can call me Marianne."

"Oh." I couldn't stop my surprise from coming out. "Really?"

Her smile, though small, was just like Jack's. Warm. Kind. "I think you are the only reason I got my Jackson back," she said. "If you hadn't come with him, I'm not sure he…" She sniffed and pulled a lily-white handkerchief from the pocket of her well-pressed slacks to dab at her eyes, though her makeup was miraculously still flawless. "Please, make yourself comfortable, and I'll go see to getting you a place to stay." She gestured toward the luscious couches then vanished down the side hall.

I almost couldn't bring myself to sit because I didn't feel worthy of such expensive furniture, but with the flight and everything, it had been a long day. I settled on a couch that was so soft I worried I might fall asleep, and then I sent a quick text to Seth before he started freaking out: *Landed in NY. Getting a hotel room now.*

He texted back so quickly that I rolled my eyes: *ROOMS, Amelia.*

I didn't even bother sending a response to that, even though technically Jack and I probably would be staying in separate rooms since he was home now. It wouldn't matter if we had to share a twin-size bed, because Seth wasn't allowed to dictate what I did with my life. I hoped he would figure that out sooner than later, before I started avoiding him as much as I avoided Steve.

"Are you Amelia?" a gentle voice suddenly said behind me.

I turned then quickly got to my feet. I recognized her from the pictures, but Jack's twenty-two-year-old sister looked even more beautiful in person, delicate and slender and none of her plain. She looked like the perfect combination of her parents, the dark hair and thin features of her father and the soft and elegant femininity of her mother. She had the same piercing blue eyes as Jack, though hers didn't have the same warmth as she looked me over.

"Hi," I said. "You must be Sara." And I held my hand out to her.

She glanced at it and lifted one thin eyebrow. "Mom says I have to bring you down to the sixty-seventh floor," she said, and she didn't try to hide her annoyance. How could someone sound so soft and so irritated at the same time?

"Oh," I replied. "Um, thanks."

Without another word, she turned with her long, straight hair swishing behind her and headed straight for the elevator.

I figured she wouldn't wait for me if I didn't follow immediately, so I grabbed the suitcase, hesitated by Jack's guitar then grabbed that too, and scurried across the large room just in time to climb into the elevator with her before the doors closed on me. I knew I should say something as the elevator slid into motion, but she had already whipped her phone out and was typing out a rapid message.

Okay then.

Upon reaching the sixty-seventh floor, she walked faster than I expected from someone who was still texting then stopped at room 6703. "Here you go," she said and started to head back to the elevator.

"Wait!" I called in alarm. "Is there a key or something?"

Sara just rolled her eyes and looked like she wanted nothing more than to leave me standing there feeling completely stupid. "That's not my job," she said with a little shrug. "Unless he's gotten lost again, Rohan should be here in, like, two minutes. Have a lovely stay at the Tower." And before I could try to stop her, she slipped back into the elevator and didn't even look my way as the doors closed.

A trickle of fear slipped into my heart as I stood in that empty hallway. I tried the door to the room, just in case, but it was most definitely locked, and I had no way to call Jack because he still didn't have a phone. I highly doubted I could search for any of the family's phone numbers on the internet, so the only way I could possibly get help if something was wrong was to try to get back down to the lobby and see if Hamish could direct me where to go. I hoped I had made a good enough impression on the old man, but it was hard to know.

Before my panic fully set in, however, a young man dressed in the crimson outfit of a bellhop—which I only knew from the movies and was moderately alarmed to see it was a real thing—burst through a door a little farther down the hall and gasped, "Oh man, that's a lot of stairs," as he leaned his hands on his knees and tried to breathe. "Good thing I was only a few flights down." Then he caught sight of me and got wide eyes as he let out a long, "Ooooooh."

I guessed this was Rohan. "Uh, hi."

Swallowing, he glanced around the hall as he approached, still heaving for air and clutching a stitch in his side. "Is Sara already gone?" he asked, and his disappointment was clear in his dark eyes.

I nodded. *Poor guy.* "I think she had things to do," I said. "I'm Amelia Blake."

"Rohan Bakshi, at your service." He shook my hand with a smile, though he still looked like he had run up however many stairs in the hopes of seeing Sara Hawthorne and was realizing his folly in not going even faster. "Well," he said, and now that he could breathe again he stood a lot taller and seemed more like the sort of person who would work in Hawthorne Tower and less like a bumbling employee in a chick flick. "Welcome to Hawthorne, Miss Blake," he said and bowed a little before slipping a keycard out of his pocket. "If there is anything you need during your stay, I would be happy to assist you."

With that, he unlocked the door and pushed it open for me so I could get into my room.

Room wasn't the right word. Immediately I realized they'd given me a full room—a suite?—complete with living room and kitchen, and I nearly dropped Jack's guitar when I caught the sheer size of it.

Decorated in golds and reds, it felt so elegant that I wondered if I would ever be able to stay in a Motel 6 again. I was pretty sure Hawthorne Tower had ruined me forever.

"I know, right?" Rohan said behind me.

I grinned back at him. "Are all the rooms like this?"

He shrugged as he glanced around. "Pretty much. The higher up you go, the nicer they get, though. The Hawthornes must like you."

"How long have you worked here?"

"My whole life. Dad had a job downstairs up until he died a few years ago, then Lucas—Mr. Hawthorne," he corrected with a look of embarrassment. "He was kind enough to take me on even though I was only seventeen at the time. I'd done enough stuff with Dad that I had a pretty good handle on the way things worked."

He cleared his throat, probably thinking he had said too much, and made his way back to the door. "It'll be my pleasure to let you into your room whenever it conveniences you, Miss Blake," he said, and though he sounded perfectly professional, he was grinning at me. "No need to worry about a key or anything. If you can't find me in the lobby when you arrive, it's probably because I'm running up the stairs or doing something for Miss Hawthorne, so just talk to Luis or Sasha. Enjoy your stay, Miss Blake."

I was worried about Jack and what he was going through as he met with his dying father, but as I wandered into the bedroom and sat on the edge of the king-size bed, my exhaustion quickly caught back up to me. He would come find me when he could, I decided, and I would just rest my eyes for a bit while I waited. Curling up on the ridiculously comfortable mattress, I let out a sigh and wished I could be there for Jack from a distance. He was going to need someone.

And I hoped that someone was me.

CHAPTER FOURTEEN

"It's good to see you, Jack. I missed you, man."

"Thanks, Rohan."

A door closed, and I forced my eyes to open, even though I could have stayed asleep in that bed forever. I barely managed to sit up right before Jack poked his head into the bedroom and grinned at me.

"I see you've discovered the exceptional mattresses," he said and leaned against the doorframe. "There's not a lot we get right, but I can admit we've done well in the bed department."

"Hey," I said, still trying to wake up. It was rather difficult with how comfortable this bed was. "How's…?"

Jack's smile faded a little, but he managed to keep it there for the most part. "Dad's okay," he said quietly. "I don't think he has much time left, though."

"Jack, I'm so sorry."

He shrugged. "It's life, Blake. Happens to everyone."

I didn't like that answer. Even though it sounded like optimism, I was pretty sure it was just resignation. "Jack, he's your dad. You can be sad about this."

Though he fought it, his little frown turned into something closer to a scowl, which I liked even less than his comment about life. "I don't want to be sad," he said, somewhat roughly. "I've spent my whole life being sad, and I…" He huffed and shook his head, softening again. "I want to think about something else. Will you go somewhere with me?"

I still had to contact Gordon, but I wasn't sure I was ready for that yet. "Where?" I asked.

Grinning, he came into the room and took my hands to help me off the giant bed. "Somewhere fun. I think you might need the distraction as much as I do." That answer made me more nervous than it should have, though I felt a little more justified in my apprehension when he added, "You ever been to Coney Island?"

"Ha!" I clenched my mouth shut after letting out that laugh and shook my head. "I'm not going to Coney Island, Jack."

"Why not?"

"I don't do amusement parks." I hadn't been on a roller coaster since I was twelve, and it had been an awful experience. It had made me immensely glad when Steve told me he thought they were boring and Jordan had found them pointless, because I didn't have to explain myself to either of them.

Jack, on the other hand…

Raising one eyebrow, he searched my face, probably for some sign that I was kidding. "First of all," he said and led the way out into the main room of the suite, "it's not just an amusement park; there's all sorts of stuff on Coney Island. Second of all, everyone likes roller coasters."

"I don't."

"Why not?"

I shut my mouth tight again. I had plenty of terrible memories of vomit and panic, and I didn't need to revisit those any more than I already had.

Jack grabbed my hands again, this time pulling me so close that our noses were only a few inches apart. "Come on, Blake," he said, almost whispering the words. "You need to learn to have a little fun sometimes. Loosen up. Let go." And when I still said nothing, he leaned even closer and ran a hand through my hair to smooth it. "Will you come with me, Amelia? Please?"

My resolve was slipping as I took in his expression. As lighthearted as he was acting, I could see in those icy eyes of his that he very much needed this distraction. And maybe I did too. If nothing else, going with Jack for the afternoon would give me a reason to avoid calling

Gordon for one more day. Besides, he'd never looked at me like this before. And I really liked it.

"Okay," I said, though my stomach started to churn at the idea. "If you need to go to Coney Island, I'll go with you."

"Thank you," he said, and he briefly touched his forehead to mine before he dropped my hands and pulled away.

If his dad weren't literally on his deathbed, I would have gotten mad at him for figuring out exactly how to get me to do what he wanted. But if I was being honest with myself, I had never made it all that hard.

For anyone.

And I was starting to get sick of it.

Coney Island was so much more fun than I thought it would be. We played arcade games and went on the rides made for kids, and we both nearly puked after going on the spinny thing. We ate cotton candy and won a teddy bear that I promptly dropped over the edge of the pier. Jack paid for everything—he wouldn't even let me touch my wallet— and he didn't have to say anything to remind me that sometimes a person needed to be needed to find a little peace. And Jack definitely needed peace, so I was willing to do whatever it took to keep him smiling.

Sure, that included the terrifying roller coasters, and Jack made me go on at least one of them. But I actually liked that part. For once, I felt free, like I was flying instead of stuck in someone else's shoes and trudging along through life.

We went on the coaster three times, and Jack's grin was worth every exhilarating moment.

Around dinnertime, we bought a couple of hot dogs and found a seat near the Ferris wheel so we could eat without the danger of dropping our food like I had done with the teddy bear prize. We sat and watched people enjoying their lives and the friends they were with, and things felt okay.

I studied Jack, and he *looked* okay. I had no idea what he might be feeling inside, but at least outwardly his expression conveyed content- ment, if not happiness. He looked lighter, the way he should look, and

I was glad I had chosen to come with him. He had needed this, and so had I.

"Thank you, Jack," I said and clasped his hand.

He smiled back at me. "It's nice to let go a little sometimes, isn't it?"

"You really are so wise, aren't you?" I didn't say it as a joke this time; I meant it. I still wasn't all that sure what he'd endured during his year on the road, but Jack had discovered so many things about life, and I wanted him to teach me all of them.

"I've learned to pay attention," Jack argued. "I was never very good at that before."

"I wish I could see the good things in life as well as you can," I said with a sigh. "I think things would be easier if I could do that."

Jack gave me an odd look, like he was both confused and amused by what I said, but he didn't feel the need to explain himself, even when he noticed me wondering. "I have an idea," he said, and he nodded toward the Ferris wheel in front of us.

The thing was huge. "How about no?"

Laughing, he held my hand a little tighter and dragged me up onto my feet. "Sorry, Blake, but you don't get a say in this one."

My hot dog began churning in my stomach as he led me to the short line to get on the wheel, and before I knew it, we had a car to ourselves and were on our way up.

I scooted a little closer to Jack, because if I was going to fall to my death, he was going to fall with me. "Why are these things so big?" I whispered then grabbed the rail as the car shook a little. I wasn't necessarily afraid of heights, but that didn't mean I liked them.

Laughing, Jack laced his fingers with mine, though it only helped a little. "Relax, Blake. It's not that high."

"Please stop calling me that," I moaned.

"Okay."

Completely distracted from the churning in my stomach, I turned to him in surprise. He wasn't laughing at me anymore, but he didn't look ashamed either. He looked…pleased? "Really?" I said, unable to stop myself. "That's all it took? It was that easy?"

He grinned wider than he had all afternoon. "You can't be afraid to ask for things you want, Amelia."

I pulled my eyebrows together, and I had to wonder how long he had been waiting to say that one. Had he noticed from the beginning how much I didn't like him calling me by my last name, or was this just a spur-of-the-moment lesson he wanted me to learn? I had no idea.

Leaning close to me and wrapping his other hand around our entwined ones, he looked me straight in the eye with an expression that told me what he was about to say was important. "When was the last time you did something for yourself?" he asked. "Really, truly, just for Amelia?""

I frowned. Every day was about myself, and I had to fight to be less selfish than I knew I was. "Everything I do is—"

"No," he argued forcefully. "I want you to really think about this one, especially because I have a feeling we're going to be stuck up here for a bit."

I hadn't realized the Ferris wheel had slowed to a stop, leaving us hanging very near the top. I was feeling nauseous again, but this time it was mostly because of the way Jack was watching me. He was so close. Like he'd been in the hotel room. I could see every little variation in his fair skin and the individual hairs that made up his mop of dark hair.

And I had the sudden urge to run my fingers through that hair, though I stopped myself. Barely. Just like I stopped myself from leaning even closer than I already was. His lips were only a few inches away from mine, his eyes locked on mine until they slowly slid down to my nose then farther still until I could hardly breathe.

There was no way he was thinking what I thought he was thinking.

"What do you want me to say?" I whispered.

His intense expression fell, which meant I had already said the wrong thing. Why was Jack so much harder to read than anyone I had ever met? He pulled his hand free and scooted a fraction of an inch away from me, and then his eyes focused on the city skyline.

Eventually the Ferris wheel moved again, and though it took a long time for us to get back down to the bottom and be let off the stupid ride, we spent all of it without saying another word to each other.

Only when we climbed in the family car to take us back into the city did I try to strike up conversation again and fill the silence that felt like it was sitting solid between us. "So why did you need the distraction so badly?" I asked warily. Likely it was just because of his dad's illness, but Jack had known about that part already. I had a feeling this was something else.

Jack glanced at the driver, Max, before he reached up and pressed a button that slid a partition in place so we wouldn't be overheard. "Back before I…" He swallowed and looked down at his lap. "Back before I left home, Dad told me something. I think he'd been wanting to say it for years, but when he realized he wouldn't have the time, he…"

I took hold of his hand as his frown deepened. "What?" I asked.

"I have a brother," he said. "Or I did. A half-brother, from before Dad met my mom and moved to New York. I went to San Francisco to try to find him, and for a long time I wasn't sure I would. And then…"

My mind immediately jumped to that picture Adam had shown me, the one with his friend who looked a whole lot like Jack and his father. But before I said anything about Luke, I wanted to know how much Jack knew. It wasn't fair for me to have more information than he did about his own family.

"I found him," Jack said, and his eyes moved to the window next to him. "I talked to so many people until finally someone recognized the name, and that led me to another person, to another, to another, until finally I found someone who actually knew what happened to him."

"The day of Indie's concert?" I guessed.

Nodding, he took a labored breath then finally looked at me and met my gaze. "I had to know for sure, before I met your family, if what I'd been told was true. So I went to the cemetery."

I definitely knew where this was going, so I gripped his hand tight.

"He died," he said, the words heavy. "Luke died saving your cousin's life nine years ago. And I don't know how I can tell my dad that there is no way he can fix his greatest regret in life."

Luke had saved someone's life? My *cousin's* life? That explained Lanna and Matthew's reaction, though I wasn't sure which of them

Luke had saved. As much as I wanted to know more, I knew I had to be careful talking about this subject. It was clearly tearing Jack up inside, and I could hardly bear to see him hurting so much.

"His name was Luke?" I asked quietly.

"After Dad," he confirmed. "He said he lost track of Luke when his mom died, and he waited too long to try to find him. Besides, that was the same time Jace and I were born, so I don't think he tried very hard. But he said… He wanted me to find him and bring him home so he could make amends. And now…"

Poor Jack. If I were in his situation, I would have no idea what to do. I only had my own experience, which was similar, if not exactly the same. Gordon wasn't on his deathbed, but he was trying to fix the mistakes of his past. "I think you should tell your dad you found him," I said, wincing when Jack's hand tightened around mine. "I mean, you don't have to tell him about, you know… Luke being gone. But tell him he's okay."

Jack frowned as a tear slipped from his eye. "But he's not okay. And I don't even know if he was okay before he died. I can't lie to my dad. Not after…"

I didn't mean to be, but I was angry with Lucas Hawthorne. I had never met the man, but I wanted to know how he could think putting this kind of responsibility on his son's shoulders was a good idea. Jack was clearly having a hard time with the whole thing, and there was little I could do to help him.

"But you can give him peace," I said. "You can help him rest. My family can probably tell you everything you want to know about your brother, but until then, you need to do what's best for your dad. Let him rest, Jack."

We pulled up to Hawthorne Tower a moment later, and the conversation ended there. Halfway to the door, we paused when Rohan hurried outside and slid to a stop in front of us.

"Jack!" he gasped. "You're here. You need to go upstairs. Right now."

Jack turned pale, and he grabbed my hand tight, though I wasn't sure he even realized he did it. "What's wrong?"

Rohan shook his head, and his expression said as much as his words: "It's your dad."

Jack moved so fast I barely realized he was gone until he was at the elevators, desperately waiting for the doors to open so he could get inside and get up to his family. Next to me, Rohan looked ready to race right after him, but the young man was professional enough that he kept himself from moving anywhere and simply watched Jack disappear into the elevator.

I had known the guy for all of five minutes, but based on the look on his face, Rohan was nearly as distressed about Lucas Hawthorne's condition as Jack was. So I put my hand on his arm and tried to send him some sort of comfort in my smile.

Rohan looked at me in surprise and couldn't seem to find anything to say.

"I'm so sorry," I said. "This must be so hard on you."

He nodded a little. "Lucas has always been like a second father to me," he said quietly. "But I'll be fine. I've dealt with death before. I'm more worried about Jack."

So was I. Optimism could only get him so far, and he had already admitted he couldn't see the bright side of his father's illness. What would happen to him when his father was gone?

"Guess you'd want to go up to your room, huh?" Rohan said after a moment.

Honestly, I wasn't sure what I wanted to do. I wished I could be there with Jack, but that would mean intruding on a private family moment, and there was no way I would do that. I was stuck in the middle of something so big, with nowhere to go and nothing to do.

I certainly wasn't about to give Gordon a call when all of this was happening.

Nodding at Rohan, I followed him to the elevator, and together we rode sixty-seven floors up to my way-too-big hotel room, where I settled on the couch determined to wait, just in case Jack needed me. Even if it took all night, I was prepared to be there for him.

I just hoped he wanted me to be.

CHAPTER FIFTEEN

Sometime after eleven, a soft knock on my door woke me as I lay on the couch, though I hadn't fallen completely asleep. Jumping up, I dashed to the door and pulled it open to find Jack with hardly any expression on his face.

"Dad's gone," he said, and he stepped inside before I could ask him if he wanted to come in. He sounded about as emotionless as he looked, and I didn't blame him. If my dad had just died... I shuddered to think about it. Maybe in the next few days I would call my parents in Denmark and see if they wanted me to come visit them.

Taking Jack by the hand, I led him to the sofa and gently nudged his shoulders so he would sit, which he did without argument. What could I say to him? There was nothing that could soothe the loss of a parent, and I wasn't good with words anyway. I wished I had Jack's ability to put my emotions into music, just so I could have a chance to express my sorrow for him.

The only thing I could think to do was sit with him and hope he would want to talk. I liked talking to Jack, and it had always been calming for me; I hoped it went the other direction as well. But until he chose to say something, I just sat next to him and took his hand, warming his fingers between my palms.

Eventually he curled himself up on the couch and dropped his head onto my lap, and though his eyes were closed, I knew he wasn't asleep. He probably *wouldn't* sleep tonight, even though he desperately needed the rest. I wasn't sure how much sleep he had actually gotten since Jace's appearance in San Francisco.

I stroked his hair, still searching for something to say, and I lost track of time as we sat there. The night just continued on until a glow of light came through the window, bathing the room in even more gold than was there to begin with.

I was exhausted. Jack was worse. He didn't even move when I slid out from under him to get up off the couch, even though his eyes were wide open. He looked like the very life of him, the spark I loved so much about him, had gone out completely.

"Jack?" I said, keeping my voice as soft as possible.

He blinked slowly.

"I know this is hard," I said. "I know you're…" I didn't know anything about what he was feeling. What would Jack say if this were me? "Your dad isn't in pain anymore, and he knows his family was all together, which is probably more than he could ever want for himself. I don't know what you believe in, but…" I didn't know much about Jack at all, if I was being honest, but I knew he was the kindest, happiest, most peaceful person I had ever known. "But I know you can get through this. I know you can because everything always works out in the end. And…"

I swallowed, and though I really didn't want to say the last thing that had come to my mind, my gut was telling me I had to say it. Things lately seemed to work out when I followed my gut. "And I need you to be okay, Jack. Please."

He looked up, meeting my eyes and pulling his eyebrows together just the slightest bit.

"I'm going to get you some tea or something, okay?" I headed to the door so I could go downstairs and see who could help me with something like that. In a place like this, I wouldn't have been surprised if there was a person whose sole job was to make the guests whatever beverages they could possibly want.

But when I pulled open the door, there was someone waiting for me.

Based on her haphazard appearance, Marianne Hawthorne probably hadn't slept at all either. "Good morning, Miss Blake," she said softly, even as her eyes slid behind me to the sofa. "I was hoping I could talk to my son."

I looked back to find him sitting up and watching the pair of us. With hardly a change in his expression, he shook his head. I bit my lip. "Um…"

I waited for her to just force her way inside, since this was her hotel, after all, but she simply nodded and folded her arms, as if she needed the comfort so badly that she would take it from wherever she could get it, even if it was from herself. "Thank you anyway," she said, and a tear slipped onto her cheek.

I spoke before I really thought things through: "Mrs. Hawthorne, um, Marianne, is there anything I can do for you?" I felt so useless when it came to Jack that I was desperate to find somewhere I could be of some help. No matter how small.

She shook her head, though her denial came with a frown. "Oh, I'm just trying to arrange everything for the funeral, so I don't think…"

I grabbed hold of her hand. "Let me help you," I nearly begged. "I used to plan events all the time back when I lived in Chicago, and you should be spending time with your family, not stuck on the phone dealing with all of this. Please."

I could tell she wanted to argue. It was right there on the tip of her tongue and in the lift of her eyebrows. But sheer exhaustion must have won over, because she nodded.

I glanced back just as Jack disappeared in the direction of the bedroom. "Um." I thought quickly about the best way to say this so I wouldn't offend her. "Give me a little bit," I said, "and I'll try to get Jack to come up with me. Is that okay?"

This time she smiled a little, and she gave my hand a squeeze before pulling herself free. "You have a beautiful heart, Amelia Blake," she whispered, and with one more glance toward the bedroom, she turned and wandered toward the elevator.

I found Jack in a chair out on the balcony, his legs curled up beneath him and a tiny notebook in his hands. I'd seen that notebook a few times, and I was pretty sure it was where he wrote all his song ideas. He didn't seem to have realized I stepped outside with him, and he kept scribbling words as if getting them onto the paper was a matter of life and death.

"Are you writing a new song?" I asked and settled in the other cushioned porch seat. When Jack shrugged, I chanced another question: "Is it about your dad?"

This time he looked up and gave me the strangest expression, though I really couldn't put any words to it. His face looked like his music, full of emotion that was desperate to be heard. He watched me for only a few seconds, and then he went back to it, writing as fast as he could and nearly tearing the page out when he quickly turned to the next.

He continued on that way for another five minutes, and then he finally grew still, taking a long, slow breath as if he hadn't even dared to breathe until he had the song written out.

"I'm going to go help your mom plan the funeral," I told him.

His gaze traveled the buildings around us, and he nodded.

"Will you come with me?"

Another nod.

By the time we got to the elevator, I worried he was never going to say a single word again.

To my utter relief, after he slipped a keycard from his pocket to light up the button for the top floor, he turned to me and said, "Thank you, Amelia." I could have cried just hearing his voice again, and maybe I did a little, because a deep line appeared between his eyebrows as he looked at me. "I mean it," he said and gently brushed my cheek with his finger. "Without you, I… I told him about Luke, like you said. And you were right. He needed to hear it."

"Good." But I was pretty sure there was something else he wanted to tell me, and I waited in silence until he found his breath again.

"There's something…" he said with a frown. He pulled an envelope out of his pocket and showed me his name written on it in a bold and strong handwriting. "Dad gave one of these to all of us. The terms of our inheritances. Apparently…" Sighing, he shoved it back into his pocket and instead took my hand. "Apparently we all have a task to complete, and Mom gets to decide if we've done it properly before we get anything from them. A last request from Dad."

That sounded either diabolical or genius; it was hard to know which. "What does yours say?" I asked, too curious not to.

As the elevator slowed to a stop, Jack shrugged. "I haven't opened it yet. I don't care about inheriting a fortune if it means my life is going to be dictated just like…" He shook his head, and the doors opened to that incredible first floor of his family's home. "Remember when you promised to call me out when I wasn't acting like myself?"

I nodded, though I was distracted by Jack's sister Sara looking up from her phone and glaring at us. Or, more specifically, at me.

"I'm going to need that now more than ever," Jack finished then made his way over to the couch where Sara sat. "Where's Mom?"

"What is *she* doing here?" Sara replied.

It was a perfectly valid question, in my opinion, but anger flashed in Jack's eyes. "She's here because I want her to be," he practically growled. "Where's Mom?"

"This is supposed to be family time."

"Is that why you're spending all your time on your phone?"

"Jack," I said gently and squeezed his hand.

He immediately softened. He wasn't kidding about how much he needed the reminder, and it made me wonder again what he'd been like before he went on the road. Jace had said Jack left a note telling his family that he didn't like who he'd become, and if this was who he was, I could well understand that feeling.

Giving me a grateful little smile, Jack pulled me closer. "I'm sorry, Sara. Amelia is here to help Mom plan the funeral."

"We can plan the funeral," said someone else, stepping down the stairs with a hard glare on his face. Jace looked pretty much the same as he had in San Francisco, only now there wasn't any trace of friendliness in his eyes. "Do you think we're all useless, Jack? It's not like I've been doing my job *and* yours for the last year and a half."

Pain filtered into Jack's eyes, and he had the look of someone who was being cornered. Probably because he was, since Sara had gotten to her feet and was staring me down just like her brother.

"This should be just family," Sara said again.

"I don't know why you brought your incompetent little overseer in the first place," Jace added.

And before I could even think about defending myself, Jack had stepped in front of me, still holding fast to my hand. "Don't you dare," he said, and though the words should have been harsh, he kept his voice soft. Gentle. "Amelia is the only reason I even came back, and you know I was terrible at the whole hotel management thing. Even Dad thought so. You're smart enough on your own, Jace."

"I think you should leave," Jace said to me, ignoring his twin even though he could barely see me hidden behind Jack's thin frame. "You don't belong here."

"Yes she does," Jack argued.

Honestly, I was about ready to turn around and leave before things got ugly. They clearly didn't want me here, and it wasn't like their arguments were wrong. I was just Jack's friend, and I didn't have any right to interrupt this family's grief.

"Your friend can go," Sara said coldly.

Jack must have felt me inching my way toward the elevator, because he pulled me even closer to him and slid his arm around my waist. "She's not my friend," he said with a little more force. "She's my girlfriend. So shut up and tell me where Mom is."

"I'm right here," Marianne replied, appearing from the side hallway in front of us.

And while I would have loved to study her expression and see if she still wanted my help, I was a little too dizzy to focus. I knew Jack had only called me his girlfriend to get his siblings to stop insulting me, but... I glanced down at his hand at my waist, wondering if there was more to his statement than I thought.

Marianne smiled at me, and though she had freshened herself up a bit and looked more put together than before, she still seemed frazzled. "Thank you for coming, Amelia," she said to me first, though there was a bit of hesitation in her words. "Sara, I need you to go find your brother. He has been hiding for long enough. Jace, they need you at the office."

Both Hawthorne children looked furious about their assignments and seemed ready to blame me for their tasks, and I shrank deeper into Jack's hold. "How am I supposed to find him?" Sara asked at the same time Jace said, "Can't they handle things themselves for a while?" and Jack took a deep breath that was likely to prepare another angry statement toward his siblings.

Luckily, Marianne raised a hand, which stopped them all in their tracks. *Impressive.* "Jace," she said forcefully, "I know this is a hard time, but we still have responsibilities. You, in particular, are especially crucial to the business now that your father is gone. Now go out and act like the professional I know you are." She turned next to Sara, who preemptively winced after listening to Jace's thorough scolding. "I'm worried about Wes, and I can't go look for him right now. I need you to step up and play an active role in this family."

Sara grumbled something unintelligible and turned to go, but Jack stepped forward and muttered, "I'll go find him, Sara. It's fine."

And while I admired Jack's willingness to help his family, if he went to search for his apparently missing brother, that would leave me alone with his family, which was downright terrifying. However kind Marianne might have been so far, I was way below her level when it came to social standing. But then, to my complete surprise, Jack quickly kissed my cheek and flashed me a grin before he hurried up the stairs.

"Excellent," Marianne said, though her eyes lingered on me longer than I would have expected as I touched a finger to the spot Jack had kissed. "That means you can help us with the funeral, Sara." Sara seemed even less enthused by this idea than going after her brother, but she was smart enough to keep her mouth shut this time. "We'll go to my office, I think," Marianne continued, and the blessed woman slipped her arm in mine and led the way before her daughter could try to complain again about my presence.

At least two of the Hawthorne clan were okay with having me around, and I would take what I could get. I wasn't here to be liked, anyway, and I hoped I could actually be of some help to this poor family who was standing stronger than I would have in their situation.

I'd never planned a funeral before—thank goodness—but there was a lot more that went into it than I'd expected. Lucas had apparently arranged everything with the funeral home, choosing his own casket and purchasing the plot and headstone at the cemetery. But we had to pick the date, arrange eulogies and pallbearers and a priest, and there were flowers to order and programs to create and people to invite. Lucas had been well-loved by his staff and had apparently had many friends and associates, so we had to find a venue big enough because the funeral home was way too small.

And somehow we managed to get it all done, down to the little details, even when Sara disappeared at lunchtime and never returned. After going all night without sleeping then spending most of the day searching the internet and making phone calls, I felt like I could sleep for a week and still be tired, but I forced my exhaustion away because I knew Marianne was still fighting to hold herself together, even if the hard part was over.

"Thank you, Amelia," she said as we made our way back to the front room around dinnertime. "I don't know what I would have done without you."

"I was happy to help," I assured her. "Really, it was a good way to spend the day."

"I worry I took you away from your business here in the city," she replied. "But I can't say I regret letting you help me. What was it you came to New York to do?"

I nearly told her it was simply because Jack needed me to come, but I knew that wouldn't have been the whole truth. But I also didn't *want* to tell her the whole truth. It felt strange, talking about a father I'd never met when she had clearly loved her husband and built a perfectly functional family with him. But then again, there was that whole thing with Jack's half-brother, Luke, so maybe she would understand.

Wait, did she even know about her husband's first son?

"I'm going to meet my father," I said quietly. "I found out about him a few years ago, and I figured it was time to get to know him a little." Although, the fact that I hadn't even called him yet to tell him I was nearby should have been a good indicator of how little I actually wanted to make that first contact.

Marianne patted my arm. "That's a lovely thought," she said then looked around the empty room. "I'll go see where Jack has run off to."

She'd only made it two steps when laughter rang down from the floor above us. Apparently laughing was a rare occurrence, because she stared up the staircase with a bewildered expression and took my hand, though I wasn't sure she realized it.

Together, we went up the stairs and arrived at what looked like the kind of kitchen Gordon Ramsay would cook in, though I highly doubted Ramsay's kitchen was ever covered with flour. I doubted Ramsay himself was ever covered in flour, unlike the two people who stopped throwing it at each other when they noticed us standing at the top of the stairs.

If not for his bright eyes and crooked smile, I would have had a hard time distinguishing Jack from anyone else when he was covered head to toe in white powder. The teenager next to him dropped his smile as soon as he saw Marianne, but there was still a hint of it lingering there despite his best efforts.

"I can explain," Jack said then laughed when the other boy slipped a little as he tried to get out from around the counter. "Wes wanted to make cookies."

Marianne still looked completely dumbfounded, and she glanced between the two of them as if she didn't know what to say. "Cookies?"

The teenager—Jack's youngest brother, Wes, I assumed, though I couldn't be sure when he was just as covered in flour as Jack—bowed his head a little.

Jack wrapped his arm around Wes's shoulders and forced him to bend down so he could brush flour out of his dark hair. "Thing is," he said, as if there was nothing unusual about the scene, "neither of us knows how to make cookies, and then Wes knocked over the flour."

Pulling himself free, Wes glared at his brother but said nothing.

Jack didn't seem to care about the silence. "Okay, so *I* knocked over the flour, but Wes threw the first handful." He laughed again and ducked as his brother grabbed some flour off the counter and chucked it at him. "Fine!" he said happily. "I threw it first. Sorry, Mom. I'll clean it up."

But Marianne didn't seem all that concerned about the mess, because her eyes were only for her sons. Mostly, she just watched Jack as he grinned every time he saw his brother's white face, and I had a feeling she had never expected to find so much happiness in such a time of grief.

"Oh," Jack added, coming around the kitchen island to stand a little closer to us, "I think Jace was looking for you, Mom." When his gaze turned to me, he got a sudden gleam of mischief in his eyes that came too quickly for me to react fast enough, and next thing I knew, I was in his arms and inhaling a mouthful of flour as I shrieked to try to get away. "That looks better," he said when I freed myself.

I knew I was covered in flour now, but I couldn't find the strength to look down and see how bad the damage was. Not when Jack was looking at me like everything was complete now that I was here. My face burned with heat, and for a moment I forgot it wasn't just the two of us there in that massive kitchen.

Then Wes coughed, and Jack blinked and stepped back a little. "Hey Wes," he said without looking away from me, "could you take Amelia up to the roof? I want to take a quick shower, and then I'll relieve you from tour guide duty."

I fought to find my voice. "Don't I get a shower?"

Reaching his hand out, he used the heel of his palm to wipe my cheek, even though his hand was still covered in flour and probably did more damage than good. "Nah," he said. "You're perfect. Is that okay, Wes?" Though Wes didn't even nod, let alone say anything, Jack took his silence as agreement and said, "Thanks," before he disappeared up another staircase.

"I'll go find Jace," Marianne muttered, and I could still hear her confusion and surprise.

That left me with the youngest Hawthorne, who seemed to be sizing me up like his siblings had as he brushed flour off his shoulders.

"Uh, hi," I said and held my hand out to him. "I'm Amelia. You must be Wes."

He shook my hand, but I was pretty sure he didn't even consider opening his mouth to say anything. At least it was a nice change from indirect—and direct—insults.

"You can just show me where the roof is," I said. "You don't have to stay with me, if you have other things you need to do."

Stowing his hands in his pockets, he shrugged then jerked his head a little toward the stairs, which must have meant I was supposed to follow him because he started walking that direction. Was this silence normal, or was it just his way of mourning?

This staircase led to a bright hallway full of what I guessed to be bedrooms, though all the doors were closed so I couldn't see inside as we passed. Wes continued to the very end of the hall and pushed open the last door for me, which opened up to yet another set of stairs, and he followed me up until I reached another door and pushed it open. A burst of golden sunlight greeted me, warmer than I expected, and I found myself on an incredible rooftop high above the bulk of the city. A large pool occupied the far half of it, and there was a gas fire pit near the hot tub and surrounded by the most comfortable-looking patio chairs I'd ever seen.

Wes gestured toward the chairs and sat after I did, and though he still said nothing, he gave me a look that was easier to read than I expected. Or at least I thought I could read it, and I was pretty sure he was trying to tell me that he didn't hate me like his other siblings did. His small smile and kind eyes spoke for him.

"Uh, thanks," I said, since that could have meant gratitude for his unspoken thoughts or just for getting me here. "It's beautiful up here."

He nodded, looking around.

The sun was low on the horizon and would set soon, and I felt like our view of the city was something very few people got to see, so I wanted to take it all in as much as I could. But I couldn't ignore Wes when he had chosen to stay up here with me, so I searched for a conversation starter that wouldn't be awkward.

"You're seventeen, right?" I said.

Wes nodded.

"So you're a senior?"

Another nod.

"Are you going to go to college after you graduate?"

He shrugged.

"What would you want to study if you did?"

Another shrug.

I swallowed the next comment that came to my head, since "sorry about your dad" probably wasn't the best thing to say to a teenage kid.

Apparently I had to stick to yes or no questions unless he decided to start talking, and I was bad enough at conversation already.

"Do you like living in New York?" I asked. "I think it's incredible here."

He thought about that one for a second, looking around at the nearest buildings, almost as if he hadn't fully realized he lived somewhere as well-known as New York City. He nodded again, but it was slowly this time. Maybe he only liked parts of it?

"Do you like being in such a big city?"

Nod. *Yes.*

"Have you been to other cities like this?"

Yes.

"Where? Boston?" *Yes.* "Los Angeles?" *No.* "Chicago?" *Yes.* "I used to live in Chicago."

That comment got me some interest as he sat up a little straighter and gave me a look that seemed to say, *Really?*

I smiled. "I lived there with my…with someone I used to know. I really miss it sometimes, and being here in New York has felt more like being home than I've felt in a while."

San Francisco had been great, but the West Coast felt so different from the other side of the country that it hadn't quite felt like home over the last couple of months. I was still trying to settle in.

"I haven't seen much of your city yet," I said, "but I really like it. You're lucky you get to live here."

To my surprise, Wes actually opened his mouth, and I was pretty sure he was about to say something when Jack appeared at the door and bounced over to us.

"You're a mess," he said to Wes, and then he grinned when he caught sight of the damage he'd done to me. "You're less of a mess."

"But still a mess," I agreed, though I was a little disappointed that Wes had shut his mouth again.

Jack reached out his fingers and brushed a bit of flour from my hair, which, I realized with horror, was probably all over the place because I hadn't done anything with it since early yesterday evening. He smiled, ran his finger down my nose to get rid of even more flour, and then he turned to his little brother as he sat next to me. "I forgot to tell you," he said to him. "Dad told me you're taking a creative writing class in school."

Wes's eyes went a little wide, but he nodded a little.

Jack grinned. "Dude, that's awesome. Didn't I tell you that was a good idea?" He must have seen something in Wes's face that I didn't, because he rolled his eyes. "Come on, man. You're going to get better. That's the whole point of practicing. Do you think I was any good at the guitar when I started?"

A glimmer of laughter lit up Wes's eyes, which were a slightly darker blue than his brother's so they stood out a little more from the flour on his face than Jack's had.

"That's right," Jack said. "I sucked. Someone even threw a tomato at me once. Don't look at me like that; it's true. I was playing at a farmer's market and trying to get enough cash to buy some of the pot-stickers I was right next to because they smelled amazing."

I was fascinated. Wes literally didn't say a word, but that didn't bother Jack, who carried on like they were having a normal conversation. Wes relaxed more the longer they "talked," and Jack somehow kept getting closer to me. Or maybe that was me getting closer to him. Eventually, I was right at the edge of my chair so I could be as close to him as I could be without leaving my chair to share his, and I just sat there and watched him connect with his brother in a way I'd never seen before.

Jack was so in tune with Wes that he seemed to know exactly what he was thinking just by looking at him, and I was pretty sure he had done the same thing to me before. Did that mean we had as strong a connection as he had with his brother? The thought made me shiver.

Jack noticed that shiver and glanced up at the disappearing sun. "You must be freezing," he said and hopped up, disappearing into a little shed-like building near the pool.

"He's different."

For a moment I was sure I had imagined the sound, but then Wes was looking right at me. I furrowed my brow. "Different?" I asked.

He nodded, glancing at the shed. "Happier. Nicer." Though he spoke softly, there was a lot more strength and depth to his voice than

I would have guessed. It lent power to his words, and I imagined he only said something if it was truly important.

Cocking my head, I shifted onto the chair Jack had been sitting in so I could get closer to the teen. "Jack's always happy," I said, though based on the way everyone was acting around him, I was really starting to think that hadn't always been true.

Wes shrugged. "He used to be arrogant. Mean."

I honestly couldn't even imagine Jack being mean. "I guess his year on the road really changed him."

But Wes shook his head and frowned a little. "Jack's always been nice to me, but I was the only… He's the only one who really tries with me. But with everyone else, he was…" He swallowed, as if saying so many things at once was terrifying. "He called me a couple of months ago. To wish me happy birthday. And he was still Jack. Cold and dark, like he usually is."

The fire pit burst to life in front of us, making me jump, and Jack stepped out of the shed with an armful of blankets. "I forgot how to turn the thing on," he said with a chuckle. "Guess I should have come up here more often when I lived here."

"Jack's different," Wes repeated even more quietly then got to his feet, pausing to gaze at Jack for a second before he disappeared through the door leading back inside.

Jack watched him go, his smile shifting into something more content than before, then he took one of the blankets, draping it around my shoulders, and settled right next to me on the same chair so we were hip to hip. He didn't have to sit that close, especially now that none of his family were around to see us, but he did. And my cheeks burned, and not because of the fire. It was because Jack reached for my hand and laced his fingers between mine as if he'd been doing that as long as I'd known him.

And I was realizing I was perfectly okay with that.

"Thank you," Jack said and ran his thumb along mine.

I was suddenly grateful for the fire and blanket as another shiver ran through me. "For what?"

"For helping my mom. For sitting with me. For talking with Wes. Everything."

"Of course," I whispered. Then I had to ask: "Um, does Wes always…"

"Sit there like a statue?" Jack finished for me then nodded. "He's been that way his whole life, and I have no idea why. I can never get Jace to shut up, and Sara will spend hours on her phone chatting with her friends or whoever. People always think Wes never has anything to say, but you just have to know how to listen the right way. He likes you, you know."

I tried to smile, but it didn't work very well. "Well, he's the only one," I muttered.

"That's not true."

I raised an eyebrow at him. "Come on, Jack. They hate me."

Jack leaned closer and gently touched his head to mine for a moment. "It's impossible to hate you, Amelia Blake. Jace just…" He sighed. "Jace thinks he needs to control everything, and he has a hard time letting go of his expectations. Plus, I think he's always resented the fact that Dad picked me to take over the business because I was six minutes older. Running Hawthorne Enterprises has been his dream. And Sara… Well, I don't really understand Sara," he admitted. "I think maybe being the only girl outside of Mom is all she's ever known, so it's hard for her to accept anyone else coming into the family."

My heart seemed to catch in my throat, though I knew Jack probably didn't mean anything by that. Not really. "Has Jace never brought a girl home?" I asked to distract my thoughts from this weird sensation in my chest that was too foreign for me to really understand. The question I *really* wanted to ask was, "Did you ever bring girls home?" But I didn't want to hear the answer to that one.

Jack laughed a little. "Jace is too focused on his career to worry about trivial things like love." Either he was oblivious to the way I couldn't seem to breathe at the mention of love, or he could see it clear as day and was kind enough to change the subject, because he coughed and said, "Have you talked to your dad yet?"

Thank you. "I haven't exactly had the time," I said with a small smile. "But also…it's terrifying."

"Why?"

"I don't know." But I knew that wasn't true as soon as I said it. "I mean, my whole life I thought I knew what my life was, you know? I was Amelia Carter, the daughter of Megan and John Carter. An only child who had her mom's brown hair and her dad's laugh. And then one day I wake up and my laugh isn't my dad's because I don't know how Gordon laughs. And I didn't get my blue eyes from my mom because they came from him, a guy I didn't even know existed until I was twenty-six. And I felt like my whole life had been a lie, and that hurt too much. It hurts too much, Jack."

I dropped my head onto his shoulder, and he put an arm around me that felt like it shut out some of the darkness that was creeping in with the twilight. "I'm not as carefree as you, Jack. I don't know how to see past all the crappy stuff and be happy even when things are hard. How do you do it?"

Rubbing my back, he kissed the top of my head and took a deep breath. "I'm not sure I'm the best person to ask," he said, which made absolutely no sense. "But I want you to listen to me very carefully, okay?" He shifted away so he could take both of my hands and look me right in the eye. "Be brave, Amelia. Let go of the past. Don't be like me and regret the time you didn't spend with your dad. I know things aren't what you thought they would be, but that's what makes it life. Life is never what you expect, and when things happen, you just have to move forward. *Let go.*"

Tears in my eyes, I nodded and reached for my phone. And when it came time to hit the call button, Jack did it with me.

CHAPTER SIXTEEN

My father was leaving the country for a few weeks, and the only time he had free for a meetup was the morning of Lucas's funeral two days later. He committed to make the drive up to New York from Washington D.C. even though I tried to say it would be easier for me to go to him, and we would meet for coffee and just get to know each other a little bit.

"I don't want there to be any pressure," he said. "This is all on your terms, okay?"

I tried to cancel multiple times, but since I was pretty much spending every waking moment with Jack, he stopped me every time.

Eventually, he straight up stole my phone. "It's for your own good," he told me and said he would give it back just before I headed to the café where Gordon and I were going to meet.

At least everything seemed to be going well for the upcoming funeral, and as I double-checked with all the vendors and the funeral home, everything was in place and ready to go. That made me feel just a little bit better about leaving, though that didn't stop me from complaining a bit when Jack walked me down to the lobby and out to the car he'd ordered for me (even though I had tried to tell him I would just get a cab).

"What if he is only meeting me to tell me he doesn't want to be part of my life?" I said.

Jack rolled his eyes. "The man would not drive all the way from D.C. to tell you he hates you."

"What if we have nothing to talk about?"

"Talk about your brother and sister," he replied. "By the way, Seth has texted you, like, twelve times, so you might want to reply before he thinks I've sold you to a cult. Now get in the car." He even pulled the door open for me.

"Okay," I said, "but first I need to tell Rohan something."

That one confused him, and he glanced back at the bellhop who was talking to another guest. "Rohan? Why would you need to talk to him?"

Was that a touch of jealousy I detected? It was almost funny, because I was pretty sure Rohan was several years my junior, even younger than Jack. Besides, I was also pretty sure he was super into Sara, anyway. He had been up in the family suite almost as much as I had, always with Jack's sister, even though she kept trying to make him leave.

"I forgot something in my room," I said. "Could you just go get him, please? You can even order him to make me get in the car if you're so worried I won't."

Jack narrowed his eyes. "I don't give orders," he said, but he turned and walked up to the bellhop anyway and spoke to him long enough that I was pretty sure he had done exactly as I suggested.

"What did you forget, Miss Blake?" Rohan asked with a smile. "I'd be happy to run up and grab it for you."

I made sure Jack was far enough away that he wouldn't hear me, and then I said, "I need a huge favor, actually. I was hoping you could help me with something, but you can't tell Jack about it."

He was more intrigued than he should have been for being a Hawthorne employee. "Secret mission under Jack's nose? I like it."

I smiled. "It's not that exciting," I said. "I need you to grab the guitar from my room and make sure it gets to that funeral. Think you can do it?"

"Easy," he replied, but he pulled his eyebrows together. "Isn't that Jack's guitar? I didn't think he was supposed to play anything at the funeral."

"He isn't, but I want it there, just in case."

"Then it'll be there."

I gave him a quick hug then slid into the car before Jack came to tell me I was going to be late for coffee. I could see him standing in the lobby frowning at Rohan, and I hoped the bellhop wouldn't crack if Jack tried to pressure him into telling him what I'd said. I was pretty sure if Jack knew I was bringing the guitar, he would tell me I was being ridiculous and a funeral wasn't the place to whip out a song, but I meant what I told Rohan. I hoped I wouldn't need it, but I wanted it close, just in case.

As soon as the car pulled out onto the street, the nerves started to set in. I was finally meeting my father. After five years of pretending he wasn't real, I was going out and having coffee with the man who had helped make me exist.

"What am I doing?" I muttered out loud.

I opened up my messages and texted Seth back to tell him that, despite his belief, I had not been left for dead on a New York City street, but unfortunately that distraction didn't last very long. It was still a bit of a drive to the café, and looking out the window could only be so diverting until my thoughts got the better of me.

But then, as I watched Central Park go by, something clicked in my brain, and I looked back down at my phone. I had had so many texts from Seth that I hadn't even paid attention to another one that was sitting there beneath them, especially because it was so unexpected that I was sure I had imagined it until I opened it up.

Why was Jordan texting me?

I have some of your stuff, he said. *Where are you living now so I can send it to you?*

"Well that's awesome," I grumbled and quickly typed out my San Francisco address.

California? he sent back immediately.

Groaning, I shoved my phone deep into my purse and slumped into my seat. This was not the sort of thing I wanted to be thinking about right now, not when I needed to be at least somewhat nice to Gordon. *He* hadn't disappointed me yet, at least.

The car pulled up outside the café way too soon, and I took just a moment to take a few deep breaths and prepare myself for a conversation that was going to be awkward no matter what. I hoped Gordon wasn't expecting me to be anything like Lissa or Seth, who were both confident and cheerful and knew exactly who they were and what they were doing with their lives. Would he be disappointed to have a daughter who didn't even have a real job? The man had been crazy successful his entire life, which was how he managed to send me such a huge amount of money willy-nilly, and now he worked for Homeland Security. There was no way he wouldn't look down on me being a manager for a musician who couldn't even afford his own place to live.

Thanking the driver, I slipped out onto the sidewalk before I could outtalk Jack's voice in my head telling me that everything was going to be fine. I really wanted to believe that, but I also really wished he could have come with me to give me strength. When Jack was around, I felt like I could do anything. But he had more important things to worry about, and I knew his mother needed him more this morning than I did. That was probably the only reason Jack wasn't standing right next to me as I gazed through the café window at the man who was so easy to recognize, even though I'd never even seen a picture of him.

Gordon Hastings looked just like his son, only not as freakishly tall and with a whole lot less muscle, though he was still impressively fit. His blonde hair leaned closer to white these days, but I could easily imagine how he managed to leave a string of women stuck raising his children on their own. In his heyday, he must have been quite the hot commodity.

"Weird way to think about your dad," I muttered then pushed my way inside.

Gordon looked up immediately and brightened when he met my gaze. "Amelia!" he said and hopped up to his feet, his hand extended. Even without his son's giant stature, this was a powerful man, and I had to silently tell myself over and over that he wasn't here to do anything to me. He was here in a gesture of friendship. "You look just like your mother," he said, and then he winced.

Yeah, that doesn't make me feel weird at all.

"Um, would you like to sit?" he asked, gesturing to the table where he'd been waiting. "What would you like to drink? Or eat? It's on me. Order anything you'd like."

When I told Lissa I was finally meeting Gordon, she warned me he would be extra generous and would fight tooth and nail if I tried to argue. So I glanced down at the menu and said, "A regular coffee is fine. I'm not really hungry."

Gordon waved down a waitress and ordered for me, and then he turned his focus to me, though he was nice enough to glance away every few seconds so I didn't feel like I was under inspection. After a few moments of awkward silence filled only with the soft chatter and noises of the other people in the café, he coughed and clasped his hands together on the table. "You'd think I would be better at this after Lissa," he muttered with a little self-deprecating smile.

A wisp of pity slid into my chest as I watched him fight for something to say, and I managed to smile back at him. "I guess I didn't really think about how strange this must be for you."

His smile briefly grew, and I could see why my mom would have been interested in him. It was a smile much like Jack's, warm and friendly. "I suppose I should start by saying I'm sorry," he said. He paused as the waitress returned with my coffee, and then he grasped his own mug with both hands. "I despise what I was in my younger years, and I'm doing what I can to pay for the mistakes of that stupid man. But I don't want you to think I'm just…" He swallowed a sip of coffee then shrugged one shoulder. "I hope you understand that I don't expect anything from you. You don't owe me anything, and I… Well, I just want to know you. And help you. If you'll let me. And if not, we'll part ways and you can go on with your life as if I was never part of it."

Well how was I supposed to say no to something like that? Sipping my coffee, I took a moment to think things through. I already had a dad who loved me, even if he lived in Denmark now. And true, I had definitely needed Gordon's money over the last couple of months, but if I had to, I could find myself a real job so I could support myself if the music thing with Jack didn't work out.

Though now that I thought about it, I wasn't sure what was going to happen with Jack now. He'd said his dad had picked him to take over the family hotel business, and even if he didn't want to, I had a feeling Jack was loyal enough to his family that he would do it if he had to. Besides, he no longer had to run away, not now that his greatest fear—his dad's illness—was gone.

What did Jack's future look like, and was I going to be in it? Would he take his own advice and let go of the past? Move on?

Swallowing, I met Gordon's gaze again and smiled. "What do you want to know?"

We went for a walk around the city after we finished our coffee, and I was quickly realizing how very much I liked Gordon Hastings. He had a sense of simplicity about him, something he said he didn't find until just a few years earlier, when he realized how much of his life he had wasted without connecting with people. It had started, he said, when Seth was still part of the Special Forces and had gotten captured by that terrorist group he had helped take down.

"I realized I had almost lost my son," he said as we strolled through Central Park. "And it could have been my fault. I'd never been much of a parent, but eventually I realized that there was no success I could have in my career that equaled the pride I felt for my son, for the man he had become, even without my help. I knew it wasn't going to be easy, but I vowed to change my ways and become better. It took me a few years before I really felt like I had made any strides, and that was when I contacted Lissa."

"She's had nothing but good things to say about you," I told him.

He smiled a little, but there was humility in his expression that made me like him even more. "When she and Steve told me about you, I felt even less prepared than I had been with Lissa. At least with her, I'd known about her for several years at that point. I'm sorry I didn't reach out, Amelia."

I shook my head. "I'm not sure I would have listened to anything you had to say," I replied quietly. "I'm learning to let go of things and be open to new realities, but it's harder than I wish it was. Scarier."

"I'm glad you decided to be brave."

Smiling, I shrugged a little. "I wouldn't have been if not for my friend, Jack," I said. "He convinced me to…" And then I froze, the blood draining from my face. "What time is it?" I hadn't even been paying attention to how long we'd been talking, and it felt later than I wanted it to be.

Gordon glanced at his watch. "Almost ten thirty. Why?"

"Oh no."

"What's wrong?"

I pressed a hand to my forehead and started looking around, trying to figure out the fastest way out of the park and to a cab. "I'm late for a funeral," I said breathlessly and started to walk the way we'd come.

Gordon was right behind me. "Where is it? Let me give you a ride."

I shook my head. "Oh, no, that's okay, I'll just get a—"

"Amelia."

I glanced at him and could see his determination, so I swallowed my refusal and simply said, "Thank you. It's at St. Patrick's Cathedral, wherever that is."

Gordon was on the phone with his driver, it sounded like, telling him where to meet us, but when he hung up, he gently grabbed my arm and pulled me to a stop when we reached the street. "You're going to Lucas Hawthorne's funeral?" he asked with wide eyes.

Of course they knew each other. "Were you friends with him?" I said, though I was having a hard time just standing still and waiting for the car to show up.

Gordon shrugged a little. "It's hard not to know people when you reach my level of, uh…"

"Wealth?" I suggested and couldn't help but smile.

"Yeah," he replied as he turned a bit pink in the ears. "Ah, here's the car."

"The car" looked like a small fleet of vehicles, and I raised my eyebrow at him as he opened the door of one of them for me.

Grinning, he shrugged one shoulder then followed me inside. "One of the perks of working high in the government," he said then nodded to the driver. "Luckily you don't have to go far."

To my surprise, several of the cars turned on flashing lights, like police cars, and the entourage practically flew across several blocks, getting me to the funeral a whole lot faster than a cab could have done it through the traffic.

"Thank you," I told Gordon as we both stepped out of the car. I gave him a quick hug, but that was all the sentimentality I allowed myself as I hurried up the steps and to the massive front doors of the cathedral. "Amelia Blake," I told the man standing guard, hoping there was some kind of list, because there were more people milling about outside the venue and wanting to get in than I would have guessed.

The guard didn't even hesitate; he simply nodded and held one arm out toward the door, telling me to go inside.

"Thank you," I breathed and slipped inside the beautiful church, where a few thousand attendees sat with their gazes fixed on the podium at the front.

Jack was just getting to his feet and stepping up to the microphone, a set of cards in his hands and the same look he had every time he was about to play a show. He may have been clear on the other end of the cathedral, but I could practically feel his anxiety as he took a deep breath and began his eulogy.

"Lucas Hawthorne was…" He swallowed. "My father was a good man. Anyone could see that. He…" I could hear him exhale a shaky breath, but I didn't think it was nerves anymore. This was something different, and he looked out over the crowd as if his words were stuck.

I searched the crowd quickly, relieved when I found Rohan standing at the back of the church with the guitar at his side. He must have sensed the same thing I did, because he looked over and nodded, unclasping the case and pulling out the guitar as I hurried over to him.

"Thanks," I whispered.

Ignoring the thoughts that ran through my mind—*you can't just walk right through the middle of the church—he's not going to want to play—what will the family think?*—I strode right down between the aisles, my shoes clacking against the floor and echoing around me. I could feel the alarmed gazes of the crowd as well as hear their whispers, but I kept my focus on Jack, who was staring at me with glistening eyes and a look that seemed a mixture of confusion and gratitude.

And when I reached him, he put his hand on my arm and looked down at the guitar with his eyebrows pulled together. "Amelia," he whispered.

"You have to play," I replied. Out of the corner of my eye, I could see Jace on his feet and Marianne with a handkerchief pressed to her mouth as she cried, but I tried to ignore the family and just keep my gaze on Jack.

He shook his head and glanced at the guests. "I can't… This isn't the…"

Reaching up, I brushed a tear from his cheek, wishing I had the words I needed. "Your music is special," I said. "It speaks to people, and you put your whole heart into your songs. I think your dad would understand that."

Though he was still hesitant, his fingers grasped the neck of the guitar, and even just that little connection with the instrument seemed to weaken his argument. A moment later, he slipped the strap over his shoulder and returned to the microphone. "I don't have the words to say how much I'm going to miss my dad," he said and took a shuddering breath. "But I know there was no better man, and I hope someday I can live to be a fraction of who he was. Dad, this is for you."

As soon as he started to play, the whispers stopped. The crowd grew still. Jace sank back into his seat. There weren't any words to this particular song, but the melody seemed to speak volumes as it filled the cathedral, like Jack's fingers had found a way to transcend human language and enter straight into the soul, touching every emotion I had a name for and even those I didn't.

I started to cry, as did many people in the audience, but it didn't feel like a sad song. It felt like a tribute to who Lucas was, a celebration of his life and an expression of how much he had affected the people who knew him. Jack played exactly what everyone needed to hear.

A hand grabbed mine, and I turned in surprise to see Wes, tears in his eyes, smiling at me, and he gently tugged me toward his seat next to his mother. Marianne shifted closer to Sara so I could fit on the row with them, and then she grabbed my other hand and squeezed it, saying things no words ever could. And as I sat there with that family, Jack looked up and smiled at me so warmly that it felt like the sun itself had entered the cathedral.

A girl could get used to that.

When Jack finished his song, he let the last few notes linger in the air like he always did. But this time he lifted his gaze to the ceiling and seemed to be saying goodbye, and then he slipped the guitar over his head and returned to his seat. The priest got up and said something brief, but he seemed to realize there wasn't much he could say when Jack's song had already said it all, so he concluded the service with a prayer and invited the pallbearers to take the casket, the three Hawthorne boys among them.

As Marianne and Sara followed with the rest of the extended family, I lingered where I was. Coming to the memorial was one thing, but I didn't feel like I had a right to attend the graveside service. That seemed more intimate, and I wasn't a part of the family.

But as I followed the crowd out the doors and onto the steps outside, I couldn't stop thinking about how much I wanted to be a part of the family. I didn't know what it was, but even if Sara and Jace didn't like me, I still felt like I could be one of them. Not because I could live their lavish lifestyle or because I wanted to be famous—I could get that from my family back in California—but there was something about the Hawthornes that just felt like home.

I got halfway down the stairs when Jack appeared out of nowhere and pulled me into a hug so tight that I thought I might snap. And yet I never wanted it to end. He tucked his chin over my shoulder, and his heart beat against my chest, and I wanted to stay there forever. I'd never been held like this, and I knew nothing in the world could compare to it.

But eventually he let go, though he kept his hands on my shoulders, and despite his tears, his smile was happy. "Thank you," he said. "If you hadn't… Thank you."

I shrugged and brushed his tears from his cheeks. "You should go," I told him, though I wished he didn't have to. "Your family is waiting for you." They were standing at the car, all four of them watching us and making my face burn.

Jack glanced back, but only for a second. "Come with me," he said, grabbing my hand.

"Jack, I don't think they—"

"Amelia, it doesn't matter what anyone thinks," he interrupted. "I want you to come with me."

And while I very much wanted that same thing, I felt like I should stand my ground on this one. "I should get back to the hotel and make sure everything is ready for the luncheon," I said and did my very best to ignore his disappointment. "I'll see you when you get back, okay?" I felt a hand on my shoulder and glanced back to see Rohan, who gestured toward a cab, silently telling me that I should go with him when I was done here.

As soon as Rohan was gone, Jack took one step down, his eyes still fixed on me as my hand slipped out of his. "Do you promise?" he asked.

I smiled. "Absolutely."

"Okay." He walked backwards the rest of the way, which was pretty impressive considering the several stairs and the sheer number of people he might have run into. But he kept those beautiful blue eyes on me until he got into the family car and disappeared.

"I think I'm in trouble," I muttered to myself, and then I hurried forward to join Rohan in the cab.

CHAPTER SEVENTEEN

When we arrived at the hotel, Rohan handed the guitar off to one of the other staff members and asked her to bring it up to my room for me. "I've never heard him play like that," he said once she was gone, though it seemed the other staff were keen on listening in to our conversation as if hoping to hear about the funeral. "That was incredible."

Of course it was. *Jack* was incredible. And I needed to distract myself before I thought too hard about the look he'd given me on the steps.

"Hey," I replied, "can you show me where the luncheon is happening? I want to make sure everything is ready."

"Of course," he replied, and he waved his hand once to the others in front of us.

Almost immediately, they all jumped into action, and I watched in awe as they returned to their computers or headed outside to greet an incoming guest. "What exactly is your job, Rohan?" I asked as we took a hallway to the right of the desk, opposite the elevators.

I could see a massive pool at the end of the hall, but before I could get a good look at it, Rohan swiped a card at a door to our left which opened up to a huge event room that was already full of beautifully decorated tables set with some impressive dinnerware. Caterers were gathered in one corner, having what looked like a quick logistics meeting before the luncheon began, and there really wasn't much I needed to do, from what I could tell.

Rohan laughed a little and straightened a fork on the table just in front of us. "I'm not sure if my job really has a specific title," he said. "I started as a regular bellhop, and that's still mostly what I do. But I make sure every guest has whatever they might need, so I'm sorta in charge of the kitchen and the cleaning and the concierge."

"Isn't there, like, a hotel manager for that?" I asked.

He grinned. "Oh, he's busy enough without having to deal with the little stuff that I handle. But maybe someday that can be me."

"Do you like working in a hotel?" Maybe I could find one in San Francisco, because Rohan's job sounded pretty fun. I could work there when Jack didn't have any shows to play. Assuming he even came back with me.

"I like working in *this* hotel," he corrected then flagged down a passing caterer as they spread out to double check the tables. "Everything good, Beau?" he asked. "Do you need anything?"

The caterer shrugged. "I think we've got it covered. Thanks, Bakshi."

Rohan offered him a salute then turned back to me. "Looks like you've done your job well," he said with a smile. "Wanna sit down while you wait for the family to show up?"

I did sit, though I didn't like the uselessness I felt just sitting here. Surely there was something I could be doing, but everywhere I looked things were perfect.

"We've been talking about you," Rohan said as he settled in the chair next to me.

"Who?" I gasped, my stomach twisting and my face flushing.

He laughed. "The other staff and me. And calm down, it's not a bad thing. You're just surprising."

All I'd done was say hi whenever I passed someone. It wasn't like I had actually interacted with anyone much. "Yeah, okay," I muttered, though I still wasn't sure if I could believe it wasn't a bad thing. I actively tried not to surprise people, but apparently I wasn't as good at that as I thought.

Patting my arm, which probably meant I looked a little pathetic, Rohan got back to his feet and said, "You're just not like the people we usually interact with. I mean, you've seen this place. The guests here mostly just ignore us. You don't. And it's nice." He wandered back out into the hallway, leaving me alone with a smile and a warmth in my chest. As often as I tried to focus less on myself and more on the people around me, it was nice to be recognized for doing something good.

Half an hour had passed, during which I called Indie and told her about the funeral, when the Hawthorne family arrived at the hotel, something I realized when all the catering staff stopped chatting and disappeared through the double doors leading to the kitchen. I jumped to my feet just before Marianne came through the opposite doors. She took in the sight and seemed satisfied that everything was as it should be, and then she came straight for me.

"Amelia," she said and pulled me in for a hug. "I can't even begin to thank you for everything you've done for this family."

"It's nothing," I said, though my words came out breathy because Jack had just come through the doors and grinned at me. What was wrong with me? I was acting like I'd never seen the man smile before.

Marianne shook her head. Pulling me aside, she made sure we were far enough away from her children, who were all talking to each other, and then she said, "No, I really mean you've done more for this family than I could even say. Particularly for Jack." She glanced at her son when his laugh cut through the growing chatter as more people filtered into the room. "I haven't heard him laugh like that since he was a boy," she said, and tears filled her eyes.

"Wait, really?" I asked. Wes had said something similar, about how Jack was so different now from who he used to be, but I couldn't imagine Jack not laughing.

Her smile turned a little sad. "Jace was always ambitious, so we never worried about him. But Jack… He had all this unused potential, and we may have pushed him too hard. As he got older, he wasn't…happy," she said. "He rarely even smiled. And no therapist or medication could do what you've done for him."

I was about to argue that I hadn't done anything, but then Jack sent me another grin that made my legs nearly give out from under me. *Oh boy*.

"I'm just glad Lucas got to see the light in his son's eyes before he went," Marianne said, and she gave me another hug as if I had helped her husband live just long enough to see Jack one more time. "Thank you, Amelia. Thank you for bringing us a miracle."

I nearly burst into tears as she returned to her children and shared an embrace with each of them before moving on to speak to other relatives. I barely held myself together and hurried for the kitchen so I could double-check that everything was going smoothly, and I spent the bulk of the luncheon helping direct the catering staff, even though I badly wanted to go sit with Jack.

I wasn't ready for that yet.

Eventually, though, there was nothing for me to do behind the scenes, so I made my way back into the event hall and found Jack in the middle without even having to search for him. It was like my eyes knew exactly where to look, and I just watched him as he chatted with uncles and shook hands with friends and endured kisses from old ladies who were probably grandmothers or great aunts. If he really had spent the bulk of his childhood depressed and quiet, I could see why this version of him would stun everyone who knew him.

This Jack radiated light. He spread his happiness with everyone he came in contact with, and the whole room seemed to glow as he smiled and laughed.

And I couldn't help but think about the warmth he brought into my life every time he looked over at me. Maybe it was just that same light he shared with everyone, but I wasn't so sure. If the rest of this room felt what I was feeling, that was going to cause some problems.

Especially because I didn't know what it was I was feeling. It was completely foreign to me, and that was terrifying. How could I understand it when I couldn't even put a word to it? Of all the times for me to be wordless...

"Hey," Jack said, suddenly appearing in front of me. I hadn't even noticed him move from the other side of the room. "Can we go somewhere for a bit, just you and me?"

I wanted nothing more. Nodding, I laced my fingers with his and followed him up to the roof.

We stood at the roof's edge looking out over the city for a long time in silence, which I didn't mind, especially because Jack still held fast to my hand even though he was focused on the cars and people below us. I was quickly becoming okay with silence, especially if I was sharing it with Jack.

"I've always loved this city," he said after a while. "There's an energy about it, you know? And there's nothing quite like it."

"I know exactly what you mean," I replied. I just wished I knew what this burning sensation in my chest meant.

Jack turned to me, and whatever he saw made him frown a little, which I didn't like. "I need to tell you something important," he said and let go of my hand.

I grabbed the cool metal rail that protected us from falling over the edge. "Oh?" I said, though it was more of a squeak.

Jack nodded. "Dad always pushed me to be better." He swallowed, as if that had been difficult to say, but then he jumped into so many words at once that I was positive he'd been wanting to say them for a long time: "He didn't do it with any of the others. Just me. And it didn't seem like anything I did was good enough, no matter how hard I tried to please him. But I knew he loved me. I never even questioned that part. So when he got sick and there was nothing I could do about it, I felt like I'd failed him worse than ever. Like it was somehow my fault, and I knew that the person I was wasn't the kind of person who could make him proud."

He took a deep breath and looked out over the city again. "That was why I left. I had to figure out the person he wanted me to be, and I thought maybe I would find it out there somewhere. My music was the only thing I had control over at that point, and it felt like if I could just find the right song, if I could find that music in my heart that was me, I could make things right. But it wasn't working. I got farther and farther from home, and no matter how good I got on the guitar, nothing sounded right. I was just falling farther behind and wasting my time, and I'd never been so miserable in my life. How could I possibly be happy when everything was wrong?"

He looked at me again, his icy blue gaze more intense than I'd ever seen it. "Then I met this girl on the side of the road who looked like she had lost everything."

My stomach twisted inside me, and I gripped the rail a little tighter.

Jack grinned. "She was ridiculous," he said and put his hands in his pockets. "Covered in mud and sitting there in the pouring rain along with all her stuff, and she had the nerve to smile up at me and say she was fine."

I had said that. That day felt like forever ago, and I could barely remember the emotions that had pushed me down into that mud. "Rock bottom," I muttered and couldn't help but smile a little. "And now I have pretty much everything I could ever want." *Almost.*

To my surprise, Jack's smile faded, and he reached out for my hand, pulling it off the rail so he could hold it again. "I stood there in the middle of a rainstorm that felt like the universe telling me I should just give up, and I thought to myself that if she could still stay positive when everything had gone wrong in her life, why couldn't I? Happiness is a choice, and I made a promise to myself that I would always be happy. No matter what. I knew it was possible because it was sitting right there in front of me. I know it's different for everyone, but for me, the secret to happiness is choosing to smile even when I know I can't. It's choosing to accept that things go wrong, and people make bad choices, and family members get sick. It's knowing that every day can be perfect even when it looks like it never will be. That soaked and muddy girl changed my life without even knowing it, and the longer I knew her, the easier she made it to remember why I wanted to change. She made me forget I had ever been anything but happy."

Leaning forward, he touched his forehead to mine and closed his eyes. "You saved me, Amelia. And you don't even know it."

"I didn't do anything," I muttered, knowing there was little point in arguing. But I really believed that. I'd been hanging on by a thread when he found me, and the only reason I even made it to California was because of him. "Jack, if anyone is a savior, it's you."

He laughed a little. "Agree to disagree. You are the most positive person I've ever met."

Okay, now he was just being ridiculous. "I'm serious, Jack."

"So am I." And as he pulled away, the twinkle in his eyes reaffirmed his belief.

"I am so far from positive," I argued. "I can't go a day without waiting for tragedy to strike."

"That's called being human, Amelia. But you put on a smile anyway."

Was he not going to let this drop? "Jack."

"Is there something I can do to prove it to you?"

I doubted that, since the most optimistic person in the world was standing right in front of me. But I could play along, because I was in a pretty good mood up here on the roof. "You mean like some sort of quest?"

Grinning, he nodded a little then reached into his pocket and pulled out the envelope his father had given him, the one dictating what he had to do to get his inheritance and make his father proud. "Good thing I've got a handy quest right here."

I raised an eyebrow, unsure how that envelope would help his case, but I was glad to have something else to think about. "That's your quest, Jack. Not mine." And I sighed as my words sank in. "It's too bad I didn't get to meet your dad. Maybe he would have known how to fix me."

"You don't need fixing," Jack replied and slid his thumb beneath the flap to break the seal. "You just need to believe. And if I know Dad…" Pulling a single sheet of paper from the envelope, he unfolded it then held it out so we could read it together.

The paper only said three words: *Follow your heart.*

We looked at each other, and Jack's expression shifted between confusion and thoughtfulness.

"What does it mean?" I asked him.

A tiny smile played at the corner of his lips, and he looked back down at the paper as if he was seeing something more there than I had. "It means we have to go back to San Francisco."

The morning was bittersweet. With all of my things packed and my hotel room tidied and clean, I was glad to no longer be an imposition to the Hawthorne family. It would be nice to go back home to my own apartment and be able to see my own family again. Seth was growing increasingly worried that I had been coerced into staying as long as I had, even though it had only been a few days, and I was hoping I could talk to him and try to better our fragile relationship. After seeing this week how much a family needed each other, I didn't want to ruin mine just because I didn't fit in.

But it was going to be hard to leave the Hawthornes behind. Marianne was such a sweet soul, and I would cherish her kindness for the rest of my life. And the many hotel staff members I had gotten to interact with had made my experience so much easier than it could have been. For such a swanky hotel, Hawthorne Tower was a comfortable and familiar place now, and I would miss it.

"You ready?" Jack asked as I came out of the bedroom. He took my suitcase from me and added his few clothes to it, and though I wondered why he wouldn't take more back with him now that he was no longer a transient, I decided not to ask. Apparently I didn't have to: "I've gotten used to the minimalist life," he said with a grin and zipped the suitcase closed.

"I hope you don't mind," he added as we stepped out into the hallway, "but I thought it would be a good idea to go upstairs and say goodbye to the family before we go."

"Of course I don't mind," I replied without hesitation.

As we stepped out of the elevator into the family's home, we came across Sara, who was deep in a heated argument with Rohan. She was saying a whole lot of words that got lost in her fury, but I guessed she was mad about something being ruined when Rohan brought it upstairs for her. Probably something in one of the several shopping bags that sat at her feet.

Rohan, I noticed with amusement, was perfectly calm and professional, and he was taking the verbal beating with impressive valor.

Only when Jack started to laugh did his sister notice us standing there, and she shut her mouth and grew silent and red-faced, apparently unwilling to keep yelling now that she had an audience. "Relax," Jack said to her and pulled her into a hug she only sort of fought against. "There will always be money to buy a new one."

"You don't know that," she mumbled, and then she hurried up the stairs and disappeared.

Rohan watched her with a smile then turned to Jack. "You're leaving already?" he asked, clearly disappointed when he saw my suitcase in his hand.

Jack embraced him too. "It's what I have to do. Take care of my sister for me, okay?"

He nodded. "Unless she kills me," he muttered and slipped into the elevator after giving me a warm smile.

Taking my hand, Jack led me upstairs to the next level, where we found Jace leaning one elbow on the kitchen island and reading some complicated-looking spreadsheet while he munched on a plate of veggies. He looked more relaxed than I'd ever seen him, and the similarities were more pronounced between him and his twin than they'd been before.

"You're going back to California?" Jace asked, though it didn't sound much like a question. "Will you at least get yourself a phone so I don't have to search for you every time I want to talk to you?"

Jack laughed, and the two of them did a fancy little handshake that made me grin. They were finally acting like brothers. "Only if you pay for it, Mr. CEO," he said. "At the moment, I'm a bit short on cash."

"You and me both," Jace grumbled.

His eyes bright, Jack leaned a little closer to his brother. "What was in your terms of inheritance?" he asked.

Jace rolled his eyes. "You know we're not allowed to talk about it. Now go find Mom before she starts to think you've already left without saying goodbye."

"I'll be right back," Jack told me with a smile, and then he bounded up the stairs.

I was tempted to go back down to the main level and wait, since Jace and I weren't exactly best friends, but then he surprised me.

"I'm sorry I wasn't very friendly when we first met," he said, though his eyes had moved back to his computer. "I think… I guess I should thank you. I can't remember the last time I saw Jack like that, and it's been nice to have my brother back."

"Everyone keeps telling me how different he is," I replied. "But he's always been like this for me."

"I think that says a lot right there," he said, shutting his laptop and tucking it under one arm. I idly wondered if he ever wore anything but a suit. Even though he looked so much like Jack, I couldn't picture him in anything but the best. "It's been nice getting to know you, Amelia Blake," he said. "Look after him, okay?"

Before I could reply, Marianne and Wes appeared on the staircase, Jack behind them, and I was engulfed in a hug by Jack's mom.

"You're welcome to visit anytime," she told me, and I knew she meant it, which made this goodbye so much harder.

Wes hugged me too, and though that was surprising enough, he said, "I'm glad Jack met you," and turned a bright red as he retreated to his mother's side.

So am I, I thought to myself. Tears welled up in my eyes as I thought about the distance we were about to put between ourselves and them, and I grabbed Jack's hand for comfort. At least he was coming with me so I wouldn't have to feel like I was leaving them *all* behind.

The journey to the airport passed in a haze of sadness and relief, and I was grateful Jack took charge so I didn't have to concentrate on anything until I was securely in my economy seat, which oddly felt so much more comfortable than the first class trip had. Maybe that was because Jack was right next to me, close enough that our shoulders brushed against each other. Takeoff was smooth, and the airplane settled into a soft roar of engines as I silently said goodbye to a city that seemed to beg me to come back. I made a vow as we got too far for me to see it anymore that I wouldn't go long before I went back.

Jack pulled out his notebook an hour into the flight and hunched over in his seat as he wrote line after line, and I wondered what this new song was about. I'd never really paid attention to his lyrics because the music was so enthralling, and suddenly I wished I had. What sort of things did Jack say that I had missed completely?

I grabbed my book from my purse and tried to read as he wrote, but just like the last time, I couldn't really focus. What was going to happen when we got back? I knew we couldn't go back to the way things had been before this New York adventure, since everything was so different now. *We* were different. And that strange warmth in my chest still hadn't gone away, and until I figured out what it meant, I wasn't sure I would know how to settle into a new normal.

"Have you ever fallen in love, Amelia?" Jack asked suddenly.

I dropped my book and turned to him. "What?" When he didn't say anything, I shrugged. "I've been engaged twice and married once," I reminded him.

"That isn't what I asked."

How was I supposed to respond to something like that? But since this was Jack, and I knew he would keep pushing until I gave him a real answer, I gave it some good thought for a moment. And when I couldn't focus long enough for that to be any help, I decided to think out loud.

"I always felt lucky Steve chose me," I said. "He made life exciting, and he made me feel like I was interesting and worth knowing, and I was just glad I got to share in his life. But did I love him?" *Well this is concerning.* "I don't think I did."

Jack nodded as if he wasn't surprised by my response. "And Jordan?"

"Jordan..." I frowned. "I knew life with Jordan would be comfortable. Stable. He was exactly the sort of husband a woman should want. But..."

"But you didn't love him," Jack guessed.

"I'm not so sure he loved *me*," I replied. "I don't think he's even thought about me since the divorce." *Except to ask me where to send my stuff.* "So I don't think I've ever been in love," I finished with a frown. Thirty years old and never fallen in love? *How sad.* "Have you?" I added, the blood rushing from my head a little.

Jack shrugged, returning to his little notebook. "I'm still figuring out what love means," he said and started to write again.

I wasn't sure why my stomach dropped—maybe there was some turbulence I didn't notice—but I spent the rest of the flight feeling slightly queasy, and I was more than happy when we finally landed in San Francisco and caught a cab to my apartment.

It may have only been seven at night, but I was exhausted when we stepped inside my little apartment. I smiled at the fancy table I'd barely been able to use yet, and I pretty much dropped the suitcase by the couch. I was ready to go straight to bed as soon as I got some food in me.

"I'm buying you some real furniture," Jack muttered, looking around the apartment just like I was. "Especially a TV."

"I thought you said you were broke. Do you expect you'll get your inheritance sooner rather than later?"

"I hope so," he replied. "I'm gonna take a shower, and maybe you can find me a show to play so we don't get bored in the next few days."

I grinned. "That's a good idea, and I'm pretty sure I'm going to have hundreds of requests after you disappeared without explanation. That little trip of ours was probably good for business."

I waited until he was in the shower, and then I pulled up my email, though I got a little anxious when I realized I was right about the number of messages I'd received over the last week. I just had to find one for now, and I could deal with the rest later.

Thankfully, I found a few requests for just a couple of days away, and I booked an easy one for tomorrow. When I called the party's host for the second, she eagerly told me she absolutely still wanted Jack to play. "My second choice was going to be terrible," she said right before she hung up, and though I was worried I had just cost some other poor musician a gig, I was too tired to try to fix my mistake.

Yawning, I figured I would at least open up my suitcase and maybe toss things into my laundry bag, but halfway there the doorbell rang. "I'm not home," I mumbled, but I couldn't justify ignoring it. It was probably one of my siblings coming to make sure I got home safely, so I ran my fingers through my hair and trudged to open the door.

My heart nearly stopped when I saw who was on the other side.

"Amelia," Jordan said, and then he pulled me into a hug I was too confused to return.

CHAPTER EIGHTEEN

When Jordan released me, I stared at him and tried to figure out if I'd fallen asleep on the couch and this was some weird dream. *Nightmare, more like.* But I could smell his cologne, and the bouquet of roses he handed to me felt incredibly real, and pinching myself didn't make him go away.

"What are you doing here?" I asked, and my voice broke. I was too overwhelmed by the last few days to deal with this right now.

"Can I come in?" he asked then stepped inside before I could say no. His dark eyes took in my sparse apartment quickly then landed on my suitcase sitting by the couch. "Did you just move in? I thought you were staying with your parents."

What was he doing here? "They moved to Denmark. Jordan, what—"

"I made a mistake, Ames," he said, pulling the flowers out of my hold and tossing them onto the counter so he could grab my hand. "I have been missing you like crazy, and I keep trying to figure out why I let you go and I just keep coming up blank. You are the sweetest, kindest person I've ever known, and my life has been empty without the light you used to bring to it."

I stared at him. "Are you serious?"

And then, to my horror, Jack appeared in the bedroom doorway in nothing but a towel and stopped dead, his eyes locked on Jordan's with an expression that said he knew exactly who was standing in my living room holding my hand. "Hi," he said, though the word came out a little strangled. "Uh, I'm Jackson Thorn."

I barely had time to wonder why he would use his pseudonym before Jordan let go of me so he could shake Jack's hand in a much tighter grip than he needed to use, which I only knew because Jack winced a bit. "Jordan Blake," he replied.

I thought I might throw up. Or pass out. One of the two. Maybe both.

"If, uh, if you'll excuse me," Jack said, and he unzipped the suitcase and grabbed some of his clothes before disappearing back into the bedroom and closing the bathroom door behind him.

Jordan was smart enough to recognize the suitcase he'd bought me, and his expression hardened. "We've only been separated for a couple of months, Amelia," he growled.

"Divorced," I squeaked. That distinction was important.

"So what, you're living with some guy now?" His eyes locked on Jack's guitar leaning against the couch, and that only seemed to make him angrier. "Can't he afford his own apartment, or is he one of those starving artist types who preys on lonely women?"

"Hey," I said, but my voice was so much weaker than I wanted it to be. I wanted to tell him that Jack was worth a hundred million dollars and was a better man than pretty much anyone I knew, but it wasn't going to work if I couldn't speak with a little confidence.

I wasn't sure if it was a good thing or a bad thing that Jack reappeared right then, fully dressed this time, and answered the question for me. "Actually," he said lightly, "I'd be living on the street if not for Amelia offering up her couch. I'm hoping she can get me famous someday, because she's a seriously good manager. I'm sure you knew that already, though." He plopped himself onto the couch and put his hands behind his head, looking completely at ease.

Jordan's anger dissipated ever so slightly, but I could see he wasn't going to drop the issue of Jack staying with me. Before he started throwing out more insults, I took him by the hand and dragged him out the front door and into the hallway.

"Look," I told him gently, "I just got back from a really exhausting trip, and I'm too tired to talk about this right now, okay?" *Please let it be okay.* "Can we talk tomorrow? We'll go get breakfast."

He didn't want to leave. I knew he didn't. But he looked at me for a long while and softened, and then he nodded. "Okay," he said and leaned down to kiss the top of my head like he used to. "Breakfast. I'll come pick you up at eight."

I wished he would just meet me somewhere, but he was already heading down the hall.

When I got back inside, Jack was stretched out on the couch and pretending to be asleep. I was tempted to ask him why he wouldn't tell Jordan who he really was, since I was pretty sure Jordan would know exactly who the Hawthornes were, but I was also pretty sure Jack didn't want to talk for a reason. So I kept my questions to myself and went into my bedroom, knowing I was not going to sleep well tonight.

I woke to the sound of Jack's guitar, though for a little bit I wasn't sure if it was real or had just been part of my dream. I'd been dreaming that I was next to a lobster tank at the grocery store, trying to choose which one I wanted to take home, and Jack and Jordan the lobsters were fighting in the middle of them. Then suddenly they were people, and Jordan was throwing wadded up paper at Jack while he angrily strummed his guitar, which shot beams of light at Jordan and made him catch fire.

The guitar that woke me up, though, was much softer, and I slowly sat up so I could hear it better. It was a melody I hadn't heard before, so it must have been new, and it was the most beautiful thing I'd ever heard, in a dark, melancholy sort of way. Creeping to the door, I ever so slightly pulled it open and caught some mumbled words, though I couldn't hear what they were. It was just after seven, but based on how easily Jack played the song, I had to wonder if he'd been awake for a long time.

After I got dressed—I didn't put a whole lot of energy into my appearance, despite how long I took—I made a little more noise as I opened my door this time, and Jack stopped playing immediately.

"Good morning," he said and smiled at me. I almost believed it, but it didn't look quite right. "How'd you sleep? Sorry I passed out so quickly last night, but it's been a long couple of days."

"Yeah," I agreed. I wanted to sit next to him on the couch, but I sat at the kitchen table instead.

"When did Jordan leave?"

I frowned. He sounded so cheery, but he certainly didn't look all that happy. "Pretty much right after he got here," I said. "I'm meeting him for breakfast this morning."

Jack plucked a few notes on his guitar, but they didn't sound like they went together. "That's really good, Blake."

My stomach twisted itself into a knot. Why did he call me that? "Is it?"

"Why wouldn't it be?"

I didn't have an answer for that, and thankfully I only had to sit in the awkward silence that followed his question for a couple of minutes before Jordan knocked on the door. "Um." What could I say to make this less weird? "I found you a couple of gigs this week. There's one tonight, if that's okay."

"Cool," he replied without looking at me. "Just let me know when and where."

Jordan knocked again.

"I'll be back in a little bit," I said after giving him the details for that night's show.

Jack didn't say anything.

When I opened the door, Jordan pulled me into a hug that was so much…more…than the one he'd given me last night. Like he was trying to say something with it, though I had no idea what that might be. He followed it with a kiss to my cheek, and he had another bouquet for me, this time with the little billowy flowers that they turned into all sorts of colors that weren't real. What were they called?

"These reminded me of you," he said, holding out the flowers. "Are you ready to go? I'm starving."

I almost looked back at Jack, but I had a feeling he was ignoring me anyway, though I couldn't for the life of me understand why. "Yeah," I said and took the arm he offered me.

Jordan took me to a little café that made me squirm, but I didn't say anything about it. Steve had always talked about this place any time we drove past it, and he had always wanted to eat here but never had because he was so busy doing adventurey things.

"Isn't this place great?" Jordan asked as we settled at a table in the corner, away from everyone else. This was exactly the sort of place Steve and I would have come all the time if we'd gotten married.

It's something, I thought bitterly. "Great," I agreed.

"You still look tired. That musician didn't keep you up with his guitar playing, did he?"

Technically, no. Theoretically? Yes. "Nope."

"So where did you go on your trip?" he asked, but then he turned to the waitress who approached us and said, "Hi, I'll have the siesta omelet, and she'll get the avocado scramble." Then back to me: "What made it so exhausting?"

I could really go for some pancakes. "A lot of things. Jordan, why are you here? Really?"

He frowned as if completely thrown by my question. "I told you. I've been going crazy without you." Reaching over the table and holding his hand palm up, he waited until I placed mine on top of it then curled our fingers together the way he always did when we went out for dinner. I had gotten used to eating with my left hand because he always claimed my right. "Amelia, my life has been all sorts of upside down since you left."

"Since you divorced me," I mumbled.

"Since I made the biggest mistake of my life. I still love you, Amelia."

I looked up, trying to understand why that sounded different from what I was used to. I'd meant what I told Jack when I said Jordan hadn't loved me, and though he had said it all the time, as a good husband should, it had never felt like it did this time.

"You mean that," I whispered, shocked to feel something spark inside of me. "You love me."

"I love you so much that I flew across the country so I could tell you," he agreed, and he suddenly looked miserable. "I wake up every morning and still find myself asking you how you slept. I grab two coffee cups from the cupboard. When I get back from taking Roxy on our runs, she still goes upstairs thinking she'll find you in the bathroom getting ready, and it kills me every time she finds it empty. The dog misses you almost as much as I do."

"The dog misses me," I repeated. This was too much for me to process, and when the waitress set my scramble in front of me, I felt too sick to eat it. "What are you saying, Jordan?"

"I'm saying I want you to come back with me. I'm saying I miss laughing together when Mrs. Gawa does something ridiculous next door or that guy runs past the house wearing those really awful short shorts. I'm saying I want to give this another chance because you and I are perfect together. Everyone knows that."

Did everyone know that? I wasn't so sure.

"Look," he said, and he reached for my other hand so he held them both. "I know it's not like we can just jump right back in. It's not going to be easy, and I get that. I'm willing to fight for us."

"I don't…" I swallowed, and it felt like my tongue was stuck to the roof of my mouth. "What would I do in Chicago?" I highly doubted my old company was in any position to hire me back after just a few months.

"I can get you a job in the marketing department of my firm."

"I thought you didn't want to work together," I muttered, looking down at my plate and trying to force my mind to work properly. "You said it wasn't professional."

"That was before I realized how much I hate not being around you," he replied. "You'd have to let someone else help that musician, Jim, get his life together, though."

I looked up, and suddenly it felt like I could think again. I couldn't just abandon Jack. It wasn't just the music thing, either. After everything we had gone through in New York, and after everything he had told me up on that roof, I was pretty sure he needed me to stay positive. No matter how determined he was to keep his smile, he still needed that reminder when things got especially hard.

I didn't know what our relationship was, but it was something, and I couldn't end it so suddenly just because Jordan had changed a little.

I believed everything Jordan was saying, I really did, and I missed the routine I had had with him. But I couldn't just drop my whole life. I had my family to think about now, and I knew they would miss me if I left California so soon. My life was finally starting to look okay again, and for once the future was looking bright. Or it had been, before Jack started acting weird. Did he not want me to stay? Was he going to go on his little quest for his dad on his own? What about proving to me that I could be positive, like him?

There were too many questions, and I didn't have enough answers on my own. "Can…" I took a deep breath. "Can I have a few days to think about it?"

"Of course," Jordan replied. "You can take all the time you need."

And though he said that, I was pretty sure he wouldn't wait forever. Jordan had always been a man who knew what he wanted, and he wasn't afraid to fight for it.

But would Jack fight back? Did I even *want* him to fight?

Initially, Jordan brought me back to my apartment, but when Jack said he needed time to practice for the show that night, I figured it was best if I left him alone. So I went straight back downstairs and hopped in my car, deciding I needed some advice from someone I trusted if I was ever going to make a good decision.

But when I knocked on Lissa's door, it was Steve who answered it. "Oh," I said and winced because going to the house where he would most likely be had been a bad idea. I should have gone to talk to Indie.

Steve rolled his eyes and rested one arm on the doorframe next to him. "That's a terrible way to greet someone, Amelia."

"Is Lissa around? I was hoping I could talk to her."

"'Fraid not."

"Oh. I'll come back later."

"Amelia," he growled.

I paused halfway down the steps. "What?"

"What's wrong?"

Yeah, coming here had been a terrible idea. "Nothing's wrong," I said and did my very best to sound carefree, like Jack. Only, thinking about Jack wasn't helping anything.

Steve let out an over-dramatic sigh then opened the door wide. "Get inside, Ames. We were together for three years, so I think I can tell when something's bothering you."

And to my utter horror, the moment I heard those words, I burst into tears and fell into his arms. He hadn't been expecting that any more than I had and nearly tumbled backward, but he held me anyway, wrapping his arms around me as we stood there on the doorstep.

Eventually he got me inside and guided me to the couch—the irony of that coming from a blind man stopped my tears, thankfully—and then he sat next to me and did his best to keep his gaze focused on me. "So what's wrong?" he said again, and this time I was ready to answer.

"Jordan is back," I said.

"Your husband?"

"Ex."

"That's what I meant. He's here in S.F.?"

I nodded then remembered he probably couldn't see that. "Yeah. He showed up last night."

"And this is making you cry because…?"

I wasn't sure how to answer that, and Steve seemed to understand my silence.

"He wants you back doesn't he?" he asked quietly. And when I still didn't say anything, he muttered, "Can't say that I blame him."

"Steve," I complained. "That's not helping."

Laughing a little, he shook his head. "I know it's not, and before you get any crazy ideas, I am still madly in love with my wife. But that doesn't mean I don't remember who you are and what you're like. Can I tell you something that might get me punched in the face?"

I couldn't even form a response to that one aside from, "Huh?"

"You have a problem, Amelia."

I swallowed, stunned into silence for a long time, silence that Steve didn't feel the need to fill. What did he expect me to get out of that? "A problem," I repeated. "Tell me again why I'm sitting here talking to you?"

"Because you have a problem, exactly as I said."

"And what is my problem, Steve?"

"You care about making other people happy."

"I think Seth is right," I muttered, frowning at him. "You're an idiot."

He laughed and ran his hands through his thick curls. I had always liked his hair, but as I looked at it now, I decided I loved Jack's more. It was wilder and had more personality to it than Steve's hair.

"Like I said, I'm fully expecting to get punched for this, but that doesn't mean it isn't true. You care *too much* about making sure everyone is happy, and you don't focus on yourself enough."

When was the last time you did something for yourself? Jack had asked me on the Ferris wheel at Coney Island. That felt like ages ago, even though it had only been a few days.

"You're a people pleaser, Amelia," Steve continued, "and that isn't always a good thing. Not when it gets in the way of your own happiness."

I let that sink in a bit, though it didn't make a whole lot of sense. "I don't know. You might be taking things a little out of proportion."

Steve raised an eyebrow at me. "Do you actually like skiing?" he asked. "Like, if you're being totally honest with yourself, and you had the chance to either go skiing or stay at home and clean the kitchen, what would you choose?"

I frowned.

"That's what I thought," Steve said, though I was pretty sure he couldn't see my expression. "And yet you went skiing with me every weekend that year we started dating. And do you remember when we went to Isla Guadalupe and I asked if you wanted to do the shark dive with me?"

I shuddered at that memory. "I had nightmares for weeks."

"So why did you go?"

My voice seemed to shrink even smaller as I said, "Because you wanted me to."

"Do you see what I mean?"

I did see, but that didn't mean I knew what to do about it. "And what does this have to do with Jordan?" I asked.

"I can't say I know the guy, but my bet is he's not very much like me. Am I wrong?"

"No," I sighed. "Are you trying to say I married Jordan because he was the opposite of you?" It sort of made sense, and I was pretty sure

I had been attracted to him in the first place because he was so different from Steve that I figured things wouldn't turn out the same way.

Steve shrugged, and his expression was one of pity. "I'm trying to say you've based your whole life on other people, and now that you actually have a choice, you have no idea what to do."

"Do I go back with Jordan or do I not," I said and sighed again.

"Those aren't your only options," Steve replied. "You're forgetting one very crucial person in this equation."

"What, you?" I laughed a little. "I thought you were madly in love."

"I am," he growled, sounding a lot more annoyed than I expected him to be. "I'm talking about Jack."

"Jack?"

"Yeah, Jack. You know, the guy who's been sleeping on your couch for the last month."

"How did you know—"

"Come on, Ames!" Steve leapt to his feet, making me jump. "This shouldn't be that hard to figure out! I'm almost completely blind, and even I could see the way you looked at the guy. I'm pretty sure the only time I've ever seen you stand up for something was when it involved him. The question isn't if you should go back to Jordan, which honestly sounds like a terrible idea, if you want my opinion. The question is more simple than that."

I stared up at him, trying to figure out how I ever thought I could have married him when clearly we weren't compatible at all. He was too abrasive, too strong-willed, and I didn't think he had ever been able to express his emotions very well. Steve was absolutely not the man for me, and for the first time, I felt like we could be friends. He was perfect for Lissa, which meant he was perfect as my brother-in-law. But realizing this didn't make his words any clearer.

"What's the simple question?" I asked and got to my feet so he wasn't towering over me.

He smiled, clearly pleased by my choice to stand. "What do you want?" he asked. "And I don't mean who do you want to be with. I mean what do *you* want?"

"I don't know."

Without a change in his expression, Steve nodded and said, "Then you might want to figure that out."

The question may have been simple, but I was worried I wouldn't have an answer.

Lissa came home a moment later, and she offered to take me out to lunch so we could chat about Gordon. And while I enjoyed my time with my sister, I couldn't stop thinking about what Steve said. Maybe it wasn't about who I wanted to be with, but it didn't feel right not including Jordan or Jack in my thoughts about what I wanted. Did I want to return to that stability and security I'd had with Jordan? Return to the man who loved me? Or did I want to risk everything and stay in my life with Jack when everything was so uncertain but absolutely comfortable, where I had what felt like a second family on the other side of the country?

Did I want to move on from the past and let go?

CHAPTER NINETEEN

I made it to the karaoke bar where Jack was playing just in time to hear his greeting to the audience as he wished happy birthday to the host. Though he caught my eye for a moment, he didn't offer up his usual smile. I didn't like that, and I settled on a stool at the bar to watch him play while my thoughts continued to spin around in my head and make me dizzy.

Why was it so hard to know what I wanted? Shouldn't everyone have had the answer to that question at all times? I used to think I knew what I wanted, so it was easy to make choices. I wanted a creative job that paid well enough for me to support myself if I had to, so I chose marketing. I wanted some excitement in my life, so I dated Steve. I wanted the dream life with the house and the dog and the successful husband, so I married Jordan.

When I met Jack, that had been the first time I didn't have a real goal for myself outside of meeting my family, and that had turned into something crazy. I had ended up clear on the other side of the country in the middle of a family crisis, and I had loved it.

I really didn't think I wanted chaos, but neither could I really say Jack *was* chaos. Now that everything was settled with his dad, he wasn't running. He wasn't hiding from his past. He had moved on.

But what did that mean for us?

"I'm scared to take that step," Jack sang suddenly, and I blinked to shake myself out of my thoughts. I'd never heard that line before, even if I'd heard this particular song many times. Had it always been there?

"This is what happens when you don't pay attention to the lyrics," I reminded myself and frowned as he kept singing. I didn't remember any of these lines. Had I really managed to be so completely riveted on the music that the words just went in one ear and out the other?

The next song was the same thing, and the next, and little lines kept popping out at me as I sat there dumbstruck on my stool.

Watching my dreams fly
into the moonless sky…

Everything was dark until I met the sun…

Give me one more smile to carry
with me into the deep unknown…

Every lyric hit me with a strange sense of loss, as if I could have had so much more in my life if I had only been paying attention before.

Hanging on an unspoken prayer…

Can you look me in the eye
and say I'm enough…

The simple moments haunt me most
I wonder how I could have lived
before I understood life…

Jack seemed to be singing right to me, even though he hadn't looked up from his guitar since he started playing.

Every choice is a path to something more.
If I made you wings, would you fly to me
or never come home?

I barely breathed as each and every word of his songs sank deep into my chest, and even when he finished playing and the party guests burst into tumultuous applause, I couldn't bring myself to move. I just sat there and watched Jack interact with his fans, smiling and chatting and looking almost normal.

He didn't play that new song he'd been writing, and I wished he would. On top of hearing that incredible music, I wanted to know what it could say. It felt important.

A woman pushed her way up to Jack, and at the sight of her I found myself moving through the crowd after her. She looked too determined to talk to him, and even if I didn't know what I wanted, I definitely knew what I *didn't* want. I didn't want anyone to look at Jack the way I did, and I didn't want him to light up when he looked at anyone but me.

"Jackson Thorn," the woman said and shook his hand with gusto. "I've been looking all over for you the last several days."

"Seems to be a theme," Jack said with his smile twisting crooked. "Well now you've found me."

"My name is Jenna Russo, and I work for West Stone Records here in San Francisco."

I stopped dead in my tracks.

Jack's eyes went wide, and he gently rested his guitar on the stage behind him. "I've heard of it," he said slowly.

Jenna got right to business: "I've heard your music, Mr. Thorn, and we want to add you to our collection."

Wait.

"Full studio album, worldwide distribution, the whole package. I can make you a wealthy man, Jackson Thorn."

Jack folded his arms and still looked a bit confused, but he had to know exactly what she was saying to him. "You want to sign me?" he said after an agonizing length of time.

Jenna gave him a wide—and completely fake—smile. "I want to give you a chance to do better than playing birthday parties and coffee shops. How does that sound?"

"That sounds too good to be true." Jack grinned.

My feet carried me out the door before I had to hear anything else, and I fell back against the wall of the bar outside, trying to hold myself together. "So that's that," I said, and I wanted to curl up into a ball and stay there until my reality returned to something I understood.

Jack was leaving. I mean, technically he would probably stay in San Francisco, but he didn't need me anymore, and that was pretty much the same thing. He'd be stupid if he didn't sign with that record label, and they would be able to take him exactly where he wanted to go. He could chase his dreams for real.

Follow his heart.

Exactly like his dad wanted him to.

I had my phone out before I let any other thoughts get through, and I dialed Jordan's number with shaky fingers. Clearly Jack was able to move on, so why couldn't I? Jordan loved me more than I'd thought he had, and he deserved another chance. We could forget what we were before and become something better. Maybe I didn't love him, but maybe I did. It wasn't like I really understood love, and maybe it wasn't some soul-changing thing that I'd thought it was.

"Amelia?" Jordan said when he answered the phone, and he sounded hopeful.

"I want to go home," I told him.

I just wanted to go home.

CHAPTER TWENTY

I was still packing when Jack knocked on my apartment door several hours later. He paused in the doorway when I let him in, taking in the boxes strewn around the apartment.

"You're going with Jordan," he said. It wasn't a question. Neither did it seem to bother him, though there wasn't a whole lot of emotion in his expression.

I shrugged a little as I stacked plates into a box. "He deserves another chance," I said. "I really think we can make things work this time."

"I hope you're right."

"You played well tonight."

Jack slid his guitar off his shoulders and settled on the couch. "Thanks," he muttered. "Do you mind if I go to bed? It's been a long day."

"Oh," I said. "Of course. I can finish this in the morning."

As he stretched out with his usual blanket, I made my way into my bedroom and looked around at my few belongings. I almost felt like it wasn't worth bringing them with me. Jordan had everything I could need, and maybe it would be better if I made a clean break with San Francisco.

Maybe I should let go.

I slipped into my bed and curled up beneath the covers, and through the blinds I had forgotten to close, I could see the lights of San Francisco. From this angle, it really didn't look all that different from Chicago or any other big city. But the longer I stared out the window, the more I realized how hard it was going to be to say goodbye to this place.

There was so much to love here, and leaving it behind would be more painful than the last time.

Eventually I fell asleep, and thankfully I didn't dream. I didn't want Jack showing up in my subconscious and making things even harder. I needed a clean break from him too. And when I woke up and went out into the front room in the morning, Jack and his guitar were gone.

"Wait, you're leaving California?" Lissa was having a harder time processing the news than I expected; Seth may not have liked the idea, but he hadn't made a scene. My sister, on the other hand, just stared at me like I'd said complete nonsense. "But you just got here."

Steve had started to pace, and try as I might, I couldn't ignore him. As soon as I'd said Chicago, he'd known exactly what my choice had been, and he wasn't happy about it. Unfortunately for him, he didn't get any say in what I did with my life.

Not anymore.

"What about Jack?" Lissa asked.

I shrugged. "What about him?"

"Who's going to be his manager?"

Probably fancy-pants Jenna Russo whose pixie cut is sharper than Steve's glare. "Jack will be fine," I said. "A talent scout from West Stone Records approached him last night, and he's signing on with them. He'll get a lot more money and fame this way."

"Where's Jordan?" Steve asked quietly.

Jordan hadn't left my side all day, and it had made me even more convinced that this was the right thing for me to do. He loved me, and that was more than a girl could ask for. "He's waiting out in the car," I said. "I really just stopped by to give you the news."

Lissa wrapped her arms around me and gave me an awkward hug thanks to her enormous belly. She was due any day now, and I was sad I would miss the arrival of my niece. "I'm just glad you came to find us," she said and brushed a tear from her cheek. "Please come and visit again soon."

"Or we'll come to Chicago," Steve growled.

"Yes!" Lissa agreed. "We're family now, so we have to stay close."

"Of course," I said and grasped her hand.

Sighing, she got to her feet and gave me another hug when I stood as well. "You have to at least stop by Indie's before you leave. She's been talking about how much she missed you when you were in New York, and I don't think she'd forgive you if you didn't go say goodbye."

Jordan wouldn't be happy about another stop before we went out to dinner, but I absolutely didn't want to leave the city without seeing Indie again. She was the first person who understood me and made me feel like maybe I could belong with this family. And maybe I would have, if I had stayed a little longer, but at this point I felt more a part of Jack's family than I did mine.

Jordan would be my family from now on.

"Thank you for everything, Lissa," I said as I headed out the door, and thankfully Steve gave me at least a wave if not a smile. "I'll see you around."

As I predicted, Jordan wasn't thrilled about the idea of stopping at a supposedly random coffee shop just before dinner, but I took his hand and told him Indie was as much my sister as Lissa was, so he relented.

Indie reacted pretty much the same as Lissa, though she didn't freak out quite as much. "Are you sure you want to leave?" she asked. "I thought things were getting better."

"They were," I agreed. In fact, they'd been pretty great up until Jordan showed up. "I just… I don't think this is the place for me anymore."

Surprisingly, she didn't ask about Jack, which meant she either already knew about his good fortune or she could tell I didn't want to talk about it. She proved it was the first when she asked when I was leaving, and after I told her our flight was in the morning, she brightened.

"Then you can come with me tonight!" she said.

"Where?" *Jordan's not gonna be happy*, I thought, but I would take any time with Indie I could get.

"Jack's show."

Or maybe not. "Oh."

"Amelia." She grabbed both my hands and held them tight as she smiled at me. "I don't know Jack nearly as well as you do, but he was here this morning."

Was he? Why would he go to Indie when he barely knew her?

"Matthew and I had a long talk with him," she continued, and there was a look in her eyes I didn't fully understand. "First of all, Artemis loves him, so that should say something about the guy. She only likes the good ones. But more importantly, I really think you need to go to his show tonight."

"Why?" And why wouldn't he tell that to me himself instead of just disappearing in the middle of the night? We had gotten so good at talking, and then something had changed when Jordan showed up.

Indie shrugged. "I'm not sure I can put any specific words to it, you know? But after talking to him, I can see what he values the most in his life. Your friendship is one of those things."

Friendship.

"Please come with me. Even just for a little bit."

"Jordan's waiting in the car," I mumbled, and if he was so annoyed by stopping to talk to Indie, there was no way he would be willing to let me cancel on him for dinner so I could go watch "Jim the musician" play his little songs.

"Then tell Jordan to come with us too. Actually, I want to meet this guy." efore I could stop her, she marched out of the shop and knocked on the passenger window of the car before I could catch up. "Hey," she said when he rolled the window down. "I'm Indie, Amelia's… uh…sister-in-law? Cousin-in…whatever. I'm her sister. And I'm kidnapping her and taking her to a concert tonight. You can either come with us or pick her up when the show's over, but she doesn't have a choice in the matter. Okay?"

Jordan glanced at me, his eyes wide and confused, but I couldn't stop myself from smiling. I wished I had Indie's tenacity. "What show?" he asked, and he sounded like he already knew.

"Jackson Thorn's," she replied with a shrug. "You in or out, Blake?"

Back when we were first married, he would have absolutely said no and convinced me to get in the car so we could stay on our planned schedule. I could see that part of him fighting to take control, but he swallowed his instinct and took a breath before he spoke. "Do you really want to go to that?" he asked me.

Indie glanced back at me and gave me a look that reiterated the fact that I didn't have a choice.

Thankfully, I didn't have to make one, because this was easier than I expected. "Yeah," I said. "I do."

And though he looked at me as if he didn't believe me—making me wonder if he knew the same thing Steve did, that I was a people pleaser—Jordan nodded and muttered, "I'll drive."

Letting Jordan drive was an awful idea. According to him, there was terrible traffic, but I was pretty sure he was driving slowly on purpose and missing lights so it would take us longer to get to the venue. I tried to ignore him, since I was sitting in the backseat so I could talk to Indie a little longer, but even she was starting to glance at the road ahead and getting confused looks on her face.

"He gets grumpy when he's hungry," I whispered.

Indie frowned. "You don't have to defend him," she whispered back. "Hey Jordan," she said louder, "how about you take a right here? I know a shortcut."

"Great," he grumbled back, but he did turn.

By the time we finally got to the club where Jack was playing, the place already looked packed, and I worried we wouldn't be able to get in. Indie must have caught my anxiety on my face, because she gave my hand a squeeze and muttered, "Jack said he would make sure we could get in."

Hang on, does that mean he expected me to come? Given the way he'd been acting the last couple of days, I couldn't really imagine that being true. Thankfully, I didn't have long to dwell on that question, because halfway to the door I realized Jordan wasn't with us.

"You go," he said through the open car window. "I'll go find a parking spot and meet you inside." Then he drove off.

"Why do I get the feeling he's going to take a very long time to find that spot?" I asked out loud.

Laughing, Indie pulled me onward, gave our names to the bouncer, and led the way inside.

Jack was already playing to a riveted crowd, and he sounded perfect. Almost too perfect. He gazed down at his guitar as always, his hair flopping into his face, but he moved so little that it was hard to believe he could be playing at all. As good as his music sounded, he wasn't putting his heart into it for the first time since I'd met him.

Something told me that was my fault, and I watched him for a long time, wishing I knew what had changed. No, I knew what had changed. I had chosen Jordan, but I had no idea what that meant. Did Jack think it was a bad idea, just like Steve did? A part of me wanted to think there was more to it than that, but if Jack thought there was more to the two of us than friendship, why wouldn't he have said something? He was always so good about being up front and honest, especially now that he didn't have to hide anything from me.

So why was he hiding now? He usually poured his whole heart into his music, but now there was a wall in between his soul and his guitar.

"That bouncer almost didn't let me in," Jordan said right behind me, making me jump. He didn't seem to notice as he narrowed his eyes at Jack up on the stage. "I had to say I was with you, and even then he thought I was just trying to crash the party. Huh, Jim's not that bad."

"You should see *Jack* when he's having a good day," Indie said and gave my hand a squeeze; I hadn't even realized she was still holding it, and I smiled at her, even though listening to Jack play without any of his usual emotion was making it hard to breathe. Was there a way I could fix it before I left? Or was this the new Jack?

When I left, would he still be able to remember why he should be happy, no matter what?

"We should get going," Jordan said after a few minutes, and he clasped my other hand and gave me a gentle tug. "We have an early flight tomorrow, and I know how you get when you don't eat well before bed."

I looked at him in surprise, though I shouldn't have been shocked. I was married to the guy long enough that he would know my little quirks, and the fact that he remembered and wanted to help me avoid a migraine and some serious grumpiness brought a smile to my face. He was a good man, Jordan. That was never going to change.

"Yeah," I said and briefly touched Indie's arm to tell her goodbye, even though I could tell she wanted to argue and keep me here longer. Staying was just delaying the inevitable, and I didn't want—

I stopped halfway to the door when Jack started playing that new song. The one that was better than anything I'd ever heard. It seemed even sadder now, and as if he'd just flipped a switch, Jack was pouring everything into that song so it resonated across the entire club.

The wall was gone.

"Amelia?" Jordan pressed, pulling again.

But Jack had started to sing, and there was no way I was going to miss a word of this song when it felt like it was written just for me.

Do you know who you are?
Afraid to open your eyes
and see how bright you shine.

Jordan's hold grew tighter. "Amelia. It's time to go."

Carnation dyed
to please the eyes
of everyone but those who can see
who you are,
that flame in your heart.
A perfectly imperfect reflection of me.

I took a step closer to the stage, but Jordan pulled me back, looking at me like I'd lost my mind.

I tried to forget you,
tried to move on,
but your song keeps me up at night.
And I will play
until you stay
in my arms, my heart, your light.

Do you know who you are?
I'll only tell you one thing:
Be brave, little flame.

"Amelia, we need to go."

"No," I whispered and reluctantly pulled my eyes away from Jack to look at Jordan.

He frowned. "What?"

"I don't want to be married to you."

"Amelia, what—"

"I want to stay here." Not just here in California. I wanted to be *right here*. Standing in an overcrowded club that smelled a little too strongly of beer and body odor. *Wait, no.* I wanted to be up by the stage where a man was playing a song for me without knowing I was there to hear it.

Let go of that fear that keeps you
from burning bright,
bright enough to light the dark
every day of my life.

Leaving Jordan behind, I hurried up through the crowd, ducking under arms and pushing people aside until I was right in front of him, and the commotion made him look up.

"*Let go*," he sang, finishing the song, and his gaze jumped to the door, where I assumed Jordan was on his way out.

The crowd burst into applause, but he only had eyes for me as those last notes filled the space between us. And while I knew he wouldn't be able to hear me because his audience were in raptures over the new song, I spoke anyway:

"I love you."

Jack's expression overall didn't change much, but I saw the fire burst to life in his eyes. Without even acknowledging the crowd, he slid his guitar onto his back and leapt from the stage, and in the next moment he was kissing me.

Jack's music was incredible. His kiss was even better. It felt like all the best emotions of all of his songs rolled up into one timeless moment of just me and him. Me and him and two lifetimes of trying to be what we thought was expected of us and forgetting to be ourselves.

Kissing Jack was like finally taking a breath of air after drowning most of my life. His lips explored mine as if he wanted to know everything I might ever say. He wasn't stealing my secrets but asking for them, every little movement gentle and hopeful and nothing like I had ever felt before. Jack didn't take command over me; he simply became a part of me.

"I didn't sign with West Stone," he said after what felt like an eternity locked together.

"I'm not going back with Jordan," I replied.

He kissed me again, but then he looked out over the crowd and muttered, "I should probably finish the gig."

"Probably," I whispered back.

He hopped back up and started up another song, one that was much livelier than my song but no less emotional, and the crowd drank it all up. Somehow I wandered back to where Indie was waiting for me with a squeal and a hug that meant she had probably been hoping this exact thing would happen. And while I wanted to tell her there was no way she could have planned any of it, I figured this was a good time to make her happy. I was in absolute heaven, so being my people-pleasing self didn't feel like a burden right now.

It felt like I was sharing a little bit of my light.

CHAPTER TWENTY-ONE

Jack and I went for a walk after the show. He put his arm around me and held me firmly against him, and I held tight to his waist, wondering how it could have possibly taken me this long to realize how hard I had fallen for this man. I'd probably been in love with him for weeks, and I hadn't even noticed.

The silence between us didn't bother me. I was content to just be there in his hold and look at everything around us as if it were the most incredible thing I'd ever seen. Everything looked different. The lights of the city twinkled, and the sounds of downtown were musical, and every person we passed was absolutely beautiful. The world looked right for the first time in a long time.

"Did you like your song?" Jack asked after a while.

I dropped my head onto his shoulder as we walked. "I've never heard anything better," I breathed. "Will you play it for me again sometime?"

He laughed and kissed the top of my head. "I'll play it every day for the rest of my life if you ask me to," he said.

"Why didn't you sign a contract with West Stone?" I replied. "They could have helped you do what your dad wanted. Follow your heart."

"Because my music will always be for you. Amelia…" He paused and stepped out of my hold so he could look me in the eyes. "Amelia, my dad's instructions have nothing to do with music. It's all about you."

My chest felt like it was ready to explode, and I sank onto an obliging bench next to me before I completely fell apart. "Me?" I whispered, only because I wanted him to say the words.

Jack understood, and he grinned at me. "I love you, Amelia. I have for a long time."

"Why did you never say anything?"

"Because if I told you I was in love with you, you would stay with me."

"Um." *I thought that was the point.*

Laughing again, he sat next to me and grabbed both my hands. "Amelia, I wanted you to do something for yourself for once. To make your own choice, no matter what that meant for other people. This was such a big decision that I didn't want to make it for you, but I wanted you to see that you deserve happiness as much as anyone else. Even though it nearly killed me to let you go, I thought it was what you needed to be happy."

"I'm happy," I told him, though the tears that filled my eyes might have given him a different impression. "Jack, you've been trying to tell me for so long, and I…" I was an idiot.

Must have learned it from Steve.

"You got lost for a little bit, yeah, but you got there in the end. That's what matters."

"Seriously," I muttered, "how did you get to be so wise? You know everything."

"You're saying this to the guy who ran away from home at twenty-four because he didn't have any of the answers. I know what I've learned. I just think you and I were meant to find each other."

I thought about that for a moment, trying to decide if I believed that like he did. Fate seemed too good to be true, and I still credited most of my life to circumstance. But maybe some things could be destined, like a guy walking down a road where a girl needed his help. I'd thought so from the first moment I knew him.

"Do you think your dad could have planned all this?" I wondered out loud. It was a ridiculous thought, but I couldn't help but think maybe it was true.

Jack smiled. "Lucas Hawthorne changing lives because he can see what others can't? Sounds about right. Come on, we're almost there."

As he took my hand and pulled me back to my feet, I furrowed my brow. "Almost where?"

Jack turned off the road less than a block later and stepped into a dark cemetery, though there was just enough city light for me to read the names on the headstones as we passed.

"I talked to your cousin Matthew for a long time today," he said, quieter now that we were surrounded by silence. The city seemed to have disappeared around us. "He told me all about my half-brother, Luke, since they had been really close friends before he died saving Lanna. He told me what Luke was like. And maybe he didn't spend a lot of time with Dad, but it sounds like they were more alike than either of them realized."

We stopped at a beautiful granite headstone, where the name Lucas Gabriel Hawthorne glittered in the stone.

Jack held a little tighter to my fingers as he gazed at it. "Hey, Luke," he said softly. "You don't know me, and I don't know you, but I'm your brother. I was born the same year Dad lost track of you, and…" He knelt in the grass and touched his free hand to the headstone. "I should probably say thank you. If you hadn't disappeared, Dad wouldn't have realized how much he wanted to be a good father. You were the reason he tried so hard to be a part of my life. I wish I had recognized that's what he was doing sooner."

I realized he said that last part to me when he glanced up at me, and I knelt next to him and slid my arm through his. "I might not have gotten to meet him," I said, "but I'm sure your dad knew how much you loved him. And he's proud of the man you've become. I know I am."

Smiling, he turned to me and brushed a tear from my cheek that I didn't even know was there. "Have I told you yet how much you changed my life that day I met you?"

"You have," I replied. "And while it took my change a little longer to come, you changed mine too."

He shrugged a little. "I'm not so sure about that, but I know you'll argue, so I'll just shut my mouth now."

"That's a good idea." I leaned in, relishing the kiss he gave me. Somehow, it was even better than the first one. *This* was what love was. And it was so easy to recognize now that I truly felt it.

"Do you know what I want?" I said after a while.

Jack closed his eyes, resting his forehead against mine. "What do you want, Amelia Blake?"

"Well, first of all I want a new last name," I grumbled.

"I can help you with that," he replied, and when I tensed, he laughed. "Relax, Amelia. I wouldn't spring something like that on you. You'll see it coming."

I really wasn't sure why he thought that made this any better, and I could hardly breathe as I suddenly thought about how much I would love being married to Jack Hawthorne. But that was for another time.

"I want…" I swallowed as my voice caught in my throat, and then I glared at him when he laughed again. "I want to go home, Jack. And I'm not sure that means San Francisco."

To my utter relief, he seemed to understand exactly what I meant as he pulled me up to my feet. "You know," he said, "I hear the music scene in New York is pretty good."

"I'd bet there are people there who could teach me what I'm doing with this whole manager gig," I replied.

"And I know for a fact my mother would love to see you again."

"And I would be closer to my dad. Get to know him better."

Jack pulled me close and had the most incredible grin on his face, one that spoke almost as clearly as his music did. "I'll buy us some plane tickets," he said and bent his head, teasing a kiss against my lips. "Because I'm pretty sure I'm about to come into a whole lot of money. Wherever you are, my heart will follow. Always and forever. But first…"

He reached into his pocket and pulled out an envelope. It looked just like the one he had shown me in New York, with the terms of his inheritance, but this one had Luke's name written across the front. I looked up at him in question, and he smiled. "There's something we need to do."

EPILOGUE
Matthew Davenport

"I can't believe you convinced me to do this." I stood at my brother-in-law's open garage, my eyes fixed on the lump of canvas that hid a beat-up white pickup. I was holding Indie's hand too tight, but I couldn't help it. And my wife didn't complain. For that, I would be forever grateful.

If she weren't here at my side, I wouldn't have been able to breathe.

"You need this, Matthew," she whispered and gave my hand a squeeze.

Maybe I did, but I wasn't sure I was ready for this.

"Dad always had a thing for trucks." Jack was the first to step forward and put a hand on the canvas tarp, gripping it in his fingers. "Seems fitting, don't you think?" He gave the tarp a tug, and it seemed to flutter away rather than slide off, as if something helped it move.

My chest grew tight as the instinct to immediately look away became too strong to resist. I shut my eyes, though it didn't help much.

I hadn't looked at that truck in almost a decade, and yet I knew exactly what it looked like, down to the dent in the passenger side door. Although, that was probably because I was the one who'd put it there. With my boot. I hadn't exactly been myself at the time, and I had never been blamed for the damage, even if I should have been. Luke had been smart enough to know my anger had only been masking pain, and he kept the dent to prove to me I was still alive.

Still alive because of him.

"Matthew?" A hand touched my shoulder, and my sister's warm voice pulled my eyes open again. Lanna smiled at me, and I was pretty sure she had no idea how much her smile gave me courage. "You don't have to do this, you know."

"Yes I do."

As Jack examined the truck with interest, Lanna's husband stepped into line alongside us. Adam had never been big on showing emotion, so it was strange to see the tears glimmering in his eyes. "I tried to sell it a few times," he admitted as he gazed at the truck. "But I could never bring myself to do it."

"It wasn't time yet," Jack said. I'd only met the guy a few weeks ago, so I couldn't say I really knew him all that well, but he had a way of saying things like they were fact, no matter how ridiculous it may have sounded. "Luke Hawthorne wasn't ready yet."

Jack was so much like his half-brother that I wasn't entirely convinced they weren't the same person. Jack was eleven years younger than Luke, and they had never met, but they were most definitely brothers. They had the same way of seeing deep into a person's soul and finding the most battered pieces in the hopes that they could fix it.

Luke was the only one who had been able to get me back on my feet, and even if he was gone, I would never forget what he did for me.

As I'd come to discover, Hawthornes had a habit of ignoring their own needs and helping the people around them. Jack's girlfriend, Amelia, was a testament to that, and she was already so much different from how she'd been the first time I met her. She was braver. Stronger. Happier.

She joined Jack next to the truck and took his hand, and her eyes glittered with happiness. "Your dad would have loved this," she told him.

He kissed her temple and grinned, far too happy for a guy who had just lost his father a couple of weeks ago. Another reason he was like his brother. It didn't matter how tough his life had been; Luke Hawthorne had spent his every moment with a smile.

"Do you have any idea how much I love you?" Jack whispered to Amelia, and then he looked at all of us in turn. "So who's driving the truck?" he asked.

His eyes seemed to linger on me, though, and I could guess why. Jack *knew*. How he knew, I didn't know and probably never would, but he knew how important this was.

"I'll drive," I said, barely managing to get the words out.

Lanna's hand tightened on my shoulder. "Are you sure? I can—"

I held out my hand and let Adam hand me the keys. Indie was right. I needed to do this.

Climbing into the driver's seat wasn't easy—not that I'd expected it to be—but I wasn't surprised when Lanna joined me and took the only other seat. My little sister was one of the strongest people I knew, and she was one of the few who truly knew how hard this was for me. Indie could see my pain, even when I didn't want her to, but Lanna *shared* it.

She'd loved Luke as much as I had.

"Are you ready?" she asked and took hold of my hand, which had started to shake.

"I'm not sure I'll ever be ready," I replied. This truck *felt* like him. Like my best friend was just outside the garage, waiting to laugh at me and tell me I was being dramatic.

He would have been right, as always. It had been long enough since he died, and it was time for me to let him go.

The truck started up with just a little coaxing, a testament to Adam's dedication to keeping it in working condition, and the rumble of the engine pulsed through me like it was alive. I would have immediately turned it back off if the radio hadn't buzzed until it found a heavy metal station.

Instead of going into panic mode, I laughed a little.

"You always did have terrible taste in music, man," I muttered and flipped the radio off.

"I didn't know that," Lanna said with a smile.

"The night I…" I swallowed. "The night we met, when he drove me to his apartment, he was playing some weird, folksy, yodeling something. I was this close to ripping the stereo right out of the dash and tossing it out the window."

"He would have laughed if you had."

Yeah, he would have. He probably knew it was the best thing to distract me from what I had been close to doing that night, and it had worked. Sighing, I shifted the truck into gear and muttered, "Never let it be known that a banjo saved my life."

Lanna put her hand on my arm. She didn't say anything, but she didn't have to. She was silently thanking Luke for saving me from my darkness and keeping me in her life. I thanked him for the same thing every day, since I would have lost my sister if not for him. He'd saved us both.

I pulled onto the street in front of Adam and Lanna's house, the others following just behind in a couple of cars. We had debated bringing the whole family, but something about having all of us here felt right. Even if they didn't know him, Luke would have loved meeting each and every one of them, and he had touched their lives. Directly and indirectly.

The autumn afternoon was absolutely perfect, and though I held the steering wheel a little tighter than I would have if I were driving my own car, it was a lot easier to be in this truck than I'd expected. Maybe that was because I had my baby sister with me to share her strength, but I had a feeling it was more than that.

Somehow, Luke was helping me yet again.

As we eventually pulled onto the winding lane that would take us up into the hills, Lanna peered out her window as the view got progressively wilder. I hadn't been up this way since I was a kid, but everything about it was familiar. The yellow grass. The green trees. The blue of the sky that was giving way to the golden light of sunset. There was something both peaceful and untamable about this place.

"It feels like him," I said, though I was afraid to break the silence, as if my voice might scare him away. *Ridiculous.* That hadn't worked when he was still alive, even when I shouted at him so furiously that I went hoarse, so why should my quiet words turn him away now?

Lanna pulled her gaze away from the window to grin at me. "Wait until you see the stars," she whispered.

At the top of the hill stood a building that, honestly, should have collapsed years ago, but the old observatory still clung to life, as if it had been waiting for us. I pulled the truck to a stop just in front and turned the ignition as the others came up behind, and then I froze.

As soon as I stepped outside this door, that would be it.

"Matthew?"

I glanced at Lanna as she stepped out. "Just give me a minute."

It didn't matter that I needed this; it was not going to be easy to stand there looking out at the world and say goodbye to my best friend. I had done that once before, when my brother died, and that had taken me a full decade to accomplish.

Luke had been gone for more than nine years now, and it still felt like he'd died yesterday.

"What if I can't do this?" I said to the empty truck. Over the years, I had gotten used to talking to the dead, and my brother's headstone had heard far more of my worries and concerns than any hunk of rock deserved. But this felt different. I always knew Ben would never talk back to me. But Luke? I gripped the steering wheel tight, because something told me he would be a lot more inclined to shout at me for being stupid than my brother.

"Get over yourself, Dav," he would have said and punched me in the arm for good measure. I could almost feel him sitting there in the truck next to me, waiting for me to stop being so pathetic.

But what did he expect me to do?

"I don't think I'm ready," I said. "I'm not sure I have the strength to let go."

That was when I heard the music.

I looked up, gazing at my family gathering together outside the observatory. Jack had brought his guitar and played a soft melody that seemed to echo the wilderness around us.

It sounded like Luke.

Though everything inside me told me to stay where I was and hold on a little longer, I slipped out of the truck and joined Indie at the edge of the group. My little girl, Artemis, reached out for me, and I smiled through the tears that were already building in my eyes. Leave it to a toddler to help me keep myself in one piece.

I lifted her out of Indie's arms and held my daughter tight as our little procession went around the back of the building, following Jack's perfect song until we could all see the expanse before us.

Lanna had painted this view once, but even though my sister was an incredible artist, I was pretty sure no one could quite capture a place like this in its entirety. The hills stretched out to the ocean, golden and soft, the trees and brambles bathed in sunlight as the sun sank lower. A stream wound its way to the coast, and it glittered like a ribbon of light.

All of it was wild, and warm, and uniquely Luke.

"I can see why he liked this place," Steve said as he wrapped an arm around his wife's shoulders.

I would have laughed under normal circumstances, since the man was almost completely blind, but I had a feeling Steve meant what he said. He must have felt the same thing I did. He cradled his newborn daughter in his other arm as Lissa leaned her head against his shoulder, and the three of them painted a perfect picture. Luke would have loved Steve, the way he used humor to brighten up the world when it got too dark. For a man whose life had gone entirely dark when he lost his sight, that was an important trait, especially for the people around him.

Me, in particular.

As if he knew I was looking at him and silently thanking him, Steve glanced over and smiled.

Beside him, Colin wrapped his arms around his wife and daughter, holding them both close. I didn't know the man well, since he was busier than the rest of us combined, but he knew the heartache of losing a loved one. His first wife had died without warning, just like Luke, and it had taken him a long time to love again. Beck had healed his broken heart, and his daughter Macy had in wisdom beyond her years helped him move on. The ten-year-old may not have fully understood what we were doing on this hilltop, but unlike the rest of us, her eyes were heavenward. Maybe she knew something we didn't.

Catherine was in tears at the end of the row, and her husband held her safe in his embrace. She had almost lost Seth back when they met, and he had been willing to give up his life to save hers. Luke probably would have taken one look at the giant of a man and seen the bleeding heart beneath the hardened soldier, and they would have been instant friends. Luke was a protector, just like Seth. And though no one else knew it yet but me, now Seth and Catherine were expecting a couple of babies, and I couldn't imagine better parents.

Even if they were terrified.

"Uncle Brenny, can I sit on your shoulders? I want to see better." My nephew asked the question quietly, but with all of us standing in silence, it was impossible not to hear Benny's request.

Thankfully, Brennon seemed more than happy to comply, lifting the first grader up to give him a better vantage point. He wasn't technically family, Brennon, but that didn't mean he wasn't one of us. He had a way of putting people at ease, just like his wife, Molly, had a knack for dredging up secrets and helping people be their true selves. I'd never really thought about it before, but they were a lot like Luke had been. In their own ways, they saw things other people didn't see and weren't afraid to coax it out of them if it meant they could be better. Brennon, especially, had managed to get me to say things I hadn't been willing to admit out loud, and he did it without even trying.

Luke would have been so proud of that.

"It's like your picture, Mommy," Benny said as he took in the scene.

As she held onto her younger son, Harry, Lanna slipped her hand into Adam's, and she looked happy despite the tears shining on her face. Of all the things Luke had ever done, I was most grateful for my sister. He had pulled her out of her shell and helped her heal from a messed-up childhood I'd been too scared to face, and in the end he had saved her life.

Sacrificed himself so she could live.

Adam and I hadn't talked about our friend since we sat in the hospital after Luke took a bullet for my sister, but when my brother-in-law looked at me now, I realized he still felt guilty. After all these years, he wondered if things would have turned out differently if he hadn't fought so hard to win Lanna's love while Luke did the same thing.

"He knew you were better for her," I wanted to say, but the words stuck in my throat.

Adam seemed to understand anyway, nodding once as tears filled his eyes. Tonight would be healing for him too.

Jack finished his song, leaving it open-ended as if he knew he couldn't play that final note just yet. He leaned into Amelia's embrace then smiled wide. "I've got something for you," he said to the hills and reached into his pocket, pulling out an envelope.

That envelope was the whole reason we were here. It contained a final instruction from Luke and Jack's dad. A final request from a man who regretted leaving his first son behind. I had no idea what it said—Jack didn't either—but we were here to help Luke make his dad proud. If we could.

"Anyone want to make bets on what it says?" Steve asked, glancing down the row with a grin. "Ow!"

Seth had thrown a rock at him because he was too far away to punch him.

But I laughed, because it was exactly the sort of thing Luke would have said if he were here.

Grinning, Jack slid his finger beneath the seal holding the envelope closed, but he paused then changed his mind. To my surprise, he held the letter out to me.

I stared at it, frowning. Of all people, Jack should be the one to read his father's letter. "He gave it to you," I argued.

Jack shook his head. "I think Dad would have wanted it to be you."

I wanted to ask why, but instead I took the letter and opened it before I could chicken out. My fingers shook, but I was a lot steadier than I expected given the circumstances. Indie helped, her arm around my waist, and my daughter had wrapped her arms around my neck as if she knew how much I needed the strength of someone else to get me through this.

There were only a few words written on the page in a strong hand-writing, and though I had to blink my tears away to read them, they immediately brought a smile to my face.

It was perfect.

"What does it say?" Beck asked from Colin's embrace.

A weight had left my shoulders, and I laughed again because I had been so worried that we wouldn't be able to help my friend fulfill his father's dying wish, and now I knew we could.

Luke had already done it.

I held the letter out to Lanna, who took it with curiosity burning in her eyes. As soon as she read what I had, she smiled as well. *"Build a family,"* she read out loud then hugged the letter to her chest. "Oh, Luke."

This big, messy family of mine, full of the people I cared about the most, couldn't have existed without Luke Hawthorne. Not only had he saved Lanna's life, but he had saved mine time and time again. He had brought me into Adam's world, facilitating a strong friendship with my now-brother-in-law. Luke had given me a reason to care about life again and find a purpose. To find the strength to do everything in my power to keep Seth and Catherine together when the world tried to tear them apart. Seth brought Lissa to Steve. Steve pulled Brennon into our family and Molly along with him. Brennon, who rallied to Beck's side as she fought to help Colin heal. And Luke was the reason Jack had come to California and met Amelia, Seth and Lissa's sister.

All of it was Luke.

As we stood there at the top of the hill, the sun sank below the clouds at the horizon, painting the sky with brilliant shades of pink and orange. It was the best sunset I had ever seen, and I had a feeling it wasn't a coincidence.

"You said you didn't paint," Lanna whispered to the sky, and I knew she was talking to Luke. Was he really up there, smiling down on his jumbled family?

"You were just like Dad," Jack said to the sky next, and he smiled through the tears that streamed down his cheeks. "I hope the two of you are getting to know each other."

The others murmured a chorus of thank yous, and as the sunset—brief as it was—started to dim, my family began returning to the cars as Jack played the last few notes of his song.

I stayed where I was and was immensely glad when Indie took my hand. I whispered my gratitude then turned back to the fading sky. "I want you to meet my family," I said quietly. "This is Indiana, though she hates when I call her that, and she is plenty good at telling me when I'm being an idiot, so you don't have to worry about that part. She's got it covered."

"Thanks for helping him find me," Indie said to the sky and leaned into the kiss I touched to her temple.

"And this is my daughter, Artemis," I continued. "She's an absolute handful and refuses to do as she's told, and you would have loved her. Indie, Artie…" I nodded to the sunset. "This is my friend…"

I swallowed. I had barely said his name out loud for the better part of a decade, though it was often on the tip of my tongue. Saying his name felt like saying goodbye, and I hadn't been ready for that. But it was time to let go of the pain of the past. Let *him* go.

"My friend, Luke," I whispered, and a shudder ran through me. Like a whole piece of me fell away. "He taught me how to value the things that matter most, and he showed me what life is really about. Life was always simple for him, because he knew there was nothing more important than love."

Pulling my daughter tight against my chest and gripping Indie's hand, I turned and left the fading sunset behind me. "Goodbye," I whispered, and then the three of us went back to the cars.

As I strapped Artemis into her car seat, I realized I could breathe again, as if I'd spent the last nine years with a bag of bricks on my chest, and I had never felt more whole.

Happy.

And I knew that was because of Luke. Even if he wasn't here, he had saved me again, just like he had from the day I met him. He had saved all of us.

"You okay?" Indie asked as we climbed into the seats on either side of our daughter in Catherine's car.

Luke's truck would stay where it was, in the place where his soul was finally laid to rest.

Before I shut my door, I looked up into the blackening sky and caught the first few stars popping up in the night sky. Before long, the heavens would be peppered with them, and I could imagine it was quite the sight away from the lights of the city like this.

"Yeah," I breathed, and I meant it. My daughter wrapped her tiny fingers around my thumb and smiled over at me, and I could have sworn she had a look in her eyes that told me she knew exactly why we had come up to this place.

Maybe she did. Maybe she had known Luke longer than I had and simply lacked the capacity to tell me how much she liked my lost friend.

"Dada," she said with a toothy grin.

I took one more look at the stars before Seth pulled away, and one seemed to glow slightly brighter than the others.

"Thanks," I said to the star, and my chest swelled with warmth. It was a feeling that was totally and completely Luke.

The End

OTHER BOOKS IN THE SIMPLE LOVE SERIES

ABOUT THE AUTHOR

Dana LeCheminant has been telling stories since she was old enough to know what stories were. After spending most of her childhood reading everything she could get her hands on, she eventually realized she could write her own books too, and since then she always has plots brewing and characters clamoring to be next to have their stories told. A lover of all things outdoors, she finds inspiration while hiking the remote Utah backcountry and cruising down rivers. Until her endless imagination runs dry, she will always have another story to tell.

9 781951 753078